THEY WERE CAGED LIKE ANIMALS—
WOULD THEY DIE LIKE MEN?

"Hugh, come here!" The Sime's grating whisper sliced through the bars of the cage. "Is this Aisha?"

Hugh drew himself to his feet and looked through the bars. In the adjacent cage, with Klyd, was a woman. He could make out the unmistakable features of the missing Aisha, but she lay as if unconscious.

"She's dead!" he blurted.

"No," said Klyd, "she lives, but seems to be drugged. When she wakes, she'll fear me—and the Raiders will gather to watch the spectacle of the kill. I won't be able to control myself and keep myself from attacking her if that happens."

Hugh opened his mouth to protest—when Aisha's piercing scream rent the air.

Novels set in the Sime/Gen Universe:

HOUSE OF ZEOR by Jacqueline Lichtenberg

UNTO ZEOR, FOREVER by Jacqueline Lichtenberg

FIRST CHANNEL by Jean Lorrah and Jacqueline Lichtenberg

To be published:

MAHOGANY TRINROSE by Jacqueline Lichtenberg

CHANNEL'S DESTINY by Jean Lorrah and Jacqueline Lichtenberg

HOUSE OF ZEOR

JACQUELINE LICHTENBERG

PLAYBOY
PAPERBACKS·

TO: *Marion Zimmer Bradley*
Robert A. Heinlein
Andre Norton

And to the many other writers who have entertained me
these many years, I offer the Sime Series as payment in
like coinage.

ALSO TO: *Sondra Marshak*
Laura Basta
Pat Zotti
Anna Mary Hall

And the many others who will soon be joining in the creation of new frontiers.

HOUSE OF ZEOR

Copyright © 1974, 1981 by Jacqueline Lichtenberg

Cover illustration copyright © 1981 by PEI Books, Inc.

Published simultaneously in the United States and Canada by Playboy
Paperbacks, New York, New York. Printed in the United States of
America. Library of Congress Catalog Card Number: 80-83565. Re-
printed by arrangement with Doubleday & Company, Inc.

Books are available at quantity discounts for promotional and indus-
trial use. For further information, write to Premium Sales, Playboy
Paperbacks, 1633 Broadway, New York, New York 10019.

ISBN: 0-872-16801-8

First Playboy Paperbacks printing April 1981.

Acknowledgment

I am very grateful to Betty Herr and Elisabeth Waters, editor and publisher, respectively, of *Ambrov Zeor*, the Sime newsletter, for pointing up a number of problems with *House of Zeor*, particularly Elisabeth's noting my error in Chapter 10 of the Doubleday edition, in which the "fundamental internal shunt" is defined as the process of transferring selyn from the primary system to the secondary system while the procedure under discussion was the transfer of selyn from the secondary system to the primary. I apologize for any confusion my error may have caused, and I thank the publisher for allowing the correction in this edition. If any other reader has corrections for me, I may be reached care of the publisher.

—Jacqueline Lichtenberg

May 1976

Preface

House of Zeor is my first novel and also the first novel written in the Sime Series—which has now become known as the "Sime/Gen Universe." There are two important distinctions here.

For most people, the word "series" implies a group of books about continuing characters that is best read in a certain order. As the dedication to Marion Zimmer Bradley, Robert A. Heinlein and Andre Norton was meant to imply, the Sime/Gen books are independent stories—occasionally using a character more than once because all the stories are set in the same universe, chronicling several thousand years of human history. The books can be read in any order; each book will reveal something new about the background.

The second distinction is the contribution of Jean Lorrah. She pointed out that since I had clearly established that the Gens are also mutated humans with characteristics as intriguingly different from the readers' own as those of the Simes, I must include the Gens in the logo or stand guilty of Sime-chauvinism!

These Gen characteristics are not too apparent in *House of Zeor* mainly because the viewpoint character, Hugh Valleroy, is Gen. He was raised in a culture that does not regard Gens as mutants, and the reader sees all through his eyes. This makes *House of Zeor* one of the easiest Sime/Gen books to read, a good place for a new reader to start.

In addition to the books, the first Sime/Gen magazine, *Ambrov Zeor,* grew from a newsletter to a full-scale fanzine, publishing everything from genealogy charts of the Zeor Farris family to Sime/Gen fiction written by fans. But then the pages of *Ambrov Zeor* became filled with such things as the reprint of my first professional sale—a Sime/Gen story called "Operation High Time" (IF, Jan. '69)—and *Sime Surgeon,* a full-length novel that was a rough draft of *Unto Zeor, Forever.* Two new Sime/Gen 'zines, *Companion in Zeor* and *Zeor Forum, Transfer for Ancients,* came into being to handle the creativity of the fans and the volumes of Sime/Gen discussions among the fans and between Jean Lorrah and me as we worked out new background material for future novels in an effort to answer all the fans' questions.

Jean, already established in Star Trek fandom for her Sarek and Amanda stories, began writing Sime stories for *Ambrov Zeor* and—because she was already a seasoned professional writer—I soon had her working on a Sime/Gen novel titled *First Channel*. She deliberately crafted it as an introduction to the Sime/Gen Universe as well as to answer the veteran fan's hardest questions without the use of technical language.

At this writing, we are now doing the sequel to *First Channel*, *Channel's Destiny*, and Jean has launched her own fantasy series for Playboy titled *Savage Empire*. (Don't miss it!) I am doing some Playboy SF originals, currently called "The Kren Series," starting with *Molt Brother*.

The Sime/Gen books will be distinguished from *Savage Empire* and Kren books by the starred-cross logo (the symbology is discussed in depth in *Ambrov Zeor*, Numbers 5 and 6) you see on the cover of this book. Watch for it carefully because some of the Sime/Gen stories will be written by Jean Lorrah and filed under "Lo-" not "Li-" in libraries and stores. Also, I can't exclude the possibility of some other fan making a professional contribution to Sime/Gen history.

At this time, Jean plans to write the prequel to *House of Zeor*, titled *Ambrov Keon*, developing the householding and channel-mutation that is the antithesis of the Zeor Farrises. When she has completed that, I intend to tackle the real sequel to *House of Zeor*, which tells of the founding of the House of Rior and the Distect philosophy as well as the details of how Klyd Farris engineers the "Modern Tecton." That novel will involve the head-on clash between Keon and Zeor, the first of a long recorded history.

There are several other book projects in the planning stages. For more information on the availability of the back issues of the three Sime/Gen fanzines and current and future books, send a legal-size self-addressed stamped envelope to *Ambrov Zeor*, P.O.B. 290, Monsey, New York 10952.

Jacqueline Lichtenberg
Spring Valley, New York

April 1980

CHAPTER ONE

Assignment

HUGH VALLEROY PACED BACK AND FORTH, HEEDLESS OF the muddy water he was splashing onto the boots of the District Director of Federal Police.

The director, Stacy Hawkins, huddled under a meager ledge watching his best field operative quietly going to pieces. The two men had been waiting in the icy October night's rain for more than half an hour. Hawkins was well aware that New Washington would have his head if this mission didn't succeed. That succeess depended on Hugh Valleroy's unflinching nerve.

Beyond the distant riverbank, a horse nickered. The flooding waters tore savagely at the tiny island on which they waited. Another horse raised an answering cry. Valleroy stopped in his tracks, head whipping toward the sound . . . on the Sime Territory side of the river.

"Don't worry," said Hawkins. "The only way onto this island is through the Ancient tunnel. Only Klyd knows the entrance point on their side."

Valleroy resumed pacing. Tonight he'd travel the other branch of that tunnel . . . into Sime Territory . . . to search for Aisha. No, he corrected the thought, to *find* her.

"Hugh, will you stop that infernal splashing!"

Valleroy brought his boots together and ceased walking. "Yes, sir."

Thirty seconds of watching Valleroy's spare frame poised as if straining for release made Hawkins snap, "Oh, go run around if it makes you feel better! But don't splash me!"

Valleroy sloshed restlessly about the small clearing, craning his neck as if he could penetrate the midnight darkness and spot the approaching Sime. "Stacy, he's not coming."

"He'll come. He's dependable as sunrise."

"He'd have to be crazy to come out in weather like this!"

"Weather doesn't bother Simes. You, of all people, should know that."

Valleroy rounded on his boss, voice dangerously low. "What do you mean by a crack like that?"

"Shove it, Mr. Valleroy. You don't talk to me in that tone."

Valleroy backed off. Hawkins had been his friend for years. But the man was still his superior officer, and Valleroy was only a field operative on assignment. "Sir. Would you mind explaining your remark?"

Realizing that Valleroy was under an inhuman strain, Hawkins spoke gently. "I was only referring to the fact that you've been our best interrogator ever since you came to work for us. You can't know a language without knowing the people who use it."

Valleroy found his sudden anger dissipated. Hawkins had avoided mentioning it as if he hadn't even thought it —what everybody else on the post called him—*Simelover*. His voice hardly more than a husky whisper, Valleroy said, "Thank you."

"Don't thank me. Who else is there to send? But just think what my post will be without you!"

"I'll be back. And *with* Aisha."

"I *know* that. But either way, I lose. I don't intend to take that reward money and come back to *work* for a living, do you?"

Valleroy didn't answer. Full retirement pension and twelve acres of land was a big enough reward . . . it was all he'd ever dreamed of having. And now he'd have it while he was young enough to enjoy it. It didn't really matter if he didn't come back . . . because if he didn't succeed, he wouldn't want the reward. There would be no reason to live . . . without Aisha.

"Look," said Hawkins, "I know how frightened you must be. But Simes are only human mutants. If you don't look at their arms, you can't tell the difference, can you?"

Absently, Valleroy answered the rhetorical question, "No."

"If Simes didn't have this instinct that drives them to the kill, there would be no reason at all to fear them, would there?"

"Of course not. But all Simes are subject to the need-cycle. And when they take selyn from a Gen, the Gen

10

dies. I've never heard of anybody choosing to commit suicide *that* way."

"Neither have I. But the channels are different. When they take from a Gen, he doesn't die."

"So you've been telling me."

"Klyd is a channel. His people don't kill. So there's no reason to fear them."

"What makes you think I'm afraid?"

"I know how it was when I first met Klyd. He doesn't look any different from an ordinary Sime."

Valleroy snapped, "I'm not scared, I tell you!"

"You don't have to shout. Your fear is like a blazing beacon. It'll bring him right to us."

"Oh, *hell!*"

"You can't fool a Sime, you know. Your emotions are an open book to them."

"You think I don't know *that!*"

"I know very well you know it."

Valleroy stalked toward the other man. "Go ahead. Say it. *Say it! Sime-lover!* Why are you so afraid to say it to my face? Everybody says it behind my back. You think I don't know?"

"Hugh, what is the matter with you? You know perfectly well you'd have to be convicted of sedition if there were any truth to what people say. If it were true, you wouldn't be so frightened that you have to charge around in the mud."

Valleroy's hand went to the starred-cross that he'd hung around his neck under his shirt. He hadn't worn it since he'd been promoted to a desk job. If Hawkins knew he had it—if Hawkins knew what it was—no court in Gen Territory would acquit him. His hand was trembling. He forced it behind his back and splashed away.

He could admit it to himself. He was frightened. But not the way most people would be. He honestly didn't know if he could allow a Sime to touch him. He only knew that all the events of his life had been leading up to this test. And now he wasn't sure he could pass it. But he had to find out.

"This is a volunteer mission," said Hawkins. "If you want to back out, there'll be no black mark on your service record."

"I'm no coward, if that's what you mean."

Over the roaring of the flooding river, a soft voice spoke disconcertingly near. "Your man is correct, Stacy.

11

A coward is one who cannot face that which he fears. This man fears prodigiously, but stands firm in spite of it."

"Klyd?" called Hawkins stepping away from the overhand.

"Were it not indeed I, it is doubtful if either of you would still live. You trespass on Sime Territory."

"That's debatable," answered Hawkins. "But when you hear why I set up this meeting, you'll forgive us."

"It is not my place to blame or forgive," said the voice. "Tell your tale, but do it swiftly. I pause in haste."

"What's the matter with you? Why so touchy?"

"Swiftly, I said."

"Well, yesterday, a band of Sime raiders attacked a tourist group at Hanrahan Pass. They left five dead and made off with the other twenty-three."

"It is to the prevention of this that my existence is dedicated. I regret there is nothing I can do to save your people. Many of us still depend on such raids."

"One of the kidnapped passengers was Aisha Rauf . . . our Treasury's chief engraver. This *might* have been an ordinary raid . . . or it might have been aimed at Aisha. If she can be forced to make the plates, your people could flood our market with bad currency . . . destroy our economy within months. With no organized resistance, we'd all be in the pens within a year."

"I begin to see the problem. You wish me to find this woman and return her to you?"

"Well, that or determine what actually did happen to her."

"Impossible."

"There must be a way!"

"To trace one particular Gen captive? No . . . unless . . . was she of courageous character?"

"Very!" said Valleroy.

"You know her, Mr . . . ?"

"Valleroy, Hugh Valleroy. Yes, I know her."

"Describe her."

"I can do better than that. I have sketches, and I can make more. She used to model for me."

Valleroy proffered a waterproofed case filled with his sketches. To avoid the other's accidental touch, he held the case gingerly by one corner.

Klyd took the case, apparently just as leery of any brief contact. "You are an artist?"

12

"He's my best composit man. That's why I want you to take him with you. He knows a bit of your language—"

"Take! Stacy, I've executed many dangerous assignments for you, but here I must—"

"Now, just wait a minute. Don't go getting that Sime temper all lathered up. Hugh's as good an operative as you are. You ought to make the best team I've ever fielded."

"You don't trust me alone with her?"

"It's not that. Any minute somebody may discover who she is and what she can do. We've got to get her out before—"

"Contrary to popular belief, Simes can't make Gens do anything against their will. If your Miss Rauf is not a traitor, nobody will turn her into one."

"She may not be a traitor, but she's only human."

"All right. I will try to find her. By myself."

"No," said Hawkins. "I insist Hugh may make the difference between success and failure. She'd be as frightened of you as of any other Sime."

"You are not in a position to insist on anything."

"Now, don't get upset! I only meant you ought to trust my judgment."

"Uh . . ." hazarded Valleroy. "I don't relish this any more than you do, but I did volunteer. You'll never find one girl among thousands with nothing more to go on than a few sketches. By the time you find her, she may have lost weight . . . changed."

"It would be too dangerous," said Klyd.

"You can protect him," said Hawkins. "You could adopt him into your Householding."

"Under what cover story? It would be more dangerous for me than for him. There may be spies even within Zeor."

"You know your people better than I do. You devise the cover."

The rain finally slackened, letting the moon through a crack in the clouds. Valleroy could make out the Sime's figure, like a gaunt-winged vampire. He dismissed the impression. Simes were only human mutants who wore riding capes for comfort.

At length, the Sime bit out an oath in Simelan and rounded on the Gens. "There is only one way. I'll have to take you in as a victim of transfer shock . . . and it will *have* to be genuine!"

13

"Don't try to scare him off! There's got to be another way."

Valleroy shuddered. This he hadn't bargained for!

"There *is* no other way. If I'd rescued him, and he was uninjured, I'd simply turn him loose as an advertisement that all Simes don't kill. The only reason I'd bring a Gen home would be to have his life. I can't imagine what excuse I could use to keep him more than a week."

"What would happen if I refused to leave?"

The Sime stopped splashing mud and stared toward Valleroy as if he could see him through the darkness. "I don't know. I suppose Grandfather would have to decide."

"How long would that take?" asked Hawkins.

"Hmmm. Maybe long enough."

"Hey, wait a minute!" said Valleroy. "I thought *you* were head of your Householding."

"Mr. Valleroy. I feel your fear of me . . . and fear brings out the beast in a Sime. There are ordinary Simes in Zeor. You'd have to learn not to fear them or be constantly in danger of attack . . . *unless* you were rendered low-field by transfer."

"You are trying to scare me off!"

"Frankly, yes. If it's ever discovered that I'm working with you, I would be executed . . . unpleasantly."

"I've never blown a cover yet, and I don't intend to start now! You may need me to identify—" Valleroy had to swallow convulsively before he could get it out— "her body."

Suddenly, the Sime stepped close to Valleroy and peered down at him, revelation in his tone. "You *love* her!"

"No. She's just a friend. That's all."

"Don't lie to me."

"Don't read my mind!"

"I can't read your mind, only your emotions! But never lie to me again. It's no foundation for a partnership."

"Then you'll take him?"

"It appears I have no choice since he loves her."

Unseen in the darkness, Hawkins smirked. He'd *known* all along that Klyd would accept only someone who had a personal reason to find her, and he'd long suspected Valleroy's interest in her to be more than casual.

14

Valleroy moved to lean against the rock face. To him, Sime ethics were sometimes more confusing than Sime temperament.

Approaching swiftly through the dark. Klyd spoke rapid words, "Mr. Valleroy, you were attacked by a Sime berserk with need. You drove him off with this." He snatched Hawkins' knife from its sheath and presented it, hilt first. "But you did not succeed before he drew selyn and burned you deeply. Here, take it."

Valleroy plucked the weapon from the Sime's grip and forced himself to breathe.

"Now." Klyd splashed restively back and forth as he spoke, his voice tense but coldly deliberate. "The fluctuating fields attracted my attention as I rode by on my way home. I found you unconscious and brought you in for treatment. When you are fully recovered, I will offer you freedom. If I don't have a good lead on the girl by then, you'll have to refuse to leave. Give me a good reason you wouldn't want to return!"

"Uh . . . I'm wanted by the law for . . . say, a murder I didn't commit?"

"Very well, then." The Sime came toward Valleroy with that disturbing swiftness so characteristic of his race. "This is going to hurt. But worse than that, it is going to frighten you senseless. Are you certain you still want to go?"

"Are you certain there's no other way to get there?"

"Yes."

"What are you going to do to him?" asked Hawkins.

"Kill him . . . almost. It is unfortunate you force this task on me tonight of all nights, but that can't be helped. I shall do my best, and you, Mr. Valleroy, must aid me by restraining your fear. You may expect to be unconscious for about three hours, and when you awaken you will not feel well."

Valleroy tried to subdue the wild pounding of his heart. His hand found the starred-cross, the talisman that had protected his mother as she fled Sime Territory. Valleroy was empiricist enough not to doubt its power to protect him against Sime attack. While he had faith in the starred-cross, he couldn't be hurt.

Klyd held out one steady hand in a matter-of-fact gesture that lulled Valleroy's distrust. An attacking Sime, hungry for a Gen's selyn—the very biologic energy of

15

life itself—didn't ask consent before moving in for the kill.

For a moment, Valleroy felt a strange confidence in the channel. Before that feeling could fade, the Sime's rain-slicked hands gripped Valleroy's wrists. Then hot tentacles twined around his forearms, pulled him forward until his lips met the hard-set Sime mouth.

Valleroy felt himself being pulled inside out. His every nerve was afire with rushing sparks of pain that left blackness in their wake . . . as if his soul was being sucked from his body into a vast black void!

He struggled to pull away, to bring up his knife. But any Sime can call up the strength of ten Gens. Valleroy was immobilized. Only his will could resist the forceful stripping of his vitality . . . surely to death.

He did resist. With all that he could summon, he strove to master that frightful outpouring. For an instant, he thought he did breast that current and seize control of it. But then it burst loose once more, sweeping him on rising tide of sparkling terror.

The last thing he remembered was Klyd's voice anxiously calling his name . . . over . . . and over . . . . and over. . . .

CHAPTER TWO

The Arensti Competition

VALLEROY FELT HIMSELF LYING ON SOMETHING FIRM BUT warm and dry.

A pungent sting in his nostrils. Hospital.

Warm light played on his eyelids. Then a voice, low but insistent in a penetrating, almost hypnotic way. A special voice that seemed to soak into his mind carrying with it an undeniable truth. "You can wake up now. You're safe. You're with friends."

Klyd's voice. It was Klyd's voice—but, Valleroy reminded himself fuzzily, mustn't recognize him.

Carefully, he opened his eyes, squinting against the bright sunlight that streamed through an open window and caromed off polished cabinets. Sunlight? He must have been out more than ten hours instead of three!

He thought of trying to get up, but he couldn't move. His whole body was a mass of pain that left him weak.

A slim girl moved to close the drapes, plunging the room into bearable dimness.

Now, Valleroy saw there were other Simes among the Gens in the room. It was hard to tell the Simes from the Gens unless their forearms are bare like Klyd's. His eyes fastened on Klyd's arms and hands. He did have to feign his reaction. He'd never actually seen Sime tentacles so close, and the reality sent his skin crawling.

Six tentacles to each forearm, two "dorsal" along the top, two "ventral" along the bottom, and smaller ones, laterals, always sheathed except in selyn transfer, along each side. Retracted, they lay along the forearms from the elbow to wrist like ropes of gnarled muscle. But when extended they were like pearly-gray snakes, supple, muscular, and hypnotically fascinating.

As Valleroy stared, heart pounding faster and faster, Klyd sheathed his tentacles and shifted the glass he held to his fingers. Then he proffered the opalescent liquid. "Drink this. You'll be feeling better soon, though you gave us a hard night."

"Who are you?"

"Sectuib Klyd Farris of Householding Zeor. I found you unconscious in the mud and brought you here hoping we could save you. Please accept my hospitality." He offered the glass again, softening the lines of his face with the barest hint of a smile.

Valleroy hesitated once more before reaching out to take the glass. But even if it killed him, it would be a welcome relief, so he took the glass murmuring an appropriate gratitude in Simelan. This raised eyebrows all around the room, but didn't keep the Sime girl who had closed the drapes from moving to help Valleroy sit up to drink.

While gulping the vile-tasting potion, Valleroy noted how well arranged the scene was. Simes and Gens mixed freely as they went about the chorus of tidying up the treatment room. The message was graphically clear—these Simes didn't kill Gens. There was very little else in the room he could understand. There were workbenches and glass-fronted cabinets filled with strange objects and weirdly shaped containers. He said, "I've heard about places like this, but I never really believed they existed. You people are—channels?"

"Some of us, yes." Klyd gestured, tentacles carefully sheathed. "Drink it all down, Mr. . . . ?"

"Valleroy. Hugh Valleroy."

"May I call you Hugh?" Klyd hooked a knee over the corner of the wheeled table on which Valleroy lay.

"You saved my life. Guess that entitles."

"The obligation is mine," Klyd said gravely. "You speak Simelan?"

"Only a little." And that was true enough, thought Valleroy. Except for interrogating prisoners, he hadn't spoken the language socially since his mother's death. And before that, only in secret moments when they were alone.

"Evahnee speaks a little of your language." Klyd gestured to the Sime girl who had closed the draperies. "I will place her in charge of you until you are well enough to leave."

"Sectuib," called one of the Gens approaching. He was a white-haired teddy bear of a man, ageless in the way Valleroy had always pictured his unknown grandfathers.

"What is it, Charnye?"

"Sectuib, you should go now. You should have gone hours ago!"

"So you've been saying. All night. But I'm required here."

"Not any more. Denrau must be worried frantic by now. You're more than nine hours overdue!"

"Ten and a half. But I'm all right."

With a short bark of gentle derision, Charnye seized one of Klyd's hands and pointed to the laterals . . . the tentacles along the sides of your arm. "Just look!"

Valleroy could see nothing odd, but apparently the others could for it embarrassed Klyd. The channel repossessed his arm and buried it in the folds of his cloak. "I know, but . . ."

"Go, Klyd. You had a bad time last month. You owe yourself. Next to me, Denrau is the best Companion in Zeor. You shouldn't make him wait."

"You don't give me orders, Naztehr."

"I do when you're in need! Why *are* you still here?

18

You're acting as guilty as if you'd burned him yourself!"

Valleroy saw Klyd stiffen at that, but the Sime covered it with a laugh. "Don't be ridiculous! Have I *ever* hurt anyone?"

"I didn't say you burned him. I said you're acting as if you had. You can't even hear straight any more. You ought to go."

Klyd rose as if aching in every joint. "Charnye, I feel responsible because it happened inside the borders of Zeor. Our situation is precarious enough as is. I don't want to lose this Gen. He could be the key to preventing Gen raids from across the river. But if he dies . . ."

"He's not in danger any more . . . though it *is* a miracle."

"True."

"So, go. You're responsible for the rest of us, too, remember. We'll need your strength tomorrow." He glanced at the window. "Today, I mean."

"Evahnee," called Klyd. "Take good care of our guest." To Valleroy, he smiled and said in English, "She is not a channel, but she is trustworthy. You will be very low-field during the next month, which means you couldn't entice a Sime to attack you if you wanted to. Rest with us securely." He strode away without a backward glance, obviously in a hurry now that he was free to go.

So thought Valleroy, a bit surprised at his ability to follow the conversation, Klyd had been in need last night! No wonder he'd seemed nervous! Even the channels who could take selyn from a Gen without killing and then "channel" it to an ordinary Sime so that the Sime didn't feel the need to kill . . . even a channel experienced a personal need for selyn, the energy of life that only the Gen body produced. And when in need, the channel was even more dangerous than the ordinary Sime—to everyone except the highly trained Companions. Valleroy felt lucky to be alive!

On the third morning, they removed the safety rails and, for the first time, he took an interest in his surroundings.

The room was about fifteen feet square, with ample closets and a private bath. In the corner near the window was a small, friendly radiator that worked night and day to keep the early autumn chill out of the air. The walls were lavishly adorned with hand-crafted needle-work, some pieces large enough to be called tapestries. One, in particular, pheasants in an autumn meadow with the buildings of Zeor in the background, spoke to the artist in Valleroy.

He read in it a deeply abiding reverance for Zeor's place in nature's scheme, and his eye returned to it again and again, searching deeper into its meaning. It seemed to Valleroy that the artist had loved Zeor with an intensity far too great to express . . . *painfully* great When he asked about it, Evahnee told him that it was a picture of Zeor done by a woman who was dying of an incurable disease. Comparing the picture with the map Evahnee provided, Valleroy decided Zeor had grown since that artist's time.

On the fourth morning, he woke feeling strong enough to swing his legs off the bed, totter to the window, and peek out between the drapes. He was on the second floor of a four-storied building that overlooked a courtyard. On the far side of the court, a Gen was sweeping leaves into a pile while a Sime scooped them into a large sack.

A group of children erupted from the doorway and scattered across the court, disappearing through other doorways. Some of them lugged musical instrument cases half their own size with an earnest determination. They bore these burdens as if they were illustrious status symbols untouchable by lesser mortals. The scene evoked memories of other autumns spent peering from other windows at well-scrubbed schoolchildren. The lucky ones. The silence that bloomed in their wake echoed louder and louder in Valleroy's ears. And, suddenly, he knew he was going to faint.

As his knees buckled, Evahnee's arms took his weight. A moment later, he found himself back in bed, where he lay too exhausted to wonder how she happened to be there at just that moment.

The next morning, the children's voice drew him irresistibly to the window, but he made it back to bed under his own power. For reward, he was allowed to sit up in a chair for an hour after lunch.

By the fifth day, he was making regualr trips to the bathroom without any trouble as long as he took his medicine on time. And on the sixth morning, he woke

20

feeling perfectly normal, but raveously hungry. His door was ajar as usual, so he poked his head out into the corridor.

The rich mosaic floor sparkled as if freshly scrubbed. A chemical tang hung in the air. At intervals between book-lined alcoves, showcases displayed everything from pre-Sime artifacts to models made by the schoolchildren. But there was nobody in sight.

Valleroy slipped into the robe they'd given him and padded down the hallway. At the end, it widened into a turquoise-floored reception area facing a high wrought-iron gate very like the entrance to a mental ward. To his right, another corridor branched off, while to his left, tall deep-set window slits filtered sunlight onto the cheerful-looking mosaic floor.

Halfway down the branching corridor, a door slid open. A wheeled stretcher surrounded by attendants emerged and glided past Valleroy. As the attendants opened the wrought-iron gate, Valleroy caught a glimpse of that patient: pale, semiconscious face, Sime arms carefully laced into restraining devices along the sides of the stretcher, pungent reek of a multitude of medications. Then the procession passed through the gate, and was gone.

"Hugh!"

"Evahnee!" In one glance, Valleroy took in the stained smock and disheveled hair. She must have been up all night with that poor fellow.

"I apologize," she said softly. "I know it's late, but Hrel has had such a hard night."

"That's all right. I've been fine." There was so much more he wanted to say—to ask—but he just couldn't find the words!

"Go back to your room, and I'll bring breakfast."

"Can I help?"

"You can permit me to eat with you."

"Yes, please do." Valleroy mulled that over. He'd meant could he help to prepare the food. He went back to his room and checked the notes he kept of their language sessions. By the time she arrived with the trays, he had found his error and constructed a speech that he rehearsed nervously while they ate.

For some strange reason, he found himself acutely self-conscious before the girl. For the first time, he was aware of her as a woman, not just a nurse. It

21

made him feel gross and clumsy next to her delicate, Sime grace.

It was a new feeling for Valleroy, who was neither large nor awkward. He stood nearly six feet tall, weighing a hundred eighty pounds, mostly well-conditioned muscle. His skin was weathered to a light brown that almost matched his hair. He knew he was handsome in a rugged sort of way, and he could pass for a rancher or a Border Guard as long as he kept his long-fingered tapering hands out of sight.

It was those hands that usually attracted more attention than his rather common features. They appeared to be grafted onto the heavy-boned, square wrists, and were really better suited to a Sime body. One of the first things Valleroy had noticed about the nurses and attendants who cared for him in Zeor was that neither the Simes nor the Gens ever stared at his hands.

Even now, as they ate together, Evahnee watched his face, not his hands. This somehow gave him courage to try out his speech. "Evahnee, I am well now. I would like to see—Sectuib Farris—and find some way to repay all of you."

"No, you are not well yet. You must stay at least another week. You still require medicine."

"I have no money. I could never repay such a debt."

"You owe us nothing. We are obligated to you because you were injured on our land."

In spite of her simplified wording, Valleroy was forced to say, "I don't understand." It had become his most useful stock phrase.

She repeated her sentence more slowly, emphasizing each word with graceful gestures of her tentacles. Somehow, Valleroy discovered the sinuous amplifications no longer repelled or frightened him but seemed to add meaning to the words.

"I meant," he interjected, "I do not understand why you are still obligated to me when I have received food, shelter, and constant care for almost a week. I work for my bread."

"But you are not fully recovered."

"I feel recovered."

"Only while you take the *fosebine*." She pushed a glass of the opalescent liquid toward him, and he downed it obediently.

22

"But if I feel well, isn't there something I can do to earn . . ."

"Sectuib has called you guest."

"But that was when I was . . ." He indicated the bed, not knowing how to say "flat on my back." "He seemed like a very nice man." Inwardly, Valleroy groaned. He sounded like a five-year-old! "If I could talk to him again, perhaps we could agree on some payment."

"Hugh, Sectuib is a very very busy person . . . *all* the time. You can't just walk into his office and expect to claim his attention. You must have an appointment."

Valleroy gnashed his teeth in frustration. He had to see Klyd and get started on the search for Aisha. "How can I get an appointment?"

Evahnee gave him a "Don't be ridiculous" look that stung him into blurting indignantly, "If I am guest, who is host?"

"Sectuib, of course."

"Out there," he said, gesturing toward Gen Territory in unconscious imitation of the Sime idiom, "a host usually sees his guests occasionally."

She peered at him closely for a moment, and then drew back, stifling a giggle. "I shall try to attract your host's attention. Such a joke just might succeed. But, remember, Sectuib is"—she groped in the air as if seeking the words—"well, he's . . . Sectuib! In many other Houses, the lesser channels carry much of the routine burden. But Klyd works dispensary every day so that each of us gets a turn with him every few months. And his touch is like . . ." She trailed off, enraptured by a distant vision of paradise.

Valleroy prompted, "Like what?"

"Oh," she said shaking her head sadly, "you wouldn't understand. But Klyd works harder than anybody else in Zeor. It's because of his touch that we are . . . what we are." She departed, leaving Valleroy seething with lonely impatience for the rest of the day.

On the one hand, he was a guest. But on the other, he was effectively imprisoned despite the unlocked door because of the role he must play. He'd been advised . . . no warned . . . not to stray too far from his room without a guide. A rescued Gen casualty wouldn't go on a snooping tour.

As the afternoon wore on, he took his language notebook to the window and sketched the mingled

23

groups of Simes and Gens as they swept back and forth across the courtyard. He tried to capture the singular atmosphere of the Householding, using Klyd's distinctive features—aquiline nose, sensitive lips, concerned brow, intense chin and jaw line—to form the outlines of the scene. The result left him dissatisfied. He tore the page to bits with growing resentment of his helplessness.

Savagely, he drew a grotesque Klyd with horns and tail, donkey ears and a goatee. He added a cariacture of himself thumbing his nose with a taunting sneer. The pencil snapped in half between his fingers. He ripped the sketch to shreds.

Tomorrow, he resolved grimly, he would force the lofty Sectuib Farris to talk to him! The channel had been badly scared that their working relationship might be discovered. That was ammunition. Valleroy intended to use it . . . if necessary.

With that decision made, he settled down to an earnest cram session with his language notes. Simelan was not quite cognate to Valleroy's native English. The syntax was often bewildering, especially in the passive voice. This, the grammar books said, was the result of the different way Simes perceive reality. But even with all their differences, Simes were still basically human. Their most frequently used vocabulary concerned ordinary human matters. With the years of formal study in the Federal Police and his childhood background, Valleroy was able to gather most of the meaning off the pages of a fifth-grade history text he found on the hall shelves.

The book told the story of the Sime wars very differently than Valleroy had learned it in school. According to the Simes, it was the Gens who caused the disintegration of the world civilization of the Ancients. The Gens had been unreasonable about surrendering themselves to the pens. So the sniping and pillage had gone on for hundreds of years, destroying almost all the Ancient artifacts and obliterating most of the Ancient knowledge. Only the Simes had gathered, cherished, and passed on some fragments of the old culture in spite of the beastly non-men who tried to exterminate them.

Puzzled, Valleroy flipped pages rapidly. Such prejudice seemed foreign to the concept of the Householdings. He found the back half of the book taken up with the same account told from a different point of view. Before the channels had arisen, Simes couldn't understand that Gens were people. Since there were still so few channels, most Simes still have to depend on the kill to survive, so they *had* to deny Gens the franchise. They *had* to ignore the fact that Gens had rebuilt portions of the world from which they'd scoured most of the Simes and established the territories.

Valleroy read on, intently absorbed now that he'd discovered the book was a comparison of two views. He'd never been totally satisfied with the history taught in the Gens' schools, which he'd attended sporadically. He'd learned to keep his mouth shut to avoid getting thrown out of such schools, but he never learned to believe all he was told.

Most of what he read now, he couldn't quite understand, but it opened vistas of thought about the Simes and the causes of the sudden, catastrophic mutation rate that had destroyed the Ancient world.

By the time Evahnee brought his evening medication, Valleroy was filled with new ideas, and he was even more eager to go out among these strange people to see how they applied their ideals to daily living.

"How have you been, Hugh?"

"Fine but . . . alone."

"Lonely?"

"Yes, that's the word. Have you seen Klyd?"

"Seen, yes. All day."

"Then you arranged it for me?"

"Sorry. No time." She dropped onto the foot of his bed as if she hadn't sat down in hours. "I shouldn't be here now, but I expect to have a few minutes."

"Busy?"

"We are working with a new member who is entering his final disjunction crisis, and you know what that"s like!"

"I do? I mean, I don't."

"You saw us take him down the hall this morning. You've been hearing him all day."

"Some noise, that's all. What's . . . disjunction?" What he'd been hearing sounded like a private quarrel.

Evahnee frowned at him for a moment, and then she laughed as much at herself as at him. "Odd. I'd forgotten you aren't one of us."

25

"Thank you," said Valleroy. For a moment, he thrilled to the idea that he could pass for one of them, but he pushed his reaction aside. "I still don't know what is disjun . . . whatever you said."

"Disjunction. The separation of a Sime from the kill. There *is* a fundamental difference between killing a Gen for selyn and taking transfer from a channel instead . . . at least so I'm told. I've never killed so I wouldn't know. But judging by our candidates' symptoms, it must be quite a difference."

Valleroy drained the medicine and then spent ten minutes on vocabulary before he felt he understood. "I see now. The Simes who live in the Householdings never kill Gens. And any Sime who wants to . . . be adopted . . . has to disjunct?"

"That's the test for any Sime candidate."

"What's the test for Gens?"

"No test. Merely to donate through the channels."

Valleroy nodded. Might seem trivial to her, but she couldn't know how the very idea petrified a Gen. And, thought Valleroy, if he had to stay here a month or more, he'd have to donate too.

Suddenly, a ragged scream echoed down the hall. Shouts rose over the noise. "Sectuib Farris! Somebody get Sectuib! Hurry!"

Evahnee jumped to her feet. "I *knew* I shouldn't have left!" She dashed into the corridor, Valleroy right on her heels. Together, they pelted down the hall and skidded to a stop opposite the grilled gate. A tiny knot of Simes on the other side of the grille stared up at a Sime who sat astride the top of the barrier. Among the commands being shouted up at the man, Valleroy deciphered only an occasional "Don't!" and "Wait!"

Presently, a mixed troup of Simes and Gens pounded from the side corridor with Klyd leading. The channel slid to a stop, looking up at the fugitive. Instantly, everyone fell silent.

The Sime perched atop the gate looked down at Klyd. Slowly, the channel straightened, as if thoroughly in command of the situation now. He motioned to the group around him, and a Gen girl glided out to stand in the open between Klyd and the gate, but a little to one side so that the three of them formed a slim triangle.

The fugitive's eyes riveted on the girl, who returned his gaze calmly. She was about the same age as Evahnee maybe twenty, attractive in a lean way, with coarse hands that bespoke hard work. He was small and wiry like most Simes, but had unusually blond hair that glistened in the dim light.

Klyd stepped forward raising his hands, laterals partially extended in invitation. "To me, Hrel. You can't hurt me. Come. Come to me."

Klyd continued his soft but insistent coaxing in that penetrating, professional voice. Hrel's face crumpled in an agony of indecision. Every time the channel drew Hrel's attention, he eyes drifted back to the girl, his obvious preference. Nobody moved as the three stared at each other, the girl calmly, the Sime hungrily, the channel persuasively.

Measuring the distances with his eye, Valleroy figured the Sime could leap onto the girl and have her dead by the time anybody else could react.

Klyd took another tiny step forward. "*I* can do it, Hrel. But you must choose me."

Feral eyes darted from Klyd to the girl, obviously wanting her but wishing he wanted Klyd. Seeing Hrel shift his weight preparing to spring, Valleroy unconsciously tensed to leap to her defense.

Klyd stood his ground, apparently relaxed. The girl waited without so much as blinking.

In a flash, Hrel was on the floor beside her, tentacles unsheathed and reaching for her! None of the witnesses moved. With effort, Valleroy checked his half-prepared lunge. The girl remained steady, neither welcoming nor retreating.

Hrel froze in mid-motion, tearing his eyes from his devised victim to see that Klyd was still there, hands outstretched, tentacles ready. Stiff-legged, Hrel jerked around and hurled himself toward the channel. Klyd's laterals twined about Hrel's and their lips met.

Valleroy wanted to watch the transfer, but Evahnee grabbed him by the shoulders and spun him around in a joyful dance while bedlam broke loose among the witnesses. Somebody swung the grilled gate open, and before he knew it Valleroy was sucked into the center of a wild celebration. One moment he was dragging chairs out of a closet, another he was spreading a banquet on a buffet table almost as long as the corridor.

Impromptu musicians tuned up exotic Sime instruments,

and somebody created a throne out of a table, a chair and a bedspread.

Bottles were opened. Somebody pressed a glass into Valleroy's hand. Then the triumphal procession entered while the musicians produced a sonorous tune, and the onlookers chanted. Ceremoniously, they installed Hrel on the throne. He seemed a bit dazed by it all, but he essayed a brave smile.

From the back of the group, somebody yelled, "Go on, Sectuib. He's ours!" Amid a chorus of affirmatives, Klyd vaulted onto the table and kneeled before the seated figure, offering a strip of ornately embroidered cloth draped over his hands. An almost tangible silence swept through the onlookers.

Hrel stretched his own hands out to join Klyd's under the cloth. Then Hrel lifted the symbol, displaying it to all those watching silently. At last, he draped it around Klyd's neck like a mantle and raised the channel to his feet. It was a clear act of acceptance of the channel's authority.

Pandemonium burst loose. From somewhere, coarsely woven replicas of Klyd's embroidered mantle were passed out. On close inspection, Valleroy could see it was the same pattern that bordered all the linens he'd been using here. The Householding crest.

A snake dance started in the center of the crowd, now so close-packed there wasn't room for a deep breath. A red-haired Sime girl flipped one of the replica cloths around Valleroy's neck and sealed the investiture with a brief but passionate kiss before he had a chance to be startled. Then she was gone into the swirling throng.

"Quiet! Wait a minute! Quiet!" It was Klyd calling out from his place on the table while Hrel stood beside him.

Silence welled up, drowning the merrymaking. Klyd continued, "Evahnee! Do you have the ring?"

She wriggled forward to present the crest ring to the channel, who promptly slipped it onto Hrel's little finger, calling loudly, "Unto the House of Zeor, forever!" Hrel repeated the phrase with just as much fervor.

In unison, the crowd took up the cry. "Unto the House of Zeor, forever!" Soon it became a chant, and the musicians added a strong rhythm that triggered the snake dance once more. Valleroy was sucked into it as the whole room seemed to be dancing.

From the door, a shout went up. "Clear the way! Space here! Move over!"

The dancing stopped while a Sime holding a tripod high over the heads of the crowd sidled into the room. He reached a point in front of the improvised dais, set up the tripod and attached a black box to it.

All at once, Valleroy knew what it was. He pushed and showed his way through the crowd, forgetting for the moment his wariness of the Simes. This he had to see! One of the legendary *cameras* of the Ancients. The Simes *had* resurrected some of the old arts . . . but *this . . . !*

After some careful preparation, the Sime instructed Hrel to pose. With a theatrical flourish, the . . . *photographer* . . . worked a lever.

Nothing happened.

Puzzled, the Sime bent over his box, tentacles flying. But after repeated failures, he announced, "Sorry, no pictures tonight!"

The disappointment of the crowd was almost palpable as the tripod was carried away.

Klyd called, "Hugh! Step over here a minute!"

Surprised at the sound of his native language after so many days, Valleroy slid through an opening. Klyd squatted down on the edge of the table. "Hugh, can you do a quick portrait of Hrel and me together? Just a sketch, nothing exacting."

"Sure, but I don't have anything to work with."

"That can be arranged." He stood up. "Evahnee, get a sketching board from the mill's drafting room. Hugh's going to make the portrait of us."

This set off a cheer that threatened to raise the roof, but presently another snake dance was started all around the throne. The songs took on a note of restrained ecstasy with the word "Zeor" repeated like an ardent plea.

A long time later, when Valleroy had decided they'd forgotten about the portrait in the wild emotional catharsis, several Simes manhandled a large drafting table into the room and set it up before the dais. Evahnee seated Valleroy on the bench with a cabinet of supplies at his left hand. "If there's anything else you need, just ask."

Valleroy kneaded his fingers wondering if he'd had too much to drink. Gingerly, he selected a likely looking piece of charcoal. The coarse paper was crosshatched with oddly patterened drafting lines. He turned the paper over and clipped it in place. The reverse was clear of lines, but very grainy. After several false starts, he found a charcoal soft enough to serve him, and then it went quickly.

As he sketched, the room seemed to shrink into the lighted bubble containing only himself and his subjects. He gave himself to the task in a euphoria of exquisite satisfaction, as if the frustrated creativity of years was suddenly pouring forth, relieving a tension he hadn't known was there. The joy of these people stirred something deep inside him, filling him until he knew he had to get it down on paper or die trying.

At last, the composition complete, Valleroy sat staring at it as if hypnotized. Klyd's voice pried gently into his reverie. "May we see?"

"Oh!" Valleroy jerked the page off and handed it up by a corner. "Don't smear it."

Klyd showed it to Hrel and then held it up for everyone to see. The gasps of appreciation were a more tribute than gold could have been to Valleroy. Someone started to applaud. Hesitantly, the others picked it up. Soon the room was filled with the roaring sound. Tears started to Valleroy's eyes.

Klyd beckoned the artist up onto the table. Willing hands boosted him while Klyd hauled. His legs were still too shaky for climbing. As Valleroy stood up, the applause crested and then died away as if on cue.

Raising his voice in formal tones, Klyd proclaimed, "We shall have this hung in Memorial Hall!"

The applause started again but Klyd held up a hand, tentacles twined in the "wait-a-moment" sign. "Shall we invite the artist to design our entry in the Arensti Competition?"

The unanimous affirmative was deafening. Spontaneous celebrations started in every corner of the room and spread rapidly. Under cover of the roar, Klyd said, "You may thank the photographer for this lucky break. Now you can stay as long as you like without question. I have twenty operatives out checking leads, but not a hint of your Aisha. This could take quite a while."

Valleroy hissed through his teeth, "Aisha may not *have* quite a while! We've got to discuss strategy. I want to get out and do some work."

"You can't. Not for at least another week." He put both hands on Valleroy's shoulders, whispering, "Hugh, God help me, Hugh, I hurt you much worse than I'd intended. If you can never forgive me, I will understand. But my House is yours until you are ready to leave." He fingered the cloth around Valleroy's neck and chuckled. "You see? They think you've joined us. An honest mistake. But you *are* welcome here. Now that Hrel has disjuncted, we have room for another Gen."

Valleroy brushed that aside, a cold rage building. "You brought me here because I *care* about Aisha. I thought that entitled me to look for her with my own eyes!"

"There isn't anything you could *do* right now."

"How do you know till I've tried? I came here to work!"

"Get hold of yourself, Hugh," whispered Klyd fiercely. "You're broadcasting anger, but this is a gathering of joy. The Sime Government may have spies in this very room who'd just love to discredit a channel for disloyalty as well as 'perversion'!"

Evahnee's voice lifted above the crowd. "Hugh! Would you sketch us too?"

"Go, Hugh. As our Arensti Designer, you'll be able to travel with me to the competition . . ."

"And just when will that be?"

"It's only eight weeks away now."

"Eight *weeks!*" Valleroy spat through a wooden smile. "When every minute counts, how can you . . ."

"Hugh," Klyd soothed, "we have no idea where to begin looking or even *if* she still lives. And we must search without telling anyone who we are looking for or why."

"You brought me here," gritted Valleroy, "to keep me from interfering! Well, I'll tell you . . ."

Evahnee's voice came again, concerned. "Hugh?" And she started toward them.

Fuming helplessly, Valleroy eased himself off the table and went to sketch Evahnee and the Gen girl who had offered herself to Hrel at the moment of decision.

As the praise for his work mounted, people formed lines to be sketched. It had been many ears since adulation had been lavished on him, and he reveled in it. But every few moments, cold guilt washed away the warmth of easy belonging as he thought of Aisha . . . out there,

31

captive in some filthy pen. He was an operative, and he had a role to play. He played it with a grim gaiety that was sometimes genuine.

With dawn paling the sky, Valleroy found himself drawing cartoons while Evahnee captioned them in Simelan. Jokes flew around the room leaving victims gasping in peals of hilarity. Most of the punch lines were obtusely Sime, and when Valleroy did laugh, he knew it was at the wrong thing . . . but laughter itself is infectious.

When it finally broke up, he was so exhausted Evahnee had to wheel him back to his room in a chair. He didn't remember getting into bed.

CHAPTER THREE

Felebo Ambrov Zeor, Martyr

DURING THE NEXT WEEK, VALLEROY WORKED AT A drafting table in the design room of the Householding factory. The buildings that housed the mills, factory, dye works, and plants of Zeor's industry were a separate complex located at some distance from the court residences.

Zeor, he discovered, made its living from weaving. Once a year, all the weavers in-Territory entered a designing contest, which was held at the city of Arensti, with the winner gaining not only prestige but also the greatest share of sales during that coming year.

As the Arensti Designer, Valleroy found himself in a position of great prestige within the Householding. He was moved from the infirmary to the bachelor's quarters, where he shared a suite with two Simes and a Gen. He was given clothes, blue coveralls with Zeor's crest neatly stitched over the breast pocket, and he was never asked if he was a visitor or a member, but simply treated as a member, though never addressed as such.

He found the innocent trust placed in him to be a serious burden on his conscience . . . so he worked relentlessly to produce a winning design. For hours at a time, he pored over the files of past Arsenti winners. He roamed all over the compound quizzing Simes on matters of taste and comparing their responses with the opinions of Household Gens. And he sketched. Often well into the early morning hours, he sketched.

And so it happened that he was returning from his drafting table in the factory complex late one morning. It was too late for breakfast, too early for lunch, and too beautiful a morning for sleeping, so he strolled out into a section of the grounds where he hadn't been before.

The nip of occasional mild frost had turned the leaves to vivid paeans of color that evoked poignant memories of lazy fall days spent roaming with Aisha. He had woven russet leaves into her shining black hair and painted her nude under cascades of bright-clothed branches. And he had loved her. Forever.

He walked down a tunnel roofed with arching branches and floored with fading color. Scuffing through heaps of leaves, he was almost able to feel her hand in his. The tree-lined path seemed to lead on to a promising future.

He tried to imagine what she would say if she were with him at this moment. He could almost hear her womanly voice filled with childlike wonder. "Where does the red in the leaves come from? Where does the green go to? Why do different leaves turn different colors? Why are some years prettier than others? Do you suppose," she would say, "the red is always there masked by the green—the touch of frost like the kiss of a Sime—and the red like the Sime in all of us, exposed to various degrees by our different responses to the kiss—and the beautiful years are only a preview of what all of us together may yet become?"

Valleroy stopped to find a bough bent low across the path. Were those his own thoughts muddled by the fatigue of a prolonged creative orgy? They'd never talked much about Simes, but her conventional Gen background had given her conventional Gen ideas. She couldn't understand Simes enough to analyze them like that. It was one reason he'd never been able to talk marriage to her . . . or to any girl he'd ever met.

But it was the kind of thing she *would* say . . . pointing out the congruencies between the physical universe and the realm of the spirit. It was the mystic in her that touched the artist in him and gave him such joy.

33

Each time they had quarreled, he had been driven to seek her out again . . . one more time . . . until he had decided he'd have to marry her. And when he went looking for her with this decision, he's found her gone . . . captured.

The emptiness hadn't eased until he'd immersed himself in Zeor's Arensti design. Here, he had found something that fed a part of him that had never been satisfied by police work. There were moments he wasn't sure he'd ever be able to leave Zeor, and there were moments he was frightened by the thought of staying.

Either way, he *had* to find Aisha. The urgent frustration grew to be a thing he shied away from. He kept telling himself there was nothing he could do but seek refuge in the creation of a winning Arensti design. But there was always the guilt that, while she suffered, he reveled in the unfolding discovery of Zeor and all its many-faceted meanings.

He snapped the bough aside and walked toward the hedge at the end of the tunnel. There was a small opening that led to a narrow, hedge-walled lane. Fresh cuttings were strewn over the leaves, and the painfully straight sides of the hedge still showed moist scars. The scent was intoxicating enough to draw him onward toward the sound of children's voices and the snic-snik of a sprinkler.

He came out through a trellis overhung with a mixture of grapes and berries, already partially harvested. The morning sun pierced Valleroy's eyes, achingly brilliant after the dewy shade.

The area before him was surrounded by a tall, freshly trimmed hedge. Throughout the grounds, dazzling greenhouses were being tended by groups of very active children who knew as much about what to do with a hose as did their Gen Territory counterparts.

Between the newly erected greenhouses, traces of summer crops could still be seen. It was a perfectly normal school garden, Valleroy told himself. Yet it was hard to believe.

All the greenhouses he'd ever seen had been enclosed by panels of glass, but these were covered with sheets of some flexible transparent miracle of Sime chemistry.

Agape, Valleroy watched a team of children directed by a heavily pregnant woman. The children wielded hammers and cutters with a professional dedication as they

34

stretched the sheeting over the frames. These children were older than some of the other groups about the enclosure. Valleroy judged them about the age of changeover, the point at which a child became either an adult Sime or an adult Gen.

In Gen Territory, children of this pre-puberty age were not trusted with hammers, nails, knives, and other dangerous tools. But here, he'd learned, children matured quickly and were ready to assume the responsibilities of an adult just after changeover into a Sime or "establishment," as the Simes termed the beginning of selyn production in the adult Gen.

Curious about this group of children on the brink of every child's greatest fear, Valleroy approached their supervisor. The Householding naturally chose the most competent teacher for this critical age group, so it came as no surprise when he recognized the pregnant woman as Klyd's wife, Yenava.

She was a tall, solidly built Gen with the strikingly handsome features of the Ancients, young and tanned, and *alive*.

Valleroy stopped a few yards away to watch while two boys cut the last piece of the flexible glazing and nailed it into place as if it were canvas. He gathered his courage and approached Yenava. "Excuse me . . ."

She turned to him with an instantaneous smile so genuine it made Valleroy want to reach for a sketch pad. Instead he said, "I'm Hugh Valleroy . . ."

"Yes, the Arensti Designer. Can I help you?"

"I'd like to ask an . . . awkward . . . question."

"I'll answer as best I can."

Valleroy cleared his throat and spoke low enough that the children wouldn't hear. "I notice a difference in the children here from those . . . uh . . . out-Territory. I was wondering if perhaps they know whether they'll be Sime or Gen?"

She laughed, a spontaneous, delicate laugh, not *at* him but in surprise. "No, of course not. A child is a child."

There was something classically beautiful about the way she folded her hands over her own child-to-be and regarded those nearly grown ones in her care. "We train them all, equally, in the techniques of surviving changeover. They have nothing to fear, one way or the other. Perhaps that is the difference you see?"

Valleroy didn't have a chance to answer, then or

35

ever. It was almost two weeks later and miles away as a fugitive trapped in an icy cave that he had a chance to think through what she had said.

At that moment, a knot of boys emerged from the completed greenhouse supporting one of their number between them. The invalid's face was pale enough that, at first, Valleroy thought he'd been injured and was going into shock. But Yenava went calmly to the group and took the patient's arm, her long fingers probing with sensitive competence.

Then she flashed that dazzling smile at the boy and said, "Congratulations, Rual!"

Still hanging limply between his classmates' arms, Rual managed a brave smile and a strangled whisper that barely carried to Valleroy. "Unto Zeor, forever!" Then he was catastrophically sick all over his teacher's shoes.

Retreating hastily, Yenava called to one of the Sime teachers supervising a younger class who were filling pots with soil. The Sime woman made a complex gesture with four tentacles entwined and said something to her class that evoked a cheer. She took a moment to get them back to work. Then she came toward the suffering boy, who was now seated on the ground nursing stomach cramps.

As if nothing extraordinary were happening, she said, "Yenava, how are you?"

"How could I be unwell on such a beautiful day?"

"Good enough. You know," she said, looking at the stricken boy, "your science class seems to have all the luck."

"I've noticed that. Must be the time of day." She looked thoughtfully at Rual. "Arriss, do you think we should ask Klyd to come out?"

A little more concerned now, Arriss kneeled beside the boy. "Feel better yet?"

"No," he gasped. "Why doesn't it stop?"

Valleroy could see beads of sweat forming on the boy's face. His own stomach seemed to be knotting in sympathy. He was a little surprised at himself, calmly watching a beginning changeover, a scene that had always gone very differently at the Gen schools he'd attended. The Sime overtaken by changeover while among Gens was doomed.

Arriss's well-trained fingers and tentacles probed all over Rual's body. Something she did made him vomit

36

again, so she held his head until the heaving subsided. Then she turned to one of his companions. "Get Sectuib. It might be an arrest."

The two women conferred again while the class went back to their tasks as if this happened every day. It probably did, thought Valleroy. The teachers were discussing pregnancy and childbirth rather than changeover while the victim himself appeared to be enjoying the surreptitious glances he was getting from his envious peers.

The morning shadows had grown six inches shorter by the time Klyd arrived followed only by Denrau, the Gen who served as his personal donor and official Companion. The channel threw the boy a searching glance, but stopped to speak to his wife first. "This is much too hard on you."

"I like fresh air, and I like to keep busy."

Klyd's voice dropped to an intense whisper that Valleroy barely overheard. The channel's attention was so totally for his wife alone that it was as if the two of them were isolated in a bubble of privacy. "We'll talk about it later. I don't want you overworking, and that's final!"

"And who's going to take my place?" Her whisper matched his.

"Zeor will survive, somehow." He kissed her firmly on the lips, a passionate tenderness betrayed by one quivering tentacle that brushed her cheek. It lasted the briefest moment, and then he was at his patient's side, intent with concern as if nobody else existed in his world.

Denrau positioned a field kit beside the patient, and the two experts went to work. They repeated the poking and prodding the others had subjected Rual to. Then they progressed to measurements with instruments unlike any Valleroy had ever seen. Under Klyd's soothing voice, Rual's suppressed nervousness disappeared. The channel's patience and confidence never wavered when the boy's attempts to follow directions only resulted in more heaving spasms, this time accompanied by much more pain.

Three times Klyd had the boy drink down some pink liquid that reminded Valleroy unpleasantly of his own medication. Three times the pink liquid came back mixed with the remains of breakfast. The fourth time the channel tried an orange-colored wafer.

As they waited to see if the wafer would stay down

and take effect, the science classes were gathered by their teachers and marched out in orderly lines laughing and shouting enviously as they passed their fallen classmate. When Klyd turned to glance at them, they straightened immediately into solemn angels murmuring, "Good morning, Sectuib."

They waited another few minutes after the last class disappeared through the arbor. Finally satisfied that the wafer would stay down, Klyd helped Rual to his feet while Denrau closed the first-aid kit.

Rual, unlike any changeover victims Valleroy had ever seen before, seemed in perfect control of himself. With only a little help from Denrau's steadying hand, he walked toward the arbor, head high, but legs trembling. Klyd paused beside Valleroy to say, "You ought to sleep."

"What about Aisha? Can she sleep peacefully?"

"No word yet. I'm doing everything that can be done, so there's no reason you shouldn't sleep."

"How would you feel if it were Yenava out there?"

Klyd raked him with a glance that seemed to strip his brain of its very memories. Then the channel did an odd thing. He shot out a hand, one lateral tentacle probing along Valleroy's neck, behind the ear. At the same time, Valleroy felt a strange buzzing in his ears.

Before he had time to move, the tentacle was gone, leaving in its wake only a hot streak on the Gen skin. Klyd dropped his hand self-consciously. "I'm sorry. But I had to know. It's comforting to have one's guesses confirmed."

As if retreating from a dreadful embarrassment, Klyd took off for the arbor at a brisk walk. Valleroy couldn't catch up without running, so he let the channel go. It *was* time he went to bed, at least for a few hours.

He paced back along the tree-lined path, but the spell of the autumn leaves was broken. It wasn't until well after sundown that he got back to work.

As the days passed, he decided his design would capture the essence of Householding Zeor. He struggled to define that essence. There was pride, yes, but a fluorescent pride masking a self-righteous defiance of Sime society's rejection of the channels and their way of life. Valleroy depicted this with sharp, bright colors.

The people of Zeor had built a wall around their thoughts, accepting members of other Householdings but not Simes who killed or Gens who refused to donate.

This was not, Valleroy discovered, without justification. Most Sime farmers wouldn't sell a Householding fresh produce or grain. Therefore, much of the Householding's effort went into farming, which forced them to turn their backs on Gens they could save because there was no way to feed them.

Valleroy depicted this conflict of the channels against prevailing Sime society with geometric lines forming a rigid pattern of three-dimensional hexagons very like a honeycomb. Here and there he allowed one hexagon to have bulging sides, as if stressed almost beyond endurance.

The detail work within each hexagon consisted of flows of color, some sharp, some pastel, and some brilliant but overlaid with pastel veils that blended the sharp differences into one another, denoting the unquestioning way Zeor had accepted him.

As he put the finishing touches on his final sketch, he wondered just how long that acceptance would last. He was still low-field. His body stored very little selyn to arose any passing Sime. But, he was a Gen, a generator of selyn, the essential energy of life. With each passing day his body produced and stored more selyn, increasing his selyn potential field. Two weeks more, and he would have to donate through Klyd or some other channel of the Householding who would then be able to transfer that selyn to an ordinary Sime whose body could not produce it.

Would he, Valleroy asked himself, be able to suppress his panic long enough to do it? He sat back to admire his design while one hand sought the starred-cross beneath his shirt. When facing a Sime, his mother had told him, you have nothing to fear but fear itself. The starred-cross will keep you safe, if you have faith in it.

Valleroy wasn't sure he had enough faith in the starred-cross, but he knew his design was a winner. It had a soothing depth, almost as if viewing fog-smeared city lights through a mesh fence, and was sure to please the eye of Sime and Gen alike whether they sought deeper meanings or not.

He placed the stiff paper-board into a folio case, tied it with a flourish, and set out for Klyd's office. It was only just dawn, but the channel would probably be at work.

Valleroy strode out of the factory complex, crossed

39

the small orchard on a brick pathway, and took a long hall passage through the buildings of the court. Frost crunched underfoot in mid-October chill, and he was glad to pass into the warmth of the main buildings.

He threaded his way through the maze of corridors expertly. He'd come this way many times. Often he found Klyd and Denrau followed by a swirling retinue. It was the pride of Zeor that here the Sectuib himself visited the aged, supervised, administrated, and settled quarrels. Yet this required him always to move in haste to get back to his main duties of collecting selyn from Gens and dispensing it to Simes who didn't have the channel's ability to draw slowly enough not to kill.

Yet, somehow, Klyd always managed to convey the illusion of unhurried concentration on each person he dealt with. For that moment, each suppliant became the most important person in all existence receiving the full attention of a Sectuib. It was, Valleroy learned, an exhilarating experience. Together with his skill at delegating authority, Klyd's knack with individuals was indeed what made Zeor great among the Householdings.

Valleroy couldn't deny that Sectuib Farris of Householding Zeor was a personage, capable, efficient, and busy. But today was Valleroy's day of reckoning. He'd been off medication for one whole day now, and still he felt as fit as ever. Today, he was going after Aisha . . . personally.

His steps echoed in the deserted corridors. Only the farmers working the harvest were up so early, and they had long since gone to the fields. Valleroy broke through the huge double doors that gave onto the courtyard he'd watched from his infirmary window. To his right, another door gave entrance to the building where Klyd worked . . . to his left, the infirmary and residences . . . straight ahead, the huge barred gates separating Zeor from the Sime city of Valzor. On this side of that high stone wall, the Householders were free to do as they chose. On the other side, any Gen not wearing collar chain and tags was fair game for a quick kill or to be sold to the pens. And out there, somewhere, on the other side of that wall—Aisha.

Valleroy breasted the wave of frigid air and plunged across the deserted court. Halfway to his goal, he heard a faint tapping sound. He stopped in his tracks, holding his breath. There was no wind to stir tree branches. But the tattoo came again, hardly more than a flutter.

Head cocked in concentration, Valleroy moved a few steps toward the outer wall and paused. Again it came, louder now. He moved toward the small postern gate at the left of the big gates. Again that pattering knock, but this time he detected deliberate urgency behind it, as if the knocker now perceived some one coming.

Propping his folio against the wall, Valleroy lifted the formidable bar that secured the outside door against Berserkers or Sime Raiders. Then he yanked the door open, half afraid of what he'd find there.

The bloody scarecrow that staggered into his arms was less shocking than the scenes he'd imagined. Valleroy eased the limp figure onto the cobblestones, almost losing his grip in the slippery blood. Around the man's waist coiled one of the Sime Raider's whips complete with inlaid handle. It seemed to Valleroy a grotesque contrast to the tattered, Zeor-blue coverall.

The man's face and torso were covered with hundreds of lacerations, as if he'd tumbled down a gravel embankment. But, Valleroy saw, most of the blood was coming from his forearms. He peeled back the sleeves to find deeply slashed tentacle sheaths from which the blood spurted rhythmically, but not as profusely as it had. It slowed visibly as Valleroy watched.

"I'll get Sectuib Farris," said Valleroy in his most assuring voice, though he knew this man wouldn't see another dawn.

"Stay, Naztehr!" husked the Sime, marshaling all his strength.

Valleroy paused, transfixed by an odd thrill at the man's use of the most intimate Householding term of membership . . . the one thing he'd never been called before. He had to bend close to hear the faint whisper of dying breath. "Tell Klyd . . . Hrel spies for Andle . . . Aisha . . . with Runzi. . . ."

The blood-soaked form went limp, eyes glazed, and Valleroy knew the blood ceased its rhythmic spurting even before he looked. He stood, repeating those strange words . . . Andle, Runzi . . . over and over to himself, fearful of forgetting the message from the edge of the grave.

A door squeaked open behind him; boots clattered, and Valleroy turned to see Klyd running toward him across the court . . . the incredibly swift charge of a Sime in a hurry.

The channel slid to his knees beside the still form, anguish written in every muscle of his back, and a strangled groan escaped his sensitive lips.

Heedless of the caked and congealing blood, the channel took the slashed arms in his hands, tentacles exploring the wounds gently before he swore. "The filthy perverted sub-men! *Feleho!* I shouldn't have sent you. It was my fault . . . mine. . . ."

Valleroy watched helplessly as Klyd collapsed across the body, sobs wracking him from head to foot, tentacles still twined about the dead man's arms. Even a channel couldn't bring the dead to life.

Stepping around the channel, Valleroy closed the outer door, sliding the bar into place with a resounding thud. It gave him no feeling of safety.

He turned just in time to see Klyd stumbling toward a sewer grating where he retched violently. Recalling the first time he'd seen a bloody corpse, Valleroy went to his aid.

"No," said Klyd, pulling himself erect. "I'm all right."

"I've seen uglier corpses," said Valleroy.

"So have I, but didn't you see what they *did* to him?"

"Cut a few arteries . . ."

"Arteries! *That* he could have survived. But the laterals, the selyn transport nerves . . ." He turned away as if to retch again, but regained command quickly. "And they say *we* are perverts! If I ever get my hands on the person who did this . . . !"

"Andle," said Valleroy, beginning to realize the magnitude of the atrocity.

"What?"

"Andle. Feleho said it. His dying words were . . . tell Klyd, Hrel spies for Andle . . . Aisha with Runzi."

"Andle! So that's it! Do you realize what this means?"

"That Aisha is with Runzi . . . who or whatever Runzi is."

"The Runzi Raiders," said Klyd with exaggerated patience, "are led by Andle's cousin. If they have Aisha, and if Andle finds out who she is . . . he could use her to smash the Tecton, and without the Tecton to bind us together . . . well, no Householding could stand alone!"

42

"The Tecton is the central organization of the channels?"

"More than that. Much more. But it's just barely legal. If Andle can prove that I've been trying to find Aisha for Stacy . . . he could cast doubt on the integrity of all channels . . . *and* the Tecton."

"Andle is that powerful?"

"Highly placed in government. He's the leader of the anti-Tecton faction. If Hrel has been spying for him, we must assume that Andle knows I'm looking for Aisha."

"Maybe not . . ."

"If not, then why was Feleho killed? I sent him to check the Iburan Choice Auction when I learned they had a consignment from Runzi's Raiders . . . and Runzi's Raiders operate near Hanrahan Pass."

"Then Feleho must have found Aisha! And they murdered him and sent him home as a warning."

"It's possible." He pondered, speaking half to himself. "That whip is the kind the Raiders use. They believe us cowards because we don't go armed. It could be Feleho was the victim of an ordinary attack. Or they might have captured him."

"How much could he tell them?"

"Nothing . . . except that I wanted the girl."

"That might be enough . . ."

"Andle has a twisted mind. He might think the Tecton wants her for the same reason he does."

"Where is Iburan? We have to go there."

"We can't. I have to stay here and deal with Hrel. You can't travel without tags, and I don't have any for you."

"If Aisha's there, we have to go. There's *got* to be a way."

Standing straighter now, Klyd shook his head. "Can't think like this. Help me get the body inside . . . the children will be awake soon."

Valleroy helped move the body to the infirmary, where he left Klyd to handle the funeral arrangements. He and another Gen went to scrub down the court. The red blood was already turning to brown stains, which they had to scour out of the stones. Valleroy worked benumbed by the rhythmic cursing of the Gen beside him. Death by injury to the lateral tentacles, the organs richest in selyn transport nerves, was the second most

43

horrible death a Sime could know. Apparently, it was so horrible that even the Gens who lived with Simes, understood some measure of Klyd's revulsion.

As the morning shadows retreated across the court, Valleroy took his folio once more, and headed for Klyd's offices. The outer rooms were deserted, all the desks draped in deep blue. He found the channel idling over a cup of tea, which was set in a small cleared space on his desk.

"Come in, Hugh. Have something to drink."

On the stack of papers before him lay a coiled whip, handle uppermost.

"No, thanks," said Valleroy, propping his folio against the side of the desk. "Things like that still affect my appetite."

"Trin tea will settle your stomach. Good for you." Klyd pulled a cup out of a drawer and poured.

"Yes, Sectuib," said Valleroy, meekly accepting the cup.

Klyd looked up sharply. "That's the first time you've ever addressed me . . . *Hugh*, that's it! You don't need tags if you wear the Zeor crest!"

"That's only for members, isn't it?"

"Well, you'll qualify in another two weeks anyway. You don't have to return a pledge just to accept our protection.

"Hey, wait a minute," said Valleroy, taking a chair near the corner of the desk. "Don't go so fast. What do you mean I'll qualify for membership in another two weeks?"

"You *were* planning to donate, weren't you?"

Valleroy could see Klyd's bewilderment. It never occured to the channel that a Gen might prefer almost any other option than donating. "Well . . . if I'm still here, I guess I'll have to, won't I?"

"You're frightened! Don't you realize that it is Gen fear that triggers the worst Sime instincts?"

Valleroy gripped the starred-cross and clenched his teeth. Nothing was going to happen to him *now*.

"That's better. You could travel under the crest of Zeor, but you'll need a Sime escort, and I'm not free until I decide what to do about Hrel."

"Everyone was so happy that night . . ."

"Yes, of course. It was hard for Hrel, harder than for most. Now we know why. He wasn't totally committed." Thoughtfully, he ran the tip of a tentacle over each fingernail. "He may have overheard our argument that night. He may have reported what he heard. They may have gotten Feleho killed. . . ."

"You mean it might have been *my* fault."

"No, Hugh. Any blame must be affixed only to the one who wielded the knife."

Valleroy took a sip of his tea. It was the hot, savory brew favored by the Simes, but it did have a soothing effect on the Gen stomach. "Do you know what Feleho called me . . . even before I knew his name or mission?"

"No. I arrived . . . too late."

"Naztehr. He called me 'Natzehr.' You know how that made me feel?"

"How?"

"As if I owed him something. Revenge, maybe. He died because he found Aisha for me. He died because I said something where Hrel could hear. So Zeor loses both Hrel and Feleho and no longer has need of me . . . a spare Gen."

"No Gens are ever 'spare.' Other Simes will come, and we'll be balanced again."

Valleroy sighed. "So what are you going to do with Hrel? If he learns you know about him, he'll be dangerous."

"Not dangerous, no. I'm more worried about the danger to him if word gets around what he's done."

"You're worried about what people might do to *him*? Klyd, if they did to him the same as he did to Feleho, it would be too good for him!"

Klyd frowned at Valleroy. "Sometimes I wonder if Andle isn't right. Gens are a disgustingly vicious people, sometimes."

Valleroy bounced to his feet, outraged. "Killing a Gen a month isn't vicious?"

Klyd laughed, a single burst of sound, hardly more than a bark. "Yes, I guess from your viewpoint it is."

"From your viewpoint, it isn't? If Hrel's a killer, and Zeor stands against the kill, then Hrel's an outsider. Why should you care what happens to him?"

Klyd leaned back in his chair looking up into Valleroy's eyes. "He's disjunct, Hugh. He's ours. Usually we discover spies before they get that far. This time we didn't, so now we've got a real problem. If I turn Hrel out, he'll be killing your people again. If

I keep him, maybe the experience will induce him to change allegiances, and then we'll have really won that round over Andle!"

"Is it worth the risk?"

"I don't know. I just don't know." Putting aside his tea, Klyd changed the subject. "What have you got here in the folio?"

"Oh, I almost forgot. I was on my way to show you this when I heard Feleho knocking. What do you think?"

Valleroy extracted the design for inspection. The channel's eyes widened in appreciation. "This . . . is . . . *beautiful!*"

"Do you think your weavers could achieve that depth effect?"

"Possibly. They're very ingenious when they decide something is worth doing. *This* is for Arensti." It was a statement of a fact so obvious it scarcely needed statement.

"Thank you, Sectuib."

Klyd froze in mid-motion to stare calculatingly at Valleroy. "Am I *your* Sectuib?"

"What does that mean?"

"Would you donate to me?"

The flatness of Klyd's tone underlined the intensity in the channel's eyes. Valleroy sat down hard in his chair. "I don't know. The last time a Sime touched me . . . like that . . . it was horrible. If I could ever trust any Sime, I doubt if it would be *that* one."

"Would you donate to Zeor through one of the other channels?"

Valleroy met Klyd's gaze, trying to avoid the sight of those restless tentacles. "I want to, but I don't know if I'll be able to bring myself to do it. I get shaky just thinking about it."

"Do you have any idea how shaky a Sime gets in disjunction?"

"Yeah. I've seen a couple. Worse than morphine withdrawal."

"Much worse. If they're willing to go through *that* in order to avoid killing your people, how much are you willing to endure in order to make their sacrifices meaningful."

"I see what you mean. I can't do less, can I?"

"Many do."

"But they live out there." Valleroy swept a hand toward Gen Territory. "And they don't even know about disjunction."

"Does your knowing make a difference?"

"Yes, Sectuib, I think it does."

"Do you know what will happen to me if it is ever known that I injured you?"

"Execution?"

"Of a kind that makes Feleho's death look easy and pleasant."

"I didn't think there was anything worse."

"Death by attrition is . . . far worse. You can't imagine."

"I'd rather not try." Attrition, thought Valleroy, would be a very slow death as the Sime body used irreplaceable reserves of selyn. Valleroy shuddered, almost nauseous.

"Exactly," said Klyd. "It is customary for the Head of Householding to take first donations. Such Heads are usually the most skilled channels in the Householding, able to withstand the onslaught of the normal Gen fears. How could it be explained that you fear me more than any other channel?"

"I see. But it's not a decision that must be made right now."

"Yes, it must, and it must be made with all sincerity. This," he said, indicating the folio with a graceful tentacle, "gives me an idea."

"What is it?"

"It won't work unless you adopt a certain attitude toward me. But it must be a true adoption . . . one that won't slip out of character under stress."

"I haven't blown the cover yet."

"Yes you did, during Hrel's party. You forget, Simes read emotions as clearly as words."

Valleroy thought about that. He had been angry when the cover called for everything but anger. "What kind of an attitude?"

"That of a member of my Householding. That of a loyal donor who would do anything . . . anything at all . . . to see that I never suffer need."

"That's asking a lot."

"It is a very personal commitment, but not an odd one when you consider that the channels are all that stand between you and death. Put yourself in the place

47

of our usual Gen recruit . . . weeks, maybe months, in the pens—and the pens *are* as horrible as rumor paints them—finally, one day, the overseer plucks you out of the press. You get your first shower in weeks, your first set of clean clothes in a year, but you can't enjoy it. Within the hour you're doomed. But the treatment in the pens is such that victims almost welcome death.

"Now consider, how would you feel if you discovered that your fate was to be *my* donor, *my* property. Despite being a channel, a filthy pervert, I'm still entitled to one donor a month from the pens. I collect as often as Zeor's space permits. But many die each year because it wasn't *I* who chose them. How would you feel about me, if you were chosen?"

"No matter how scared I might be," said Valleroy thoughtfully, "you still wouldn't hurt me?"

"I have never injured accidently. I can guarantee that I'll never hurt you again."

Valleroy considered. "Two hundred Simes of Zeor *don't* kill more than two thousand of my people a year. I guess I owe a lot to Zeor . . . when the times comes."

"If you travel with me, as my Companion, we can. go to the Choice Auction. Maybe we'll find Aisha there. If so, I'll buy her, and that will be that."

"Companion! What makes you think I could impersonate a Companion? I'm nothing like Denrau!"

"Denrau is exceptional. You're good enough."

"That's ridiculous. I'm not even an ordinary donor, let alone one who serves a channel's need!"

Klyd braced his elbows on the arms of his chair and steepled his fingers, tentacles weaving an intricate dance through the spaces while his eyes remained on Valleroy. "True, you're not *yet* an ordinary donor, but eventually, if you choose it, you can be a more popular Companion than Denrau."

"How do *you* know! The very idea scares—"

"Do you question my professional judgment?"

There was enough pride in Klyd's tone to make Valleroy feel he'd demeaned the integrity of Zeor. "Of course not, Sectuib. I wouldn't think of it."

The channel nodded, contuining to weave patterns through his fingers. "For the present, a good act will do. But it must be based on a firm decision for Zeor."

"I pay my debts."

"This will take more than that."

Valleroy stared at the folio propped against the side of the desk. He knew the design within that case, and he knew intimately what each line symbolized. Zeor had become a part of him, if only for a brief moment. It remained for him to become a part of Zeor, if only for a time.

He raised his eyes to the channel, the exotic creature that had changed his life one dark, rainy night. Seated behind an ordinary desk amid piles of documents in an ordinary office smelling of fresh ink and furniture polish, Klyd was altogether too prosaic to be feared. Yet there was something in his eyes, in his voice, in the way he walked, that said he was one of the most important men alive; he knew it, didn't particularly like it, but he accepted it.

And Valleroy accepted it, too. There was nothing wrong with a man taking pride in his accomplishments. Valleroy knew that pride was only the armored shell Klyd had grown around himself to protect . . . what? Valleroy would never know unless he became a part of Zeor, and suddenly he realized he *wanted* to know what lay beneath that shell.

As Valleroy studied the channel, the dancing tentacles stilled and retracted into their sheaths. The steepled fingers remained steady, but the channel's eyes searched Valleroy's face, probing each nuance of emotion that accompanied the Gen's thoughts.

As steadily as he could, Valleroy said, "Unto Zeor, forever."

Momentarily, Klyd blinked as if in relief. When he opened his eyes, he affirmed, "Unto Zeor, forever."

"But I still don't know why you think I can impersonate a Companion."

"Let's just say that in your place I could do it for Yenava. Four days from now, we may be back here with Aisha, and all will be settled."

"When do we leave?" Privately, he wondered if all this was worth the homestead Stacy had promised him as reward. If Aisha were already dead . . . he refused to think about that.

Klyd reached for a stack of papers. "Tomorrow morning, after the funeral. It's a two-day ride to Iburan so we should arrive just in time for the Choice Auction."

"Why not leave now?"

"Hugh"—Klyd gestured helplessly at the work piled

49

before him—"I will be lucky to get away tomorrow without hurting Zeor. Also, Grandfather must be consulted."

"Grandfather?"

"Of course. I must have permission."

"What if he says no?"

Glancing through the folder before him, Klyd continued absently, "Technically, I've been running Zeor for the last four years. But it is good for him to retain some authority. Uselessness is the worst part of old age, even for a Gen, but do you know what it does to a channel?" The question was rhetorical, and Klyd answered it himself with a shudder as he snapped the folder closed. "Come, bring your design, and we'll ask him now."

Klyd took the papers he'd been reading while Valleroy followed with the folio under one arm. As they walked down the hall, Valleroy drew abreast. "What about Hrel?"

"Maybe Grandfather will have something to say about him." He led the way through a narrow door at the end of the hall, and then up a steep, twisting stairway.

At the top landing, they stopped to gaze at the view. They were now in a penthouse set well back from the parapets of the tallest building at the western side of the court. From the wide windows, along a closed-in colonnade, they could look down on the buildings, the courtyard, the front gate, and beyond to the adjacent town of Valzor.

Valleroy could now see patches of new roofing and off-color stone work where repairs had been made on the court buildings. The Householders didn't often speak of the pogroms against the "perverts," but the building themselves bore mute testimony.

When Valleroy had caught his breath from the climb, the Sectuib led the way along the colonnade, and then through hangings into an antechamber lined with plush red draperies. And there, pacing back and forth in front of the inner door, was Yenava. She was carrying a folder in one hand and, Valleroy noted, she was wearing new shoes.

She turned, barring Klyd's entrance.

He stopped midway. "Is something wrong?"

"Entran," she said, tight-lipped. "Denrau's with him now."

"How long?"

"He must have been like that all night. You know him. He wouldn't call anybody if he was dying!" Valleroy could see she was on the verge of tears.

"Entran isn't that serious."

Hands on hips, she gave a ladylike snort, "Humph! When was the last time the Master Sectuib"—she looked him up and down—"went through it?"

"The way I work, I have the opposite problem."

"Do I ever have to sit up all night holding your hand?"

"You're in a fine mood this morning."

Valleroy could see the unshed tears swimming in her eyes, and it embarrassed him. If it weren't for the peculiar way Klyd had of creating an island of privacy in full public view, he'd have tiptoed out of the hot domestic scene. But then Zeor was very much like a big, quarrelsome family.

After holding her breath as long as she could, Yenava burst out, "Some morning! First Feleho and now Grandfather . . ."

"He's not going to die. Denrau is perfectly capable."

"He wouldn't require Denrau if you'd just let him work a little once a while."

Summoning a ragged patience, Klyd shifted his folder to three tentacles and took her shoulders in his hands while with the tentacles of his other arm he tilted her chin up. Two rivulets of tears wandered down her cheeks as he said, "Naavina, you know as well as I do it's not a question of 'letting.' We must face it, sooner or later. He's *old,* too old to be trusted with the donors. And as for dispensary, his sensitivity is so low that he wouldn't be able to satisfy anyone. He's done all he can do for Zeor. Now it is Zeor's turn to do for him."

For a moment, Valleroy thought she'd accept that. But then she threw the folder she'd been carrying to the floor at Klyd's feet and broke loose from his grasp. "You . . . unfeeling . . . *beast!*" Without waiting for a reply, she tore out into the colonnade and was gone.

Klyd parted the hangings she'd left swinging in her wake and called after her, "You're tired. You'd better get some rest!" He stood in the archway gazing after her as if undecided whether to stay or follow.

Wishing he hadn't come, Valleroy kneeled to gather the papers that had scattered from her folder. They were pictures. A series of drawings made by school-

51

children. Careful lettering on each one made it obvious these were get-well offerings from a class in Zeor history.

Each of the sixty drawings represented some event during Grandfather's time as Head of Zeor. There was battle, carnage, and destruction depicted with an unglazed honesty foreign to the children Valleroy had known. There was a wedding scene, festivals, the dedication of a new building, a disjunction party portrait, a family-tree diagram, even a collage of mementos.

As Klyd turned away from the colonnade, Valleroy tapped the papers into a neat stack and inserted them into the folder. "I think these must be for Grandfather."

Klyd riffled through them absently, nodding. Then he tucked them under his arm with the other folder. Valleroy asked, "Is he really very sick?"

"I trust Denrau. But at Grandfather's age, any little thing . . ."

When Klyd didn't finish, Valleroy said, "What's entran?"

As if glad of the opportunity to lecture clinically, he replied, "The channel has nerve systems absent in the ordinary Sime. They are those used in the selyn-channeling techniques. When these systems are not properly exercised, they can produce very . . . painful cramps. Entran is not lethal, but the complications can be."

"And your Grandfather can't use these systems any more?"

Klyd nodded. "After so many years, the channel's nerves become accustomed to the load. When the work load is removed, the problems are . . . endless."

Klyd fell silent, looking at the inner door. Valleroy fidgeted uncomfortably, not knowing if he should stay or not.

At last, the door opened. Denrau stood framed by a shaft of sunlight. He looked at Klyd for a long time as if sharing a somber awareness.

Klyd stirred. "How was it?"

The Companion frowned. "Rough. He's all right now, but his reflexes are . . ." He closed his eyes and sketched the barest shake of his head.

"Did you tell him about Feleho?"

"I had to. I'm still . . ."

From within the room, a cracked voice interrupted testily, "Don't whisper like that! I'm not dead yet!"

52

Klyd fixed a smile on his lips and called, "Your pardon, Sectuib. But after you're dead, voices won't disturb you."

"Get in here where I can hear you!"

"Yes, Sectuib," said Klyd, grabbing Valleroy by an arm and thrusting him hastily through the door. "Hugh, when Grandfather orders, *move!*"

Valleroy found himself standing in the middle of the floor of the most extraordinary room he'd ever seen.

Directly in front of the door, a canopied bed stood on a dais raised two steps above the floor. Three walls of the room appeared to be nearly all windows overlooking Zeor's fields and factory complex . . . a sprawling U of buildings set amid a parklike forest. The air in the room was alive with the freshness of autumn, but Valleroy could find no open windows.

The heavy drapes were drawn back admitting sparkling sun. One warm puddle of it lapped at the toes of Valleroy's shoes. Overhead a skylight was draped so that the full heat of the sun wasn't focused on the bed. But at night, Valleroy was sure, the stars lit the room magnificently.

Wherever there wasn't a window, case after ceiling-high case of books lined the walls. The wall behind Valleroy was one enormous, unbroken bookcase except for the huge double door by which they'd entered. And most of those books, thought Valleroy, looked old enough to be from the Ancients.

His hands itched to explore them, but his eye was drawn to the withered figure that lay amid the billowing quilts on the bed. With Denrau on his right and Klyd on his left, the old man shook a newspaper under their noses as if it proved conclusively the world was going to hell. "And just what do you say to this!"

The only newspaper Valleroy had seen in Zeor was the *Tecton Weekly*, put out by the Householdings. But from where he stood, Valleroy couldn't see what scandalous article was being discussed.

Klyd said, "Probably the same thing you said when you first read it."

The old man looked up slyly. "Then you agree with me?"

Klyd looked at Denrau holding a perfect deadpan as he said, "Only when you agree with me, Sectuib."

The three of them exploded in laughter at a long-

53

shared family joke. Valleroy relaxed. Suddenly, Grandfather was just as human as Klyd.

Denrau and Klyd seated themselves on benches near the foot of the bed where the reclining patient could see them. For the moment, Valleroy was left standing on the vast expanse of carpet between the door and the foot of the bed. But, apparently, Grandfather couldn't see that far.

Klyd presented the folder he'd brought up from his desk. "These are the reports you asked for. I hope you find them satisfactory. Production was up ten per cent last months. Sales were seasonal."

"That's not good enough."

"But next year we'll be doing much better. I have the design that's going to win at Arensti this year."

"Well, it's about time. Let's see it. Zeor's reputation, you know."

Klyd motioned to Valleroy, who extracted the design from the folio. He had to step up into the dais at the foot of the bed so Grandfather could see it.

The old man squinted at the design, obviously struggling not to gape. One irrepressible smile quirked the corner of his mouth, but then he got hold of himself. "Might do at that. See what the mill can do with it. I want a complete bolt by the day after tomorrow."

Klyd exchanged indulgent glances with Denrau and signaled Valleroy to put the folio away. "Yes, Sectuib."

"Don't think, youngster, that I'm going to forget what day it is!"

No indulgent glances this time. Klyd said, "Yes, Sectuib."

"Was there anything else?"

"Yes, Sectuib."

"Out with it!"

"I'd like to go to the Iburan Choice tomorrow."

"Whatever for? With Feleho gone, we're Gen-high."

Klyd threw Valleroy an apologetic glance and plunged into his explanation. What it amounted to, as far as Valleroy was able to follow the rapid-fire Simelan, was that, since Valleroy had created such an enviably great Arensti entry, Zeor ought to do all it could to keep him. Since he wasn't married, the first thing Zeor had to do was to provide him with the wife of his choice. He hadn't found anyone within Zeor, and rumor had it that Iburan's Choice this month would be very close to Valleroy's requirements. It was an intricate argument that balanced economic factors against moral obligations and projected profits from the winning Arensti design . . . and presumed future winners yet to be created.

At length, Grandfather held up a quavering hand to stem the flood of statistics. "But what about Yenava?"

"We'll be right back, Grandfather . . . weeks before she's due."

"Klyd, you went against my advice marrying a Gen. Now she's giving Zeor an heir. She'll die if you're not here to supply that baby with selyn when Yenava's delivered."

"Yenava is a well-trained Companion. I don't expect much trouble."

"Nevertheless, she'll need you. That's one of the obligations . . ."

"I'll be there, I promise."

"I'm an old man. Nobody listens to me any more. When I was running Zeor . . ."

"You still run Zeor, Grandfather. I just attend to the details."

"An heir isn't a *detail!* The gene runs in the family. Zeor must have a Farris heir."

"Yes, Sectuib."

The old man glared at Klyd's bowed head. Finally, he threw himself deep into the pillows and sighed. "You are at least traveling with a Companion?" he asked sarcastically.

"I've selected Naztehr Hugh since he must approve any purchase made in his behalf. I'll leave Denrau in case you require him."

"I won't require him. You might."

"In any event, Denrau will be your donor this month. Naztehr Hugh will take care of me."

Valleroy's command of colloquialisms was still sketchy enough that he distrusted his understanding of that. He might be able to act the part of Companion, but he certainly couldn't serve any channel's need. Klyd knew that. Valleroy hardly had time to frame an objection, though. The old man propped himself up on his pillows and let loose a stream of colorful invective new to Valleroy . . . but he did recognize it as the kind of language nobody else in the Householding would dare to use to Klyd.

The channel took the caustic abuse with bowed head. "Yes, Sectuib."

Breathless, Grandfather sank back into the pillows. "But you're going to do it?"

"I must, Sectuib," said Klyd, both humble and stubborn, a combination Valleroy had thought impossible.

"Well, then promise you won't try to qualify him unless Denrau is standing by—just in case . . ."

"You will have Denrau low-field by then."

"No I won't. Charnye will serve me, just as he always has."

"Denrau has more experience in—"

"And *you* require his experience more than I! *You* are Head of Zeor. *You* are Sectuib here whether you like it or not. All the rest of us depend on you . . . and *you* depend on Denrau. It's about time you learned when to take the best for yourself!"

"A lesson," said Klyd softly, "which you learned many years ago but have forgotten."

"Nobody depends on me any more."

"I do, Grandfather."

"Hah!" It was parody of a laugh. "When have you ever taken my advice?"

"Now for example."

"About Denrau . . ."

"No, about Hrel."

"Who?"

"Our newest disjunct."

"What's he got to do with Denrau?"

"Not with Denrau, with Naztehr Hugh."

"Naztehr . . .?"

"The Arensti Designer, our newest candidate."

"The Arensti Designer is a Gen?"

"You authorized it yourself, Grandfather."

"I did?"

"Besides," said Denrau, "you liked the design he's submitted." Surreptitiously, the Companion motioned Valleroy to hold the board up again.

One wizened hand came up, ventral tentacles waving at the design. "That one? But wasn't that last year's winner?"

"No, Grandfather. It's the one you authorized for this year's entry."

"Oh, yes, definitely a winner. Day after tomorrow. I haven't forgotten. But what has that to do with Hrel?"

"We have reason to believe he's been spying for Andle."

"Ridiculous. Disjuncts don't spy. They have to be loyal or they'd never make it."

"So I have believed. But Naztehr Hugh is the one who discovered Feleho this morning . . ."

"Dead?" said Grandfather as if he still couldn't believe. "Our little Feleho, slaughtered!"

"He wasn't dead when Hugh found him. He had a message."

"He told who killed him?"

"Perhaps. He said, 'Tell Klyd, Hrel spies for Andle. . . .' It must have been that discovery that earned him martyrdom."

"*Andle!*" breathed the old man, suddenly sharp-eyed. "So, Andle killed our little boy! But are you *sure?* This new Gen, he might have mixed up the tenses, spies for spied?"

"I know it seems impossible, Grandfather, but it can be no other way. It was something Hugh said at Hrel's disjunction party that made me send Feleho into Andle's organization. The only way he could have been caught is if Hrel overheard and reported to Andle . . . *after* disjunction."

"It was a genuine disjunction?"

"I served him myself. It was genuine."

"Then Hrel killed Feleho."

"Apparently."

"But we *can't* turn him out."

"No, we can't."

The old man lay back with a sigh. "Times are changing. People are changing."

"How many times have you told me people don't change?"

"That's true. They haven't."

"I don't know what to do with Hrel. I seek guidance, Sectuib."

"For once, perhaps, you'll take some advice?"

"You have a solution?"

"Appoint Hrel to officiate at Feleho's funeral."

"But that honor belongs . . ."

"Usually. But this is a special case. You can handle the details, I'm sure."

"Yes, Sectuib. And it might work . . . no"—he warmed to the idea—"it *will* work! I can see that!"

"Good. Now, while you are busy respecting my genius, perhaps you'll consider my advice about Denrau."

"If Charnye can serve you, he can serve me."

"Charnye is getting old."

"My point, precisely. You require Denrau's flexibility."

"So do you!"

The two glared at each other for several seconds, anger fairly sparkling in the air between them. Then, simultaneously, they burst out laughing. There was no mirth in that exchange, but it said only that they weren't on opposite *sides*, merely in disagreement about method.

Grandfather caught his breath. "What Zeor needs is a new top-ranking Companion. No, make that two new Companions and a good channel."

"Exactly," agreed Klyd. "Which is why I must qualify Naztehr Hugh. Zeor is growing. We are far too dependent on key individuals."

"*Hugh?* Isn't that the name of the Arensti Designer?"

"Yes, Grandfather. It is the same man, the one for whom we must purchase a wife so that he will stay with us."

"A good plan. I'm glad I thought of it. Decently talented Companions are hard to find. Tell me, how do you know this one will work out?"

"His perceptivity tested in-range, and we are attuned. We have already achieved an unusual selur nager . . ."

"When was this?"

"When I was treating Rual in the school garden the other day. I have the greatest confidence in Hugh."

"Confidence isn't enough. Is he well trained?"

"He is totally untrained. He is from out-Territory . . ."

"*Out*-Territory!"

"But he is the Aresnti Designer, Grandfather."

"Impossible!"

"So I had thought."

"People *are* changing."

"No, I think they are still the same as ever . . . surprisingly different from each other."

"A traitorous disjunct and a Companion from out-Territory . . . all in one month!"

"He is not a Companion yet, Grandfather."

The old man frowned, deeply worried. "Promise me, Klyd, promise me in the name of Zeor . . . don't attempt to qualify this Hugh unless Denrau is standing by—*close* by—monitoring everything and ready to step in if necessary. We can't afford to lose you."

Klyd was silent.

"I may not live long enough to see that you do it, so promise me, Unto Zeor."

"I can't promise Unto Zeor, Grandfather. But I will promise you."

"Stubborn child."

"Apparently. It runs in the family."

"Humph! Well, am I allowed to meet this candidate, Hugh?"

"He is somewhat more than a candidate. He has vowed Unto Zeor, yet he has not pledged or donated yet."

"I'd still like to meet him."

Klyd beckoned hastily to Valleroy to step up beside him. "I thought you would, so I brought him along."

As if perceiving another presence in the room for the first time, Grandfather measured Valleroy with a sudden penetrating gaze. "So you're all three of these remarkable young Gens from out-Territory I've been hearing so much about. Give me your hand."

Valleroy drew back, a thundering fear pumping his heart faster and faster. The old man's hand flashed out to grab Valleroy's arm, pulling him forward at an awkward angle.

Out of the corner of his eye, Valleroy saw Klyd motion to Denrau, who reached across the bed to intercede. But Grandfather impatiently shook off the Companion's grip. "I won't hurt him! What do you think I am, a junct?"

Heart pounding irregularly. Valleroy saw two protectors trade glances and back off.

"Tell me, youngster, what makes you want to be a Companion?"

Fighting down his fear, Valleroy could think of nothing but the truth. "I'm not at all sure I do want to."

"Aha! Such wisdom is rare in the young. But my grandson has some damn fool notion of running off to Iburan. You go with him, take care of him, and I won't worry so much."

"Yes, Sectuib."

"But, for the honor of Zeor, don't let anyone see you're not our best Companion. We'd be disgraced for letting Klyd run around unprotected."

"Yes, Sectuib."

"You have a dependable feel to you, son. I've always preferred a Companion with a solid nager. When you've qualified, be sure they leave a place in your schedule for me."

"Yes, Sectuib."

"Now get out of here, and let an old man get some well-earned sleep. Had a hard night."

"Yes, Sectuib."

The wrinkled hands loosened and fell away, asleep almost before they touched the quilts. Dazed, Valleroy followed Klyd and Denrau out of the chamber.

Outside, the channel, exchanging relieved glances with Denrau, leaned heavily against the closed door. The Companion glanced at Valleroy, and then he said to Klyd, "Solid nager! *I* could have felt the oscillations all the way across the room! Klyd, he's senile."

"I know. I thought he'd never make me promise!"

"You handled him just right."

"Nobody handles Grandfather. He's still got the best mind in Zeor. Hrel conducting Feleho's funeral!"

"I admit that's pure genuis, and it might even work, but by tomorrow he'll have forgotten who Hrel is."

"That's why he requires you, not Charnye."

"Are you sure you want to risk traveling like this?"

"I don't see any other way. We'll be back in plenty of time to take all precautions with Yenava."

Denrau shrugged. Then he turned to Valleroy and said in nearly flawless English, "I don't think we've been formally introduced, but Zeor doesn't practice much formality."

"So I noticed. I'm very honored to meet you."

"And I, you." He indicated the Arensti folio he'd picked up inside. "I'll take this to the mill office. It really is one of the greatest pieces I've ever seen. A sure winner."

"Thank you. I hope so . . . for Zeor's sake."

Denrau headed for the colonnade, but just at the hangings he turned and smiled. "I'll be looking forward to your pledge party. It should be quite an affair." Then he left.

"I get the impression," said Valleroy slowly, "he doesn't have much faith in me."

"Neither do I at the moment. Listen, Hugh if you want to complete your assignment here, you'll have

60

to master that fear reaction. Here . . ." He took Valleroy's hands, twining tentacles around the Gen wrist. "You see what I mean?"

Valleroy flinched away from the Sime's hot touch, his heart again racing painfully. The muscular, handling tentacles were covered with an incredibly soft, dry, smooth skin like a velvet sheath over steel. They left a lingering sensation on Valleroy's skin that made his hair stand on end.

"Hugh, I'm *only* reading the gradient . . . without even token lateral contact! What could you possibly be frightened *of?*"

Valleroy tried to force his heart to slow down.

"If you're going to travel as my Companion, you're going to have to get used to touching me."

"The Householding rule is to avoid contact . . ."

"That's for untrained Gens. A Companion is supposed to know when it is permitted and when not . . . without being told."

"Well, I'm not trained."

"So, I'm telling you. Because of your . . . accident . . . you and I are in-phase. As my Companion, you'll be entitled to the same liberties as Denrau would."

"I don't know how to behave like a Companion."

"For performance in front of the juncts, there isn't much to it. Just stay close. You'll learn."

As he followed Klyd down into the court, Valleroy wasn't at all sure he wanted to learn . . . but he wasn't sure he didn't want to, either.

CHAPTER FOUR

Count the Days of My Death as I Counted the Days of My Life

DAWN FOUND THE CENTRAL COURTYARD OF THE HOUSE of Zeor filled with the largest gathering Valleroy had yet seen there. He thought all four hundred-odd members, all their children, and most of the candidates were there. But the mood was somber, infused with a smoldering indignation held in check only by the overwhelming grief . . . Feleho had been a greatly loved son of Zeor.

Very conscious of the Zeor crest ring now weighing down his right hand, Valleroy shared their feelings. Strictly speaking, he wouldn't be entitled to that ring until he'd donated to Zeor through Klyd. Privately, Valleroy still doubted if he'd be able to do it. But, because of the ring, those around him assumed that he'd returned a formal pledge, joining his life to Zeor forever. That awakened in him the same thrill of daring excitement that Feleho's greeting as Naztehr had.

It felt good. But at the same time it made him feel guilty. One ought not to feel *good* on such an occasion.

Resolutely, he fixed his eyes on the casket that lay on a hastily constructed bier in the center of the court. It was draped with a cloth of plain blue . . . Zeor's blue. The sun was already rising into the clear sky.

Hrel stood beside the bier. He was draped in an ankle-length cloak of Zeor blue richly embroidered with the Zeor symbols. He read from a prepared text. "This is the dawning of the First Day in the Death Count of Feleho Ambrov Zeor. Let it be recorded that he gave himself in an effort to save a donor from the pens. Let it further be recorded that he died because his laterals were severed above the . . ."

Hrel choked on the words, and a gasp rippled through the audience. Valleroy saw mothers clutching their children as if to protect them from a like fate.

Klyd stepped forward. He laid a hand on Hrel's shoulder. Hrel coughed once, cleared his thoat, and continued. "Since the time of Rimon Farris, atrocities have been committed upon us to keep us from attaining our goals. To the roll of martyrs, the name of Feleho, who of his own free will became Ambrov to Zeor, is added. Let not his death break our spirit. Let us lift his burden and carry it on so that his death will be imperceptible to his enemies."

There was a moment of silence. Then, in various places around the court, soft chanting began. It was a melody filled with all the grief humanity had ever known.

Valleroy couldn't made out the words until those near him took up the song. It was a simple refrain repeated over and over to variations on the basic melody.

"Today is the First Day in the Death Count of Feleho Ambrov Zeor."

As the sun cleared the roof, sending its first rays probing into the courtyard, the bearers lifted the casket. In orderly rows, the crowd followed the draped coffin through the buildings, along the same route Valleroy had followed the previous morning just before meeting Feleho for the first and last time, and then out into the freshly harvested fields.

It was a long walk, farther into the Householding grounds than Valleroy had yet been. He hadn't realized how extensive the lands were. They passed the factory complex and emerged onto a dirt road that led through cultivated fields, mostly barren now after the harvest. Topping a gentle rise, the procession entered the cemetery of Householding Zeor . . . a much larger area than a group of four hundred ought to need. It was a well-kept spot, shaded by tall trees and guarded by a neat white fence with an arched gateway.

The grave had been freshly dug the night before and a marker had been prepared. Surveying the neat rows of graves, Valleroy saw that about half the markers were of the three-lobed symbol like Feleho's, but the others had only one lobe.

Each of the mourners deposited a shovel of dirt over the coffin. Then Hrel and Klyd finished the job together, heedless of the flying dirt that speckled their clean blue cloaks.

Valleroy stood aside while Feleho's widow, a homely but well-scrubbed, hard working Sime, thanked Hrel for officiating and took her three-year-old son back to the Householding.

She was allowed to walk alone before anyone else left the cemetary. Valleroy thought it must be the loneliest walk of a lifetime, and he resolved to kill the man who made it necessary if it took the rest of his life.

The widow's distant form was swallowed up by the hulking shadows of the factory complex. The others began to stir toward the cemetery gate after visiting the graves of others who had been dear to them. One by one, they offered a few words to Klyd, pledged undying loyalty to him, thanked Hrel, and left, walking that dusty trail alone or with small children.

At last, Hrel turned toward Klyd to speak the words of the pledge, but Klyd held up a hand, tentacles

63

gesturing toward Valleroy. Having listened to several hundred repetitions, Valleroy managed to get through the formula without stumbling, but while his words to Klyd were spoken with real sincerity, they became meaningless noise when spoken to Hrel.

The Sime didn't seem to notice. His whole attention seemed to be turned inward even as he pledged his loyalty to Klyd and took the trail homeward.

"I see what you mean about Hrel," said Valleroy when they were alone at last. "It just might work. But does he know that he may have been the cause of Feleho's murder?"

"We had a long talk. If he was the cause, he knows it."

"I'm glad I'm not him!"

"And he's glad he's not you."

Valleroy fingered the grave marker. "Tell me, why the two kinds of markers?"

"The trefoil is used to mark the graves of martyrs."

Valleroy whistled. "So many!"

"All gave themselves for our principles. It is a high price to pay in any currency. They will not be forgotten."

Uncomfortably, Valleroy changed the subject. "How much of this land is part of Zeor?"

"In that direction," said Klyd, indicating the south where Gen Territory lay, "all the way to the river. Over there, the hills mark our border. On the other side of the court buildings lies the city of Valzor. From Valzor to the river, only our fence line marks Zeor's border."

"But only this small portion is cultivated."

"We expand every year, but it is slow because of the law. We can take in only those we can feed. And there is a head tax on every Gen we keep. *That* money goes to support the pens. The number of Simes who join us is very small. But in spite of it all, we grow. One day, all the Territory will be disjunct. There will be no fences, no borders and no perverts." He took a deep breath, as if gathering himself back from the fringes of a distant dream. "But that day is a long way off, and we have a job to do today, this First Day in the Death Count of Feleho Ambrov Zeor."

As they took the path back toward the court, Valleroy said, "I went by the stables this morning. Our houses will be ready about now. You run a tight organization."

"That's what it takes, Naztehr," answered Klyd, striding ahead to walk alone as had the others. It was a strange custom to Valleroy, but he honored it as he had all the others. No doubt the meanings would become clear to him one day. He followed, glancing up at Grandfather's sparkling windows, certain the old man was watching him despite being nearly blind.

Dressed in Zeor's traveling livery, with sturdy mounts from the Zeor stables, they took the road across the fields of Zeor northwest toward what Klyd called a main highway. When they reached it, about noon, and turned due north toward Iburan, Valleroy was a little startled to find that the highway was a graveled road laid along what must have been a way of the Ancients. It was either straight or very gently curved, and it went exactly where it wanted to, even biting deep into hills to stay level. The surface was a strange, powdery substance apparently designed to dry quickly and to provide good footing for horses without trapping wagon wheels. Only in the center of the wheel ruts was the gravel base exposed. The Gens, thought Valleroy, could certainly learn a thing or two from the Simes about road building.

They rode steadily, side by side, as they passed an occasional wagon or fellow rider. Once they had to leave the road while two heavily laden grain wagons passed each other. And more than once their blue Zeor cloaks attracted stares of curiosity or lips curled in open disgust.

Every other Sime they passed was armed with the Sime weapon-of-choice, the long supple whip curled at his belt. These juncts raked disdainful glances across Klyd's bare hip while the channel ignored their attitude with a patently false innocence.

Along this major artery, on both sides, farmhouses dotted the landscape, with occasional clusters forming small towns. Valleroy saw the green pennant flying over one such cluster and knew that it signified the presence of a Pen. In the far distance, on the slope of a hill behind the pennant building, he saw green-clad workers harvesting grain—Gens raising their own food, breeding stock.

Tales rose out of his childhood to haunt him. He asked, "Is it true that they use drugs to make Gen women bear more children in the pens?"

Klyd threw him a sharp glance, obviously sensing Valleroy's roiling emotions. He pulled off the road, dismounting and loosing his horse to graze before answering. Valleroy followed suit. They had been riding steadily for hours. He was hungry enough to eat despite the memory of the funeral.

"Those Gens are well treated," said the channel as he dug his lunch out of a saddlebag.

"Well treated?" snorted Valleroy.

"Certainly. They are valuable property, aren't they?" Klyd took the canteens and settled down among some rocks overlooking a placid pool on the edges of a stream. Only the sound of an occasional rider marred the stillness of a warm, Indian summer afternoon.

At Valleroy's incredulous look, Klyd continued, "It is only during the last few months, after they are marked for distribution, that their health and welfare is no longer important. Even then, they are well fed."

"You're as bad as all the rest of them! You talk righteously about disjunction, and then discuss *them*"—he waved toward their backtrail where the green pennant could barely be seen over the rise, unconsciously imitating the Sime gesture—"as if they were just cattle!"

Imperturbably taking a bite of a roll of black bread, Klyd chewed and swallowed methodically before answering. "Those people *are* nothing more than animals." At Valleroy's indignant rise, the channel gestured impatiently. "Sit down and eat. Maybe you'll learn something if you can be quiet long enough to listen."

Sullenly, Valleroy sat and bit into his roll. The cakelike bread was moist with flakes of nut meats and chunks of fruit throughout. He found the canteen filled with a rich, syrupy drink that satisfied hunger without filling. Between bites, he said, "I'm listening."

"Those people over there"—Klyd gestured toward the distant pennant with a graceful tentacle—"are not and never have been your people. They were born in the pens. They have no language to speak of . . . no culture . . . and no art. They have no religion, and little in the way of morals guides their behavior. They are almost literally animals."

Klyd paused to let that sink in while he swigged at his canteen. "That is the main reason that most Simes out there"—he made an expansive gesture to include all Sime Territory—"don't really believe Gens are peo-

66

ple. If Gens aren't people, then there's no reason not to kill them as *you* slaughter animals to eat. If Gens aren't people, then Simes who interbreed with them to produce the incredibly skilled donors like Denrau . . . and *use* those donors to avoid the kill . . . are certainly perverts of the worst sort. If Gens aren't people, it follows that the wild Gens are to be hunted down and used in whatever way seems convenient.

"Until the channels came along, it was sincerely believed that all Gens were merely animals . . . anthropoid copies of people. But then we found that your people, left to yourselves, develop language, culture, art, religion . . . everything that we have and maybe a bit more. Still, it is *true* that those bred and raised in the pens for generations don't have these attributes. I *know* this, Hugh, because it is my job to take them and turn them into people.

"And, Hugh," said the channel, leaning forward impassioned, "we *do* succeed! We have shown over and over that the most dull-eyed denizen of the pens can blossom into a real human being given the right circumstances. *That* is the reason Andle and all his followers are frightened of us. Simes are no more fond of murder than you are."

"What happens to the ones born in the pens who go through changeover?"

"Most of them die in changeover . . . from the drugs they've been saturated with all their lives. The few who survive are trained to become keepers of the pens . . . they have little memory of their childhood and very little intelligence. They rarely live as much as ten years after changeover."

Cynically, Valleroy smiled. "Oh, a necessary evil?"

Klyd didn't answer, avoiding Valleroy's gaze. For once, Valleroy wished he could read Klyd's emotions. "What about the captives? Don't they teach . . ."

"Captives are never mixed with stock. It was learned a long time ago that that only produces violence."

"So Aisha couldn't possibly be there?" Valleroy couldn't drag his eyes away from the pennant.

"No, not a chance. That's a government-supported operation. If she was taken by the Runzi, and if she's still alive, she's either in a Raider's pen somewhere in the wilds, or she's been placed for auction."

67

Valleroy mulled that over as he chewed on a fresh, crisp apple. Klyd knew more about the distribution of Gens for the kill than anyone from out-Territory could. They were following the best lead that had turned up. As frustrating as it was, there was absolutely nothing more they could do. Considering Feleho's death following this same lead, it just might be the right one.

Nevertheless, Valleroy felt guilty for just sitting in the shade placidly eating an apple while Aisha was, perhaps, screaming for help . . . somewhere. As long as he was moving or engrossed in some project, Valleroy could rest satisfied he was doing enough. But the moment he stopped to rest, his mind would conjure up torturous nightmares that made him want to jump up and run to her rescue . . . but he didn't know which direction to run!

He took a deep breath and stretched out, leaning against the tree behind him. Klyd sat, tailor-fashion, watching a flock of migrating birds so high in the blue sky Valleroy couldn't tell what they were. The Sime appeared not to have a care in the world at that moment, yet Valleroy knew that Klyd walked the most dangerous path of any of Stacy's agents. "Tell me something, Klyd."

"If I can."

"Why do you do it?"

"Do what?"

"Oh, everything . . . I guess it amounts to collaborating with the enemy. Working for Stacy. Searching for Aisha. Sending your friends into danger and not even telling them why. No other Sime is doing any of those things. What makes you different?"

"Oh, I guess it's the way I see history, or rather my place in it. Only a member of a Householding *would* do any of those things . . . and only a channel *could*. It has to be a channel whose Householding borders Gen Territory . . . in this district, that means Zeor. It has to be a Head of a Householding because only a Head could put together an information net useful to Stacy. And it has to be somebody who has a contact among the Gen authorities. I don't know anybody else in that position."

"Since you're the only one who could, you must? That doesn't seem very logical."

"It is if you grant that somebody must provide a bridge between us and them."

68

Valleroy didn't even notice that Klyd had said "us and *them*" rather than "us and *you*." He still wasn't satisfied. "How did you come to meet Stacy?"

The birds had long since disappeared into the distance, but Klyd still gazed upward, as if some scene played itself out against the sky. "I was out checking a stand of timber on Zeor's western border . . . the one on the bank of the river. We thought it might be ready for some selective harvesting. I was riding alone since I didn't plan to go off the holding. I was about to light my campfire for the night when a very exhausted Gen staggered into the clearing . . . right into my arms. He was being chased by a young Sime, just through change-over and berserk with need. That was the first time the river tunnel had been used in generations."

"The Gen was Stacy?"

"And the young Sime was Stacy's nephew. The boy joined Zeor, and Stacy and I became friends."

"I must have met him, then, and never known it."

"No. Duvan was a martyr of the last pogrom. He had no children."

"Oh." It was all Valleroy could think to say. Klyd's tone bespoke a deeper tragedy better left buried. He gathered his things. "We'd better get going."

It was well after sundown, and the horses were blowing frosty clouds by the time they reached the Halfway House, which Klyd insisted was the only safe place to spend the night.

The building was a converted mansion apparently reconstructed around a prewar frame. They paid the stable fees for the horses and trudged, bedrolls in hand, through the front door.

Inside, warm air welcomed them. The large central room was a parlor, with a crackling fire laid in the stone hearth at one side. A handful of fellow travelers sprawled in the scattered lounge chairs, toasting their feet or dozing. A homely couch that might once have been red plush was piled with a salesman's sample cases. In one corner a card game attracted several onlookers. All of them, Valleroy noted, were Sime. And all of them were watching him with that spring-steel alertness only a Sime has.

He moved closer to Klyd while the channel signed the register, obtained a room key, and performed some ritual involving finances. It was the first time that he had

seen Sime money, and it made Valleroy aware that he
had none.

Following Klyd up the stairs to their room, he
shrugged. If the stares from the Simes around the room
meant anything—particularly that of the salesman—
Valleroy knew that without Klyd he wouldn't last long
enough to require money.

While they unpacked, Valleroy surveyed the room. It
was dingy and threadbare, but clean. On one wall a
small painting of a sunset looked like it had been done
by a child. There was a chair, lumpy with broken
springs, and a single sagging bed. "I guess I'd prefer the
floor," said Valleroy, picking a spot.

"Oh, no! What if the maid should 'accidentally' walk
in? Blow the cover clear to the moon! A channel's traveling Companion always sleeps in the same bed, eats
at the same table, and stays within arm's reach of the
channel."

"Why? I'm supposed to be a person, right?"

"It's the *image*. The Householdings are trying to sell
the idea that a Sime can associate with a Gen without
killing. You have to convince them, by concrete actions,
that you are not afraid of me . . . that you protect me
of your own free will. I will never order you to do anything where they can hear. Do you understand?"

"I think so."

"Good." Klyd winked conspiratorially. "I'm going to
get something to eat."

"Me too, then," said Valleroy, following back downstairs.

The thunderous silence that fell as they passed
through the parlor raised goosebumps on Valleroy's neck
—especially the oily way the salesman pivoted to watch
them pass. But he played his part, keeping his head high
and trying to be the pride of Zeor. They marched, sleeve
to sleeve, through the double doors that led to the dining room.

The long dining table was deserted, but the cook had
set two new places for them. Steaming soup dispelled
the last of the stiffness from the day's ride. Savory potatoes, fresh salad, fruit-nut bread, the bread deep
fried and swimming in a heavy sauce, completed the
most lavish meal Valleroy had eaten since crossing the
river. Klyd pointed out, discreetly, the foods not for

Gens, commenting that the cook expected him to take double the Sime portions.

The door to the parlor had been left ajar. The stares of the Simes spoiled Valleroy's digestion. He said in English, "Every time I pick up my knife, I get the distinct impression the whole room is going to jump me!"

Chuckling, Klyd replied in English, "Speak Simelan, it's more impressive."

"Well," said Valleroy, switching languages with an ease that surprised him, "are they?"

"They find the sight of a sharp tool in the hands of a Gen . . . ummm . . . disturbing."

Valleroy was about to answer that when a gust of chill wind from the front door stopped him. Two figures stumbled into the parlor, blinking at the bright light. Valleroy dropped his knife, stunned.

The first figure was a Sime dressed in plain riding breeches and a short jacket, unadorned. Behind him, on a chain welded to an iron collar from which dangled three green tags, was the sorriest-looking Gen Valleroy had ever seen. He was hardly more than a boy, thin and undeveloped. His skin was tanned against his white knee-length tunic. Under the tunic, he wore nothing but goosebumps.

The Gen was practically blue with cold but didn't seem to be aware of the warmth of the hearth. He stood quietly, eyes downcast, like a trained animal without the will to move unless pulled.

As the door clattered shut behind the pair, Klyd half rose out of his chair, eyes locked on the Sime. "Hugh, that boy's in need!"

Valleroy wrenched his eyes from the Gen to inspect the owner. "He's trembling. Looks pretty weak."

At that moment, the Sime's eyes met Klyd's, slid over Valleroy respectfully, and locked again with the cahnnel's. Leading his Gen, the Sime started toward Klyd. Halfway, he stumbled . . . something Valleroy had never known a Sime to do.

In a flash Klyd was at his side, assisting him to a chair, deftly inserting his own body between the Sime and the Gen. Valleroy hastened to his channel's side, not knowing what would be expected of a Companion under these circumstances.

After a moment, the boy regained his breath. "I promised my mother, on her deathbed, this time I would not

71

kill. But . . . can't. Zeor is too far. . . ." With a sudden surge of strength, the Sime tried to lunge to his feet. "Must . . ."

Klyd moved with that incredible Sime swiftness to wrench the chain from the boy's hands. He handed the end to Valleroy as the Sime struggled to reach the Gen.

But Klyd's superior strength held him. "I am Sectuib Farris of Householding Zeor. Come upstairs with me. I will serve you. It's not far. Just up the stairs. You can make it that far, can't you? You've come such a long way. It's cost you so much agony. Only a little farther, and you have succeeded."

"Zeor?" asked the Sime bewildered. *"Sectuib . . . you . . ."*

"I am, and I will if you come upstairs." As he moved for the stairs, still carefully between the Sime and his intended victim, Klyd continued to croon encouragement in that same professionally persuasive voice he used on his patients.

Valleroy brought the Gen on the chain. Just as he placed a foot on the third step, the old woman who worked at the desk cried out, "No! I won't allow any filthy perversions on my premises!" And she started after them.

Suddenly angered, Valleroy wheeled on her. "You won't *allow . . . !* And just how are you going to stop Sectuib Farris?"

Valleroy felt the other Simes in the room tense. They could wipe him out in five seconds, but he'd gone too far to back down. He took a wild stab in the dark, trusting that Klyd wouldn't do anything illegal. "The boy asked for the Sectuib's help to avoid killing this one." He held up the white-painted chain for all to see. "Sectuib is within the law in providing that help wherever and whenever it is sought! We rented a room. What we do there is our own business as long as we obey the law!"

The electric tension in the room was poised to destroy him. Defiantly, Valleroy thrust his chin high and marched up the stairs pulling the Gen behind him. He could almost feel that salesman's eyes boring holes in his back. As he topped the stairs, the Simes below broke into furious argument aimed just as much at each other as at the arrogant Gen.

By the time Valleroy reached their room, it was all over. The Sime boy lay on the bed, curled on his side

72

sobbing fitfully. Klyd let them in, then went to hold those seemingly fragile shoulders until the sobbing ceased.

"What's your name, boy?" asked Klyd gently.

"Heshri Sikal."

"Why is it that you wanted so to please your mother?" Heshri's eyes bored into the channel's, searching for something.

"No, Heshri, I mean no disrespect. But the determination you have shown is rarely mustered to please someone else. It must come from within. Why do *you* want to disjunct?"

"I have seen the numbers of Zelerod. It is frightening. If he is right, I will not live to help my mother's grandchildren through changeover."

Klyd rose and paced across the room to where the Gen crouched in the single chair, feet drawn under him, dull eyes downcast. Looking down at that pitiful form, the channel said, "He is right, Heshri. Zelerod is . . . terrifyingly . . . right."

The silence lengthened until Valleroy hazarded, "Who is Zelerod, and what is he right about?"

Shaking himself as if rousing fom a dream, Klyd said, "He's the mathematician who predicts that within a hundred years, perhaps less, the human race will be extinct because of the increasing proportion of Simes living longer adult lives, killing so many Gens that there won't be enough to keep us alive. Zelerod shows mathematically that the only survival is through the channel. We have known that for generations, but the juncts wouldn't accept it . . . until one of their own predicted it and died in the attempt to disjunct because he was too old."

Klyd turned to look at the boy, who still sat on the bed. "Now they accept it, and a few of them, one at a time, come to the Householdings. The more who accept it, the more frightened and desperate Andle and his followers become . . . and the more dangerous.

"Heshri, this is my Companion, Naztehr Hugh."

Jumping to his feet as if confronting royalty, Heshri half bowed as he said, "I am most honored . . ."

It startled Valleroy after the beating his ego had taken from the juncts downstairs. He said, "Not as honored as I . . ."

Klyd chuckled. "Sit down both of you. The one who deserves the most honor hasn't even joined us yet." The channel squatted down to bring his face within the Gen's field of vision. He passed his hand in front of those staring eyes. The Gen didn't even blink when Klyd touched his nose with a ventral tentacle.

"Well, after a few weeks at Zeor, he'll wake up."

"He looks drugged," said Valleroy. The Simelan word he used was closer to "medicated," so he added the English word he'd intended.

"That's part of it," agreed Klyd, "but even without the drugs he'll be a long time developing. Even so, there's hope. I've seen worse."

"Sectuib," said Heshri, "he's yours for your services."

"Heshri, you've got to learn that he's nobody's property." The channel grunted as he attacked the fastenings of the boy's metal collar. "He's a person. Think of him as sick, or mentally disturbed, but still a person."

'Yes, Sectuib."

The collar came off with a metallic snick. Klyd wound the chain around it and put it on the dresser. "We'll call him Norbom until he can choose his own name."

"Then you will accept me into Zeor?"

"No. It's not a matter of me accepting you. Rather it is you who must accept us. You will not be ready to make that decision for many months. Disjunction is neither short nor pleasant."

"I feel . . . normal . . . now."

"Now, yes. But after six or eight months, it may be different. In the meantime, you will be welcome at Zeor. I'll write your entry form in the morning. You'll take Norbom and carry a message home for me while Hugh and I ride to Iburan."

"Gladly, Sectuib."

"Go downstairs and get something to eat. I'm going to require Hugh's services here. Do you have room fees?"

"I think so, Sectuib."

"Here." Klyd fished some coins from his pocket and pressed them into the thin hand. "Head high. You represent Zeor down there, and they all know it. Watch out for the salesman. Andle uses his kind."

"Yes, Sectuib." Pulling himself to his full height, the boy gathered his pride and left, acutely conscious of his new status.

When the door had closed, Valleroy prompted, "My help?"

"Yes. In spite of the drug, Norbom may panic when I initiate transfer. I want you to stand by to do whatever seems necessary."

"Klyd, you know I'm not trained in this sort of thing!"

"You did all right handling that crowd downstairs."

"You heard?"

"Couldn't help it. You had me frightened there for a minute."

"I told you, I'm not . . ."

"At any rate," said Klyd firmly, "I would require the assistance of my Companion for this, so I could hardly send you with Heshri, could I?"

"If you're going to require help, maybe you better not do it."

"I must. I gave Heshri almost two thousand dynopters from the accounts of Zeor . . . that must be recovered from the Gen he was assigned. Besides, I can't send him out there with a high-field Gen in tow, can I?"

"I wouldn't know. It's your move. What do I do?"

"Just stand by." Klyd took the Gen by the hand. He moved docilely to the bed. Laid out against the spread, the slight form looked so fragile Valleroy felt sorry for him.

Klyd began to croon softly, no words that Valleroy could isolate, but a reassuring sound. Slowly the channel seated himself, took the boy's hands, searched out the nerves of the forearms, and made the vital contact with his laterals.

The Gen's eyes widened. Klyd hesitated, still talking to lull the incipient terror. Then, as if at some signal, the channel bent to make lip contact. The boy stiffened, real terror penetrating his drugged haze.

Valleroy was certain he ought to *do* something. Enviously, he remembered the calm competence of Denrau aiding Klyd. But Valleroy had no idea what Denrau's well-schooled motions actually *did*. He took half a step toward the channel, but almost as soon as it started it was over.

Klyd rose and moved wearily to the chair. "Hugh, take care of him." He closed his eyes.

Not knowing what else to do, Valleroy dressed the boy in one of his own changes of clothing, using several pins scrounged in an empty dresser drawer. Throughout this operation, the boy remained passive. When he'd finished,

Valleroy stood the Gen in front of the mirror. "Well, now you look like Norbom instead of a number."

"He certainly does," said Klyd, rising to examine the Gen.

"I thought you were asleep!"

"We ought to be. Let's take him to the toilet and wash. Heshri will be back pretty soon, and we can all get some sleep."

"Flip you for the chair."

"What?"

"The children get the bed, don't they?"

Klyd mouthed the English word. *"Flip?* Doesn't that mean turn over?"

"Yeah. Flip a coin. Gamble."

"Oh. No. Gen society does indeed have its cultural priorities, but they differ radically from those of Sime society. You'll still have to share the bed with me, and you'll have to make it seem like routine."

Valleroy shuddered. "Yes, Sectuib. But that old bag downstairs isn't going to rent the kids a room. Even Gen eyes can see that."

"True. She'd probably throw us all out if her husband would let her."

As they made their way down the hall to the washroom, Norbom between them, Valleroy asked, "Why wouldn't her husband let her?"

"He knows many of his guests stop here on the off chance of seeing one of us perverted freaks. When they get home, they can embroider fanciful tales about the harrowing things those 'filthy people' do. Tonight's incident will enthrall many a fireside gathering this winter . . . and it will bring a wave of new business here."

They took turns managing Norbom and were on their way back to their room when Heshri joined them. Sharing out the blankets, they bedded down for the night, the two Simes falling instantly into a deep sleep while Valleroys lay self-consciously stiff.

Valleroy's fingers sought the starred-cross that nestled on his breast. It helped. If only Aisha had such a secret weapon!

CHAPTER FIVE

Choice Auction

NOON OF THE NEXT DAY FOUND VALLEROY RIDING BE-
side the channel while trying to avoid the carts and
wagons that jammed the streets of Iburan. Unlike Gen
towns, Iburan had no wall and no apparent defenses. It
sprawled chaotically in every direction, reeking with the
pungent scents of Sime living . . . a veritable metropolis
compared to Valzor.

During that long ride through city streets, Valleroy
was slapped with wet laundry from a second-story
clothesline, clouted by a workman's ladder, which Klyd
avoided with uncanny grace, pelted by thrown mudballs,
and subjected to lewd jeers from street urchins who scattered at Klyd's merest glance. Valleroy endured stoically.

As they neared the auction, the indignities ceased.
Here, the buildings were newer, the people brighter, and
the streets quieter. At the end of a side alley, they found
a stable where the horses would be cared for. From
there they made their way on foot toward the stands
that were already filling with spectators and purchasers.

The auction occupied a bowl-shaped amphitheater
surrounded by tall buildings that seemed to crowd up
to the wall and peer into the arena. The circular stone
ledges that served for seats were unpadded except in
the lavishly appointed boxes reserved for dignitaries. As
they picked their way down through the occupied areas,
Valleroy was glad for the way the Simes fastidiously
withdrew from contact with the perverts. It left room
to walk even in the crowd.

Pausing to survey the scene, Klyd pointed out the
representatives of the Householdings in a segrated area
near the stage. Stepping carefully, they made their way
down toward them. Klyd marched right to the center of
the Householder's section, nodding cordial greetings and
exchanging comments with his peers.

Valleroy tried to acknowledge each introduction with

due courtesy but found his eyes constantly drawn to the stage. Three silvery cages arranged in a triangle displayed three lovely Gen women, impeccably groomed and implacably defiant.

Here were no vacant, staring eyes or blank minds. These were people! People who were for sale to be killed in exquisite luxury . . . but nevertheless to be killed.

Klyd's hand on his arm brought Valleroy into a seat, but he continued to stare. In English the channel muttered, "Snap out of it, Hugh, this isn't the first time you've attended an auction with me, remember? Or do you want to be answering questions until the net of lies chokes us both?"

With an effort, Valleroy dragged his eyes away from the girl in the center cage, a redhead dressed in scintillating green and white with what looked like emeralds around her throat. Klyd turned in his seat, scanning the ranks of the crowd behind them. "You take the right, while I check the left."

Obediently, Valleroy began scanning the right portion of the crowd. "What am I looking for?" he muttered barely moving his lips. The audience seemed a cross section of wealthy Simes, well dressed, well groomed, and, Valleroy noted, well armed with jewel-handled whips.

In an "of course" tone of voice, Klyd said, "The highest-ranking buyer who appears to be in greatest need."

"Oh," said Valleroy, as if that explained everything.

"Never mind. I've already checked your section. But you must at least appear to be doing your job."

"Yes, Sectuib."

Turning back to face front, Klyd bent close as if to hold a conference. "When I move over to talk with Sectuib Nashmar, you search my section until you find the woman dressed all in red. She's Deference Bidder since she is in greatest need. That means we can't outbid her. Until she makes her buy, I want you to watch her as if you were reading her bids and reporting them to me. Got that?"

"Got it. Seems there's more to being a Companion than I ever thought."

"Much more, Hugh. Much more. Let's just hope Lutrel doesn't take a fancy to Aisha . . . if she's here."

Klyd moved over two seats and went into conference

with one of the other channels, Nashmar, wearing the green livery of Householding Imil.

Examining the man closely for the first time, Valleroy noted he must have had at least one distant ancestor who was oriental and one who was black. His face had the classical broad, flat oriental features, but his skin was an earthy brown. It contrasted oddly with the typical Sime build, wiry yet powerful despite the lack of obvious muscles. But the most startling thing about Nashmar was the blond hair and blue eyes so incongruous with the rest of him. Valleroy couldn't help staring several moments longer than he should have.

Nashmar's Companion was no less interesting. He appeared to be a nearly pure-bred black, a rarity such as Valleroy had never seen before.

With difficulty, Valleroy tore his eyes from the conference and squirmed around until he could see the woman in red. He couldn't see any obvious difference between her and the others in the stands . . . except that she was perhaps, a little richer . . . but he kept her hands in sight ready to report every motion she made.

Amid a flurry of drums, the auctioneer came onstage and began a rapid-fire patter that made little sense to Valleroy. The audience settled down while Klyd unobtrusively covered Valleroy's hands with his own, tentacles entwined among Gen fingers. Valleroy managed to suppress his reaction long enough to see that the other Householders had assumed the same position. He tried to relax and keep on eye on Lutrel. At least half the audience was watching her.

The three women were quickly sold, and three men were brought out. They were muscular specimens of hale manhood, fettered by chains that were much more than decorative. Bare torsos gleamed with oils that highlighted the contours of their well-developed muscles. Around their throats, cruelly barbed collars lay ready to pierce their necks if the slightest pressure was applied to the chain. A second spiked harness encircled their loins so that any sudden movements would be sheer torture.

The men stood still, eyes, flashing defiance, but helpless. Klyd muttered, "Zeor could use a few like them. I hate to attend these affairs when I'm not free to choose from the best offered."

Valleroy was about to frame an acid retort condemning the channel for a cold-blooded Sime bigot, but instead he warned, "She's bidding now."

Klyd's eyes flashed to the hands of Nashmar, who was getting Lutrel's bid from his Companion and repeating it for Klyd's benefit. As soon as the Deference Bidder's hands moved, all the other bidding ceased. The second male captive's sale was the quickest up to that point.

"She's leaving now," whispered Valleroy. "One of her attendants is coming down to take possession. She must really be *somebody!*"

"You don't know? Hugh, that's *Lutrel.*" At Valleroy's blank stare, he elaborated, "Andle's wife!"

"Oh? Oh. Do you suppose she recognized us?"

"Probably not. Her need was intense enough to be thoroughly distracting. But you can be sure that at least one of her servants will be reporting directly to Andle. We must walk with extreme caution."

"You think Andle is directly responsible for Feleho's murder?"

"It's very possible. Zeor is a political keystone. Destroy us and the whole Householding Tecton could collapse. Look! That girl resembles . . ."

Valleroy's eyes shot back to the stage, all thoughts of Sime political intrigue driven from his mind. But none of the three dark-haired beauties that stood there was Aisha. "The one in the middle resembles her somewhat, but Aisha is shorter, with a more oriental caste to her eyes."

"Well, that's only the third group. Nine more to go. Deference Bidder is now the man dressed in black, the one in the box at the top of tier three."

"The dark-skinned one?"

"Right. Keep an eye on him."

Valleroy shifted in his seat until the new Deference Bidder came into his line of sight. "Klyd, what reason did you give Nashmar for requiring his signals?"

"The usual . . . that I was training you in a new system and wasn't sure if we had it right yet."

"Stacy was right about you. You're good in the field."

"He was right about you, too, or we wouldn't have gotten this far. I just wish you had a little more self-control."

After the man in black purchased a hulking giant of a man, there were no more Deferencee Bidders.

Valleroy was allowed to reposses his hands as the auction took on some of the aspects of a free-for-all. Fortunes were changing hands, for the sake of one Choice Kill. As the seventh group—three stunning blondes tauntingly dressed in Zeor blue—were displayed, Valleroy said, "Why are these people willing to pay so much when they could get a Gen from the pens for practically nothing?"

"For exactly nothing, and that about all they're worth. There's a certain status in being able to afford the best, and, in this case, quality is proportional to the degree of defiance the victim can muster."

"There's more of a thrill in conquering a fighter?" Valleroy knew his disgust was showing, but he didn't care.

"Not conquering, frightening."

"You ought to know!"

In that soothing, professional tone he'd used on Norbom, Klyd said, "I wouldn't know since I've never killed. But this I do know . . . disjunction is not merely physical. The kill touches deeply rooted psychological traits. It actually warps the personality. That's one reason only the young can come to us."

Valleroy greeted that with silence. The auctioneer, a wizened leathery-skinned Sime, completed the sale of the third man in the eighth group. It seemed to Valleroy that each sale was contested interminably now that there was no Deference Bidder. At least it gave him time to learn some of the auctioneer's tentacle gestures.

Group nine consisted on three petite, dark-haired beauties, each baring a striking resemblance to Aisha. Valleroy began to wonder if Feleho had mistaken one of these for her.

Group ten slowed the bidding to a crawl, Each of the three men, hardly more than boys really, was a clearly handsome specimen of a pure race . . . one Oriental, one Caucasian blond, and one Indian. The auctioneer seemed to value them higher than the bidders wanted to go.

Group eleven, the last group of women, were all statuesque blondes. Valleroy's heart collapsed. Here was the disappointment he'd been nerving himself to face. Yet Aisha was a fighter at least equal to any of these. She would be Choice for some dignitary . . . somewhere.

He watched in grim silence while Nashmar fought

a hotly contested battle for the last three men, who appeared to be brothers. They were tall, superbly muscled Gens with hatred in their cold blue eyes.

Every time Nashmar's opponent raised the bid, Klyd muttered a string of imaginative maledictions that amazed Valleroy in their scope and depth. There came a long pause after the last such raise while the auctioneer called for further bids. Nashmar sat silently, lips compressed.

Valleroy said, "What's the matter?"

"That's Tyte Narvoon bidding against Nashmar," said Klyd, as if that explained everything.

Valleroy twisted around to take another look at the opposition. The auctioneer had attempted to speed the bidding by offering the lot of three together, but this man was blocking the effort. "He looks frightening but what makes him different from anybody else?"

Klyd favored Valleroy with a sharp glance, seeming to consider the wisdom of explaining. Then he gave an almost imperceptible shrug. "I guess you're an adult even by Gen standards." He looked toward Nashmar. "Narvoon is what I would term a real pervert, but I don't know the English word for it. He prefers men instead of women. Nobody would mind except that he buys Gens for his purposes. The kill is one thing, legalized torture is something else. Haven't you noticed that even the nonbuyers have been bidding against him all afternoon?"

Valleroy looked around at the others in the audience, most of whom had come for the show rather than to buy. It seemed they agreed with Klyd. "I suppose," said Valleroy scathingly, "you don't get people like him in the Householdings?"

"It's extremely rare among Simes. Narvoon is from out-Territory originally. I'm told he had a partcularly hard time of it, and he was warped by the experience. Some say he hates himself for being Sime, and can't stand the thought of having children. Others say this is his way of committing suicide, and it's working. I don't know, but he certainly isn't well."

Valleroy looked again at Narvoon, seated a little apart from the others around him. He was a veritable skeleton of a man, with sunken cheeks and hollows at the temples that gave him a death's-head aspect. When Valleroy looked back at Klyd, he found the channel exchanging signals with Nashmar under cover

of his cloak. Nashmar nodded and signaled the auctioneer a double raise.

Narvoon rose jerkily and stalked out of the amphitheater, cloak flying behind him like bat wings. There
was a stirring among the rest of the audience that
Valleroy interpreted as a surprised approval of the Householding's move. Evidently, Nashmar gained some public
sympathy for the Tecton along with three raw recruits.

But to Valleroy it was a chill victory. From a grand
total of thirty-six Gens auctioned, only seven had gone
to the Householdings.

The crowd's buzzing rose to a full crescendo as
groups formed and drifted toward the exits. Numb
with the realization that it was really over, and Aisha
was still missing, Valleroy sat staring at the empty stage.
Around him, the Householders began to gravitate toward
Klyd, forcing Valleroy to resume the role of Companion.

He watched Klyd pass something to Nashmar. It
looked like a small purse, but Valleroy wasn't given a
chance to ask. One of the other channels, wearing a
cinnamon brown livery, greeted Klyd expansively and
then said, "You surprise me! Not one purchase for
Zeor? Was the grain harvest so poor?"

Chuckling, Klyd introduced Valleroy, saying, "The harvest is ample this year, Siml, but Zeor is Gen-high at the
moment."

"Then what brings you to Iburan?" asked one of
the Companions.

"The pendulum always swings. A talented Gen must
be retained against the day of need."

"Aha!" exclaimed the Companion, grinning. "Wife-
hunting are you?"

"Must I answer that?" said Klyd.

"No," said Nashmar reasonably, "but answer me this.
What is this great talent that must be retained?"

"Such talent cannot be described in words, my dear
friend. But you shall see with your own eyes at Arensti."

"Zeor plans to win again this year?"

"No way we can avoid it," declared the channel.

The glances that were exchanged after that solemn
pledge left no doubt in Valleroy's mind about the high
position of Zeor in the Tecton.

"Naztehr," Nashmar said to Valleroy, "you are a
designer?"

"And artist, Sectuib."

"But you are Zeor's Arensti Designer?"

"Zeor has so honored me."

The looks of pure respect that that earned Valleroy gave him a little shock. If he'd known the degree of confidence Zeor had placed in him, he might have refused to try. In fact, at that moment, he suddenly felt like withdrawing his design, afraid it would tarnish Zeor's illustrious reputation.

But he wasn't given time to think about it. Nashmar drew Klyd to one side as the company began to disperse. "House of Imil would like to submit a proposition for Zeor's consideration."

"Zeor listens," said Klyd formally.

Taking his cue from Nashmar's Companion, Valleroy assumed a station to one side and slightly behind the channels. He listened quietly to the conversation, straining his brain to infer the gaps in his vocabulary.

"Imil requires the services of an exceptional artist to do the catalog for the spring collection. So we would like to borrow your Aresnti Designer for a few days."

"Well, I don't know about that. Zeor has much work for him. . . ."

"We can pay well to a Gen-high Householding. The prestige of putting out a catalog done in the hand of the winning Arsenti Designer would be worth, say, a young channel at least." Nashmar abandoned all pretense of bargaining. "Just think what this will mean for the Tecton! A Householding triumph at Arensti, a superb spring collection bound to sweep the field also done by a Householding, *and* a catalog of that Householding's collection that will win prizes for sheer artistic perfection, designed, executed, and printed by *our Gens!*" He emphasized the last two words, leaving no doubt that it would be a historical achievement proving that Gens are capable of higher creativity.

Frowning, Klyd said, "You have a point, Nashmar. However, despite my confidence in Zeor, the judging at Arensti isn't over yet. By the time the winner is announced, Naztehr Hugh will be deeply engaged in Zeor affairs. . . ."

"By then it would be too late for us. The catalog must be completed before the Arensti winner will be determined. Imil is willing to gamble on Zeor's chances."

"It would be no gamble. Win or lose at Arensti, Hugh is still the best artist this side of the river."

"Then we must have him at all costs. Come to Imil with us now so we can discuss terms in a more congenial atmosphere."

Klyd hesitated.

"Where else can you stay the night? This must have been the longest action on record, and it's nearly a seven-hour ride back to Halfway House. There isn't a hotel in Iburan that would have you. And," he intimated slyly, "Imil has many marriageable daughters suitable for a Companion."

"True, but . . ."

"Besides that, I have three high-field Gens to transport. I could use an escort."

"Thodian road isn't safe any more?"

"Andle and his holier-than-thou's have been agitating in that quarter of the city. No place is safe since Zelerod published that paper."

"Yes still we grow. In the last year, Zeor gained fifteen Simes."

"And Imil, ten. It's been a record year, and I expect the rate to increase. You'll require another channel, soon, so why not buy one with a few days' time?"

"It's a tempting proposition, Nashmar, but . . ."

"So let yourself be tempted into a night's lodging and some serious bargaining."

"Well," said Klyd, glancing helplessly toward his Companion, "I do owe you the escort."

"Good. Get your horses and meet me at the pick-up block around back. My wagon's with Tubrem Stables."

They parted company, Valleroy resuming his place at his channel's side, filled to bursting with objections that had to be swallowed whole.

CHAPTER SIX

House of Imil

THE TRIP TO IMIL WAS THE MOST EXHAUSTING TRIAL Valleroy had yet faced. He rode beside the flat-bed wagon on which the captives, fetters removed, sat in a securely locked cage. From time to time, the three glowered resentfully or spat lurid profanity at him.

Klyd rode beside him, physically near yet so abstracted in his own thoughts as to leave Valleroy alone to bear the brunt of verbal assault. And never had Valleroy felt so alone.

All his life, he had hidden behind a cloak of Gen conventionality. It was such a deep-grained, well-constructed front that even the people who called him a Sime-lover didn't really believe it.

Still, every interrogation assignment opened a crack in that front. The day-and-night questioning of a Sime prisoner, sometimes lasting almost a month, always left him feeling more sympahy for the prisoner than for the Gens the prisoner had killed. He'd never been able to bring himself to watch a prisoner die of attrition.

When that time came, he would go to Aisha, depressed and guilt ridden . . . even though he hadn't understood the magnitude of the horror the Sime faced. She'd never called him a traitor because of that guilt.

They'd talk and talk, sometimes all night while the prisoner died in some faraway place. By tacit agreement, they never spoke of Simes. Yet he knew that she regarded Simes as people, and the torture of Simes as degrading to Gens.

On such occasions, he was never able to make love to her, a fact she accepted without question. Now, Valleroy wished they'd talked about it. He wished he'd been able to explain why he'd never asked her to marry him.

If a child of his turned out to be Sime, he wouldn't have been able to destroy it. Then, Gen law would have turned against him, leaving his wife a widow. But if his child were Gen, he'd be unable to teach him a proper hatred of Simes . . . and the traitor in him would be revealed.

He'd be savagely glad for that, thought Valleroy, because it would settle things once and for all. His own doubts would be gone. Or would they? Here he was, dressed like a Sime, riding within touching distance of a Sime, while his Gen allies sat caged and humiliated beside him. Yet something deep within him refused to admit that what the captives said about him was true.

After a long period of silence, one of the captives called to Valleroy, "Hey, Turnic . . . you with the Sime hands . . . come over here!"

Even if "turnie" wasn't the most polite form of address, it was the most civil thing they'd called him so far. Valleroy nudged his horse a little closer to the wagon.

"Hey, Turnie, you do speak English, don't you?"

"Everyone in this party speaks English."

"Yeah? You'd never know it," said one.

"Shut up, Grenel," said another, gripping the bars and staring at Valleroy's hands. "A guy shouldn't have to go his grave thirsty. Even a turnie ought to see that."

"You're not going to any grave, only to Householding Imil. And there, people ask politely for what they want."

The third captive staggered to his feet on the swaying wagon bed and bowed mockingly toward his brother. "Vrian, may I have the pleasure of killing you?"

The others laughed raucously at Valleroy's discomfort while Vrian rose and bowed smiling. "Not if I can kill you first, Prins."

Angered, Valleroy said, "You ought to be grateful Sectuib Nashmar brought your freedom!"

The first captive gripped the bars, fine muscles bulging. "Grateful! If I can just get my hands on him, I'll break every bone in his skinny body! Nobody buys the Neromein brothers!"

As if that were on old rallying cry, the three chanted, "Death to all Simes!" One of them added, looking straight at Valleroy, "And all cowardly Sime-lovers and Judas-goats. Tell me, Turnie, how many Gens have you trapped for them?"

"*None!*" spat Valleroy.

"What do they pay you with, Turnie?"

87

Prins rattled the bars at Valleroy. "They'll kill you, too, you know."

"These Simes don't kill!" shouted Valleroy.

"You don't really *believe* that?"

"It's true!"

Vrian elbowed his brother out of the way. "You'll find out the hard way, Turnie, but then it will be too late. Get us out of here, and we'll see how many of them we can get before they kill us. Give us a fighting chance, and we'll know you're no turnie."

Disgusted, Valleroy spat. "Go to hell!"

"Nothing doing! It's hot there, and I'm too thirsty already."

"Bloodthirsty, you mean," said Valleroy.

"Just gimme that canteen and I'll show you what I'm thirsty for."

Valleroy looked around at the other members of the party. Nashmar and his Companion, Loyce, riding on the other side of the cage and the two Simes driving the wagons were too far away. Klyd was near, but wrapped up in some world of his own. All were steadfastly ignoring the exchange. On impulse, Valleroy unlimbered his canteen, nudging his horse in close enough so he could lean out to hand it over.

Reaching for the canteen strap, muscular fingers closed on his wrist and jerked!

He fell, scrabbling for a hold on his saddle. His fingers slipped off the pommel. The slick material of the Zeor coverall slid bit by bit as he tried to grip with his knees. Frantically, he grabbed for the bars of the cage to keep from falling under the wagon's wheels. His boot caught and twisted in the stirrup.

He hung suspended between horse and wagon, fighting desperately to keep his hold as one of the captives secured a stranglehold on his throat. Klyd's voice, shouting, was only a faint sound behind the buzzing in his ears.

The wagon slowed for what seemed like forever. Finally it came to rest. Sime hands and tentacles dragged him loose. He sat on the ground rubbing his neck. Klyd's tentacles poked and probed at his injuries. In Simelan, the channel muttered, "Wild Gens are dangerous animals. Now maybe you've learned that lesson?"

Only the crooked grin on the channel's face kept Valleroy from punching him in the nose.

"The rule, Naztehr, is to ignore then until they've been civilized. It doesn't take too long."

Valleroy pushed the Sime hands away. "I'm all right. Let's go." He climbed back on his horse, and they resumed the ride through sparsely settled countryside.

When they arrived at Imil, the horses and the captives's wagon were taken around back of the court buildings . . . very much like Zeor in appearance . . . and the riders entered through the main gate.

Having missed lunch, Valleroy was very glad to be greeted by a lavish table set along one side of the main cafeteria. They arrived just in time for the last dinner shift, but most of the department heads had waited for Nashmar's return.

Though glad of the food, Valleroy wasn't in the mood for social conversation. He addressed himself only to the meal and steadfastly held his peace. In this company he was a respected craftsman whose services came at a high premium. He'd sustained enough abuse that afternoon to make his status here terribly important to him.

"Hugh," said Klyd softly, "it's been a long day. Wouldn't you like to get some rest?"

Valleroy looked up dazedly to find the long banquet table deserted but for the remains of the meal. He gulped the rest of his drink and rose. "Guess I just failed my diplomacy exams."

"Eccentric behavior is expected of artists. You'll feel better in the morning."

As Klyd and Valleroy moved out into the corridor, the kitchen staff swarmed out with clean-up wagons as if they'd been waiting for the visitors to leave.

"You must know this place pretty well?"

"Imil is laid out very much as Zeor, except it is oriented west to east and in mirror images. We'll have the guest suite overlooking the main gate."

"I've never been up there . . . I mean in Zeor."

"You will, no doubt, be pleased to note that the suite has two large, separate bedrooms."

"Oh, it wasn't *that* bad." Valleroy blushed pink under his tan. He had lain stiff as a corpse the whole night, afraid Klyd would make some unthinkable advance.

Turning into a wide staircase, Klyd laughed. "If Yenava knew what you were thinking, she'd faint! Channels are virtually incapable of anything but a vigorous, if intermittent, heterosexuality."

"You must be reading my mind."

"Of course not. But your emotions are a blazing beacon to anyone who has studied Gens as intensively as I have."

At the third floor, the stair led into a richly hung hallway lined with sculptures that seemed to be genuine antiques. They marched the gauntlet of pre-Sime statues acutely aware that their common ancestors had created these masterpieces.

The artist in Valleroy hungered to study them more closely, but his eyes were too heavy with sleep.

Klyd ushered him into the guest suite. "That will be your room. I'll take this one."

Nodding blearily, Valleroy made his way to his bed and fell into a sound sleep that was broken only by bright sunshine and a persistent knocking on his door.

"Naztehr! Naztehr!"

It was an unfamiiar voice and an unfamiliar title. Only half awake, Valleroy growled, "Yes? What do you want?"

"Naztehr Hugh, Sectuib Farris requests your attendannce in the Sectuib's office as soon as possible."

"What time is it?"

"Almost noon, Naztehr."

Valleroy groaned. He'd slept the clock around and more, a very rare thing for him to do. "Tell him I'll be there as soon as I get dressed."

"Thank you, Naztehr."

Valleroy wasn't accustomed to veneration. Coupled with the luxurious surroundings, it made him uncomfortable . . . as if he'd stepped far out of his class and was about to be caught gate-crashing. He hauled himself out of the cozy bed to face the day, whatever it might bring.

Half an hour later, scrubbed, shaved, and immaculately attired in clean Zeor coveralls that had been laid out for him . . . new and apparently tailored to an exact fit . . . he presented himself at the office of the Sectuib of Imil.

He was shown into the inner sanctum immediately, as if he were somebody important. The young women working in the outer offices turned appraising eyes on him as he passed. It all made him very nervous.

The inner office itself was very like Klyd's . . . clean, businesslike, well organized, and overflowing with work. But there the resemblance ended. One wall was hung

90

with layer upon layer of life-size fashion sketches. In the corner near the court window, a manikin was dressed in a flowing evening gown, while behind the door posed a well-dressed athlete manikin resplendent in iridescent shirt and incredible tan. They were, Valleroy noted, Sime manikins.

But the most startling thing in the room was the fact that Nashmar leaned against a bookcase while Klyd lounged at ease in the chair behind the desk. Valleroy gaped at this reversal of roles. To cover his reaction, he said, "Good morning, Sectub . . ." and then realized he didn't know the plural of the title. "Uh, Sectuib Nashmar, I'm sorry if I kept you waiting."

Nashmar exchanged a cryptic glance with Klyd and said, "You needn't be overly courteous, Naztehr. Klyd?"

Flowing to his feet, Klyd paced around the desk. "Hugh, of course the final say is up to you . . . but I've agreed to trade four days of your time for a young channel of Imil named Zinter. Starting today, if you concur."

Valleroy searched that dark face for some cue, but found none. "You expect to leave me here for four days?"

"Oh, no!" sputtered Nashmar hastily. "Imil would never *think* of separating a channel from his Companion. Don't worry, Naztehr, we are an honorable Householding!"

"Oh," said Valleroy, trying to look relieved. "Sectuib Farris, this is in the best interests of Zeor?"

"Sectuib Nashmar *knows*"—Klyd emphasized that word delicately—"that Zeor must have someone just like Zinter . . . young but with great potential . . . and Imil must have that catalog. This seems like the most natural solution to both problems."

"If it is in the best interests of Zeor," said Valleroy, copying a phrase he'd heard many times, "then it follows it must be in my own best interests." He turned to Nashmar. "I am at your service, Sectuib."

Nashmar laughed, that short tense laugh Valleroy had come to associate with the high-pressure administrators of Householdings. "You needn't go to work until you've had breakfast . . . or lunch, whichever your prefer. I'll notify Brennar to prepare your offices."

"While you are about it," said Klyd to the Head of Householding Imil, "don't forget to dispatch that messenger to Zeor for me."

"I'll send him around to pick up your letter. He'll be at Zeor by tomorrow night at the latest."

"Fine. Hugh, I could use some lunch."

"Sounds like a good idea."

They left together and headed for the cafeteria. "Four days!" said Valleroy when they'd rounded a corner out of earshot. "Stacy will have my hide if . . ."

"Not here! Remember Hrel?"

Looking suspiciously at the massive stone walls, Valleroy said, "How could I forget? Do you think . . . ?"

"If they can do that at Zeor, they can do it anywhere." He added for the benefit of passers-by, "I know what you're worried about. How can Zeor get along without me for another week? Well, that's just exactly the reason we need Zinter. Yenava is due to give birth in a few weeks, but it will be twelve years and more before the child will be able to assume any of my responsibilities. Zinter is already mature. He can be trained quickly."

As they rounded the corner leading to the cafeteria, Valleroy muttered in English, "You know damn well that's not what's worrying me. *Four* days!"

Stopping in his tracks, Klyd turned and backed Valleroy against the wall, gripping the Gen hands in a peculiar hold. Then, under cover of the din from the kitchens, he said, "Hugh, I couldn't help it. It was give in or blow our cover. Nashmar *knows* us, and he knows I've had my eye on Zinter for a very long time."

Valleroy tried to squirm loose. "Let go of me! I've half a mind to saddle up alone and scour the countryside for her!"

"Be still damn it! You're my Companion. Act like it!"

Suddenly shaking with a cold fury, Valleroy spat, "Let go of me, *Sectuib*. You don't frighten me!"

"Calm down! Like this, we have a minute to talk privately. Nobody would dare interrupt!"

Subsiding, Valleroy tried to wrench a hand free. "What are you doing?"

"Faking it. Now listen to me . . ."

"Faking what?"

Exasperated, Klyd snapped, "Entran. If I hadn't been faking, that blast of hatred you just threw at me would have put me in the hospital for a week." He switched to English. "You've got a role to play, mister, and you better measure up or neither of us will live long enough to report to Stacy. Is that clear!"

"Perfectly. But I can't help what I feel."

"You'd better learn to help it. Now get this. Nobody here knows where you came from or when. Zeor's reputation rides on your shoulders. I intend to write Yenava that you are providing for me as well or better than Denrau ever has. You'd better make sure she never hears otherwise, or I'll have your hide. *Do you understand me?*"

The tirade beat aside Valleroy's anger. For a moment, he had a flash of insight into the risks that the channel was taking on Aisha's behalf. One slip on his part could blast the whole Tecton to pieces, and maybe end the human race for good. He wondered if Stacy understood the stakes in this game quite that way. But then he remembered why Aisha was important to Stacy. If she was forced to help break down the Gen monetary system, organized Gen resistance would collapse . . . and *that* would increase the number of Simes by however many a month didn't get killed by the Gen Guard. Either way, it was a race to oblivion.

Sobered, Valleroy said, "I'm sorry, Sectuib."

"Let's have lunch."

That afternoon, Valleroy found that his "offices" were really an immense salon surrounded by eight extravagantly appointed studios where a contingent of models and secretaries swarmed about as if organizing a state visit. His job consisted of sketching pretty girls and ruggedly handsome men (all Simes) dressed in colorful, but unconfining, garments.

The only difficulty he experienced was with the positions of the tentacles. For a while, he was afraid someone would notice that he was very experienced at drawing Gens but not Simes, so he tore up all the false starts.

But nobody stopped to peer over his shoulder without invitation. They were all too busy rushing from room to room, dressing and undressing, or marshaling racks of exotic clothing from place to place. When he did turn out a reasonably satisfactory sketch, the breathless gasps of genuine appreciation made him feel more confident.

After a few hours, he began to enjoy himself. He had dinner brought in so he could continue to work on his sketches after everyone else had gone. He couldn't imagine how four days could posisbly be enough. But when he asked, he was told that part of the catalog had been done by lesser talents while another part would be done by the photographer. Somehow he got the impression that that lofty personage ranked considerably below the artist. But he was too busy even to think about investigating photography.

As one of the leading fashion designers and tailoring houses, Imil put out a line of elite ready-to-wear for all occasions. In the short time he was there, Valleroy saw more different costumes than he'd seen before in his whole life. Many of them were cleverly tailored to use Zeor's Arsensti winners of previous years. Much of the cloth used, Valleroy discovered, actually came from Zeor's mills.

On the next day, all Valleroy saw of Klyd was an occasional glimpse in the corridors or through open doorways; for a few minutes he listened to the channel lecturing an enthralled audience of adults assembled in the big auditorium of the school. All Valleroy could make out was that Klyd wanted the Tecton to set up a new Householding that would be nothing but a school for channels. It would be supported by contributions from all the Householdings so they wouldn't have to farm. The major objection seemed to be that such a concentration of channels would be too vulnerable, especially if they had to depend on supplies that were shipped in.

Another time Valleroy saw Klyd seated on a classroom floor, surrounded by a group of very young Simes. He was teaching them to play the shiltpron—an arrangement of rods held by intricately twined tentacles and then shaken against each other to produce harmonic hums that were damped by a touch of a tentacle. It was a complex exercise.

Valleroy watched for a few minutes, but the class was so engrossed, he tiptoed away without disturbing them. He went back to work, glad that Klyd was enjoying himself.

By late afternoon of the third day, Valleroy was exhausted, physically and emotionally. Never had he worked so hard on so many diverse projects. When the models quit for the day, he decided he needed a break himself. He tossed his charcoal aside and wandered out into the corridors.

In the distance, he could hear Imil's school band practicing. He passed the school auditorium where the dance classes were limbering up while a choral group was trying to sort out different-sized robes from a backstage locker.

Three students went by carrying a spattered ladder and a bucket of poster paint. There was an undercurrent of impending festivities in the air.

It was later the next day that he discovered the celebration was in honor of Householding Frihill's establishing a daughter Householding. One of the top Companions in Frihill who would become the Companion of the new Head of Householding would be visiting Imil on a recruitment tour.

Valleroy overheard whispers among his models about Frihill's internal politics. "There just isn't *room* for two really great Companions in one Householding." And he learned a lot about the close relationship between parent and daughter Householding. For the moment, he just wanted to get away from people.

He took a turn and then another turn. There was a stair leading down. He was too lazy to decipher the signs, so he just opened the stairwell door and went down.

Imil was built on the side of a hill so that the ground floor at the front was the fourth at the back. As he went down, he realized he was on this lower side of Imil, in an area that seemed completed deserted.

It suited his mood, so he stopped to look out a window, enjoying his solitude. It seemed that his breathing echoed down the silent well, which was cut off from the rest of the building by heavily fortified doors . . . two sets of them . . . guaranteed to stop any invaders.

From the window, he could see harvested fields, as barren as he felt. The sun was just dipping behind a distant rise. He watched it wondering whether Aisha could see it, whether she was able to appreciate it.

The thought spoiled his mood. He turned restlessly to explore the lower floors. Between landings, he came to a heavy door with a double-glassed round window set into the wall over a widened step. The sign said INSULATED LABORATORY. He had no idea what that meant, but it sounded formidable enough to keep him out. It seemed to occupy space set into the side of the hill Imil was built on. All he glimpsed through the window was a long empty corridor with a strip of light bulbs down the center of the ceiling.

He went down to the next landing and tried the exit doors. They led him into a corridor filled with the angry shouting of deep male voices. The sound of English in this strange place drew him onward.

The floor was made of some hard material that seemed to absorb the sound of his steps. The walls were freshly painted, but Valleroy could see vague outlines of murals under the new paint. Widely spaced doors indicated large rooms behind the walls He stopped for a drink at a fountain, peered through a window into an unused, bare room, and then continued toward the muted sounds of anger.

He passed a door marked lavatories, and then turned a bend to find his way barred by two massive, swinging doors. The top half of the doors consisted of a heavy screen sandwiched between panes of glass. The handles were secured with an intricate lock mechanism that refused to move when he tried it.

He wasn't sure he should even *be* here, but he stepped up to the doors and peered beyond. This was definitely the source of the noise. The corridor continued after the doors, but what had been an infirmary or school became a prison.

The door to each of the rooms had been cut in half. The top portion had been replaced with bars locked into place with devices similar to that on the swinging doors blocking Valleroy's path.

The first three rooms were occupied, two on one side and one facing. Valleroy could see Gen hands gripping and shaking those bars as their owners raged inarticulately. In the corridor between the prisoners, Nashmar, his Companion, and Klyd stood conferring earnestly.

Valleroy told himself sternly not to jump to unwarranted conclusions. He waited to see what would happen.

He didn't have long to wait. Klyd suddenly turned to look at the doors, saw Valleroy, and came toward him, smiling broadly.

Straight-arming the door as if it were locked, the channel came out into the relative quiet of the hallway. "I'm glad to see you here. Maybe you could help us out if you havee a little time?"

"Help you out?"

"The three Nashmar picked up at Iburan have proved more spirited than he expected."

"Why don't you just let them go?"

"Hugh," Klyd reproached, "you know better than that!"

"No I don't! What right have you to keep people prisoner?"

Klyd paused, looking hard at the Gen, totally bewildered. "We do not keep anyone *prisoner*. What would happen to them if we took them to the gate and shoved them out—even gave them horses?"

Valleroy looked sullenly at the channel.

"Hugh, could you live with a thing like that on your conscience?"

Gracelessly, Valleroy conceded. "I don't think I'd want to try. But we got them here, we could get them to the border."

"Do you know how long Imil would survive after we did that?"

Valleroy, remembering the scarred buildings of Zeor, looked at Klyd's grim expression. "About twenty-four hours?"

"Less."

"So why do the Householdings buy captives if they won't co-operate?"

"They are usually more reasonable when they find they've been given a chance to *live*, if only within the Householding. After they first donate, they have several weeks to become accustomed to us, as you did."

Valleroy wasn't so sure he *was* accustomed yet. "So turn them loose in the Householding and let them see for themselves."

"We can't do that until they donate. These three are brothers, the last survivors of their family. They're firmly convinced all Simes are killers and ought to be killed."

"I see. But surely they must have seen enough by now to know that Imil isn't . . ."

Klyd gestured through the door's window. "There you see Nashmar and Loyce, living testimony to what Imil *is* . . . but the brothers will have none of it. You've absorbed your share of punishment from them already. I'm not asking you to go back in there with me . . ."

"But it would be proper behavior for a Companion?"

"Uh . . . yes, it would."

"Let's go." Valleroy watched closely as Klyd gripped the door's handle and pulled it open. He *knew* that door was locked, but he'd seen it open without any resistance.

From the inside, he watched it shut and then tried pushing it open. It wouldn't move.

"Turnie! We thought they'd killed you for sure! Where've you been?" called Vrian.

"Working," said Valleroy, facing him. "Paying my own way with honest labor, which is more than you can say for youreslf! And I'm no turnie!"

"It was a turnie just like you that got us into this mess. Guess I know one when I see one," said Grenel.

"Shut up, Grenel," said Vrian from Valleroy's right. "What are you doing here, Turnie? Want another throat message?"

Valleroy essayed a wry smile.

"Just step in here where your friends can't interfere, and we'll see how long you'll smile."

"And what will that prove?" asked Valleroy. "That one Gen is stronger than another? I admit you're stronger than I am. Now are you happy?"

"I'll be plenty happy when I get my hands on one of them slimy snakes you call friends."

"Is that how you pay for your room and board, with insults?"

"Or die trying. We wasn't asked if we wanted to stay here."

Valleroy turned to Nashmar and said in English, "Sectuib, I guess that's it. There's no hope. These three are freeloaders who won't do an honest day's work for their keep. You may as well turn them loose and let the juncts kill them."

Nashmar's blue eyes widened for a moment. Then he caught on to Valleroy's tactic. "I can't do that. We've already made much too large a capital investment in buying them."

"No use throwing good money after bad," said Valleroy "They are costing you . . . how much per day?"

Nashmar considered, examining each in turn, and named a figure.

"Over a month's time that adds up to quite a lot. Maybe you could harness them to a plow or something?"

"Horses are more efficient."

"Hmm," said Valleroy, looking at Grenel thoughtfully. "How much did you say your head-tax on them was?"

"The three together come to about five hundred a month."

"That's in addition to room, board, clothing, and incidentals, isn't it?"

Nashmar nodded.

Valleroy looked at Klyd. "I doubt if Zeor could absorb that kind of a loss. There are plenty of other Gens willing to work for their keep. I'd advise getting rid of the freeloaders as soon as possible."

Grenel could stand it no longer. *"Freeloaders!* Freeloaders are we?"

As Grenel strangled on his own anger, Valleroy seized the bars of Grenel's door and faced him nose to nose. "Yes, freeloaders! Where would you be now if Sectuib Farris hadn't helped Sectuib Nashmar outbid Narvoon for you?" Valleroy went on to tell them in graphic detail just what their fate would have been. He moved from barred door to barred door, embroidering in the strongest language he knew.

The three brothers, hulking specimens of raw manhood toughened by a lifetime of frontier living, stood transfixed in utter amzement. The captives' silence only led Valleroy to new passion as he went on to describe the marginal economy of the Householdings as they strove to save one more and then one more Gen despite the Sime laws.

"And after they've done so much for you," finished Valleroy, "you repay them on with insults! Well, I work for my keep, and I won't work to support a freeloader!"

Grenel spat. "And *I* won't support no turnie!"

"Shut up, Grenel," said Vrian. "No turnie calls me a freeloader and gets away with it!"

Valleroy whirled on him. "A freeloader takes but never gives. You've taken a helluva lot from Imil, but what have you given?"

"I have nothing, so I ask nothing. I'm no freeloader!"

"You have plenty. You have so much to give that Sectuib Nashmar has to protect you with bars and locks so nobody will steal from you. You're not only a freeloader, you're a selfish miser hoarding treasure worthless to you just so nobody who can use it can get it."

"Hoarder, am I? Why you skinny little runt . . ."

"You'll show me? Come on, then, let's see you pay your debts, miser!"

Knuckles white, Vrian gripped the bars and stared at Valleroy. In the harsh world of the Reconstruction, the Gens valued only a man's willingness and ability to pay his own way . . . in that order. There was no deadlier insult than "miser," one who was able but unwilling to pay.

The two Gens faced each other, eyes locked in mutual loathing. Vrian knew the coin he'd have to pay in was selyn, even if he didn't know the word for it. Valleroy knew that Vrian knew.

Very softly, Valleroy breathed, "You're scared. You're scared sick."

Vrian matched his tone. "I'll show you who's scared!"

"So get out here and donate to Sectuib Nashmar. I'll believe it when I see it."

"You first," said Vrian coldly.

"I already have. I'm so low in potential they don't even react to me. See?" He moved to place a hand on Klyd's bared forearm.

Grenel said, "All I see is a turnie coward bought by promises of immunity."

"If I can do something you're scared to do, who's the coward?"

Vrain said, "We're not scared to die?"

"No," said Valleroy, "you're scared to live, *miser!*"

Fury building visibly, Vrian stared at Valleroy. Suddenly, Nashmar moved to Vrian's door and pulled it open as if it had never been locked. Wordlessly, the channel watched the captive as if waiting for some sign.

Out of the corner of his eye, Valleroy saw Loyce take up a position between Nashmar and Vrian, but a little to one side. Behind him, Klyd faded back toward the outer door while the confrontation grew ever more tense.

Some signal must have passed between Nashmar and Loyce, for just when Valleroy thought Vrian would attack the channel, Loyce took the Gen hand and joined it to the Sime's, sliding his own hand from between the two with a peculiar caress.

A moment later, Nashmar made full contact. Vrian endured that embrace as if paralyzed. Nashmar was almost as tall as the Gen, but only about half his weight. Neverthless, as Vrian began to struggle, it was obvious the Sime was the stronger. It was only at Nashmar's will that the contact ended.

Vrian staggered back, suddenly off balance. He fetched up against the doorjamb and wiped his mouth on the sleeve of his overall. He couldn't take his eyes off the channel, who stood impassively before him. "I didn't feel a thing. Why didn't you do it?"

"I did. You may go now."

"What?"

The cafeteria is now serving dinner. If you ask him nicely, Naztehr Hugh will show you the way."

"I'm not going anywhere without my brothers!"

"Where they go is up to them," said Nashmar, turning to the third brother, the silent Prins. "You want to try it now?" Without waiting for assent, Nashmar pulled open the door and stepped into the room beyond. There was the sound of a few footsteps and then silence. Prins was the youngest of the three and, thought Valleroy, had probably been willing all along.

Presently, Nashmar emerged followed by Prins, who stood before Vrian, head hung like a little boy caught in mischief.

Now the channel stood before Grenel, who still scowled fiercely. "Not me!"

Vrian shoved Prins aside and confronted his captive brother. *"Shut up, Grenel! You want to spend the rest of your life in there?"*

They glared at each other for a moment. Then Nashmar pulled open Grenel's door. Grenel backed away, crouching like a wrestler looking for a hold. Nashmar threw the door shut with a clang. "All right. If that's the way you want it, we can do without you."

"Grenel," said Vrian, "don't be a fool!"

Grenel straightened, coming back to the bars. Nashmar opened the door to let him out. Smoothly, Loyce interposed himself and made the contact.

From the first instant, Grenel struggled, but against a Sime he had no chance. When he was ready, Nashmar let the big Gen go. From these unwilling general-class donors, a channel drew selyn only very slowly and only from the very shallow, surface levels. Thus, he could reduce their field to the comfort range while not causing the donor any sensation at all. Even so, the selyn thus gleaned was sufficient to support an ordinary Sime for nearly a month because the channel's method wasn't as wasteful as the kill.

"You see," said Vrian, "now we can all go." It was obvious even to Valleroy that Vrian had something other than dinner in mind. Nashmar seemed to realize

101

this. "Even Gens of the Householdings aren't safe out there. Your bills are paid, and you are now low-field. You're welcome to try your luck. But why don't you come upstairs and have some dinner first."

Prins nerved himself to speak. "I don't know about you, but I'm hungry. I'd rather not get caught on an empty stomach."

Using this as assent from all three of them. Nashmar herded his recruits through the outer doors. "Good. I'm sure you'll like us much better once you get to know us. After dinner I'll take you all on the grand tour, and . . ." The doors closed behind them.

Valleroy turned around to find Loyce watching him closely. "Naztehr, that was brilliant! We guessed from your accent you must be a specialist in their psychology . . ."

"Oh, it was nothing."

"Far from it. Now I can see the real purpose behind your gambit on the road . . . the way you flirted with danger when you knew that Klyd and Nashmar were so busy masking the captive's gradients that they couldnt protect you! I can see why Zeor prizes you so highly!"

"Uh . . . thank you," said Valleroy, totally non-plussed by this interpretation. It gave him a lot to think about, but Loyce didn't allow him a moment.

"But we're glad you haven't been at Zeor long enough to have absorbed *all* their ways."

"Oh?"

"Yes, because I can see you're going to have a night ahead of you."

"I am?"

With an eloquent shrug, the dark-haired, coffee-skinned Companion gestured toward the hall beyond the double doors. Valleroy could just see Klyd leaning against the wall waiting. The back of his head was against the wall. He seemed to be examining the ceiling intently.

Loyce put an arm around Valleroy's shoulders and walked him slowly toward the double doors. "Entran is no joke. Oh, I know you two have been doing one of those famous Zeor denial exercises. You people get to be pretty good at it, and I suppose it really *is* the source of the Zeor excellence. But I'll tell you this. I'm glad I'm not the one who's changing his name to Ambrov Zeor!"

"Oh, I don't know . . . you performed very competently just now."

Loyce chuckled dryly. "I thank you, Naztehr. Zeor is rarely so generous with compliments. But Loyce Ambrov Imil is good enough for me."

"Actually you're right that I haven't been at Zeor very long." At that moment he recalled how carefully Klyd had avoided using Valleroy's last name. Since only the Farris family retained their last name within the Householding, everybody had, no doubt, assumed that Valleroy had already pledged Ambrov Zeor. He tried it out for flavor. Hugh Ambrov Zeor. It felt very strange.

They reached the doors. Loyce stopped, turning to Valleroy. "Perhaps you won't feel offended if I offer some professional advice?"

"Isn't the sign of a true professional the ability to take good advice no matter where it comes from?"

"Yes, well, as I was saying, entran is nothing to fool around with . . . especially for a Farris. And you *know* how stubborn Klyd gets. But . . . he's Sectuib. The whole of Zeor depends on him. You owe it to Zeor to make him behave sensibly even if he doesn't want to."

"You know about how far I'd get?"

"Don't I! We tried all day yesterday to get him to work an hour in dispensary . . . or something . . . *any*-thing. He wouldn't, and now look at him! Just watching Nashmar functioning has tied him in knots. How long do you think he can go on like that?

"I couldn't guess."

"How long do you think *you* can stand it?"

Not knowing what he was supposed to be enduring, Valleroy made a noncommittal noise.

"I know what you mean. Listen, Hugh, you're his Companion. You have ways of dealing with him that nobody else does—"

"Oh, I'm not—"

"I know, it's not exactly ethical. But there are times we have to take certain liberties. They always thank us, afterwards, don't they?"

Valleroy squirmed uncomfortably. "I'm not that—"

"It's about time you learned to be, then. Just look at him! How long were you intending to wait?"

"I wasn't—"

"Good. You'll take care of it tonight, and we'll all

103

rest better." Using a metal rod hanging beside the door, Loyce tapped on the grass.

When Klyd failed to respond to the faint sound, Loyce cocked an "I-told-you-so" brow at Valleroy and tapped louder. Pulling himself out of his reverie, Kyd moved to open the door, and the three of them went up to dinner.

All during the meal, Valleroy watched Klyd. The channel's appetite was even scantier than usual. He seemed to move in a daze, almost unable to focus his eyes. Valleroy decided that something really was wrong.

As they were bussing their dishes, Valleroy saw Nashmar watching from the new candidate's table where a select group of members were welcoming the newcomers. Valleroy smiled. Shifting his gaze from Klyd, Nashmar smiled back in what seemed to Valleroy genuine relief.

Both the top channel and the top Companion in Imil seemed to think Klyd was in serious trouble. Valleroy, as limited as his experience was, concurred.

But Valleroy was no true Companion. He didn't know what to do about it. He didn't even know if he *could* do anything. So it was that he found himself alone in his darkened room dressed for bed and pacing back and forth. Grandfather had made him promise to take care of Klyd in spite of himself, and not to let anyone suspect that Zeor would send an unqualified Companion with their most valuable channel.

Entran. Yenava had been so upset about Grandfather suffering from it while Klyd escaped completely. Valleroy wondered if maybe Klyd was punishing himself for some imagined wrong to Grandfather.

Or maybe Klyd was afraid of him because of the anger he felt when Klyd had been faking entran to gain them privacy. Well, thought Valleroy, that would be a switch . . . Sime fears Gen.

Still now knowing what he was going to do, Valleroy pulled on his nightrobe and crossed the suite to Klyd's door. On impulse, he opened the door without knocking and went in.

The room was dark, draperies drawn so even starlight was cut off. "Hugh! What . . . ?"

Homing on Klyd's voice, Valleroy struck out across the floor. "Sectuib, I have a grave matter to discuss with you. A matter involving the pride of Zeor."

"What's happened?"

"Nothing yet. That's the problem."

"I don't understand."

"Neither do I. Tell me what is it a Companion can do to make a channel listen to reason?"

"Oh . . . now I see. Nashmar and Loyce have been after you!"

"Just Loyce. He seems to think the situation is critical."

"These people are Imil, not Zeor. They have little conception of what we can do when we want to."

"I'm thinking, perhaps you don't really *want* to . . . or you wouldn't go around looking like an incipient disaster."

Klyd was silent, invisible in the dark. Valleroy thought he wasn't going to answer. But then the channel got up and went to the window, drawing open the drapes. The stars were bright and clear. The moon cast long shadows across the fields and illuminated the room.

"Entran is painful, isn't it, Sectuib?"

"But trivial."

"Not for Farrises, according to Loyce. What makes Farrises different?"

Klyd opened the window so he could breathe deeply of the cold night air. In the dimness, Valleroy could just see that the channel was drenched in sweat. When he spoke, his voice was low, almost too controlled. "There is a theory that the Sime mutation is still evolving. We've classified eight distinct Sime variants, none of which is ideal. The Farris family produces the channels of the highest capacities and greatest tolerances. We also suffer from the widest range of ailments unknown among others. Entran complications are only a minor part of that."

"If Denrau were here, wouldn't he do what was needed to avoid complications?"

"You're not Denrau."

"I know." Valleroy sat down on the bed. He found himself wishing forlornly that his mother hadn't fled Sime Territory but had joined a Householding instead. Watching the channel, Valleroy saw him start to shiver in the cold air. He went to the window, hand out to close it. Klyd's hands were there before his. The sensitive laterals were half extended, seeking the cold to numb the pain.

The contact was made before Valleroy realized

105

what was happening. Klyd's hands closed over his, tense but gentle.

Valleroy said, "I promise not to be angry this time, if you promise not to fake it."

With a swift surge of movement, Klyd turned full toward him, gripping his wrists in that peculiar hold. He laid his head on the Gen shoulder, face averted, not seeking the fifth contact point of transfer. Valleroy almost staggered as the channel's full weight came against him. He didn't feel anything happening except the nearly imperceptible vibration of the moist laterals against his skin.

An instant later, Klyd stood erect. "How did you . . . ?" He shook his head, bewildered. "I thought you didn't know how to induce—"

"I *don't* know," said Valleroy, shaken. "If there's anything more I should do, you'll have to tell me . . . before Imil finds out I didn't do it."

"You *wanted* to do that to me, didn't you?"

"I don't know what you mean."

"No, of course you don't," said Klyd wonderingly. "Not yet." He sat down on the bed.

"Stop talking in riddles."

"There's another theory," the channel continued, as if he hadn't heard. "The theory of the symmetry of nature. If there are so many different types of Simes, there must also be different types of Gens."

"I don't follow you."

"No, I don't suppose you do. Perhaps it's just as well. Right now, you'd better get some sleep."

"You do feel better?"

"Yes."

Valleroy retreated to the door, still not sure what exactly he'd done. As he opened the door, Klyd called, "Naztehr . . ."

"Yes, Sectuib."

"Thank you. Denrau couldn't have been better."

"You're welcome," said Valleroy, surprised to find that he really meant it.

The next morning, as Valleroy worked his way from one studio to the next, he often caught glimpses of Loyce studying him covertly. During the noon break, Valleroy wiped his hands on a rag and approached the Companion. "Good morning."

"It certainly is!" Loyce agreed. He glanced around to

make sure there was nobody within earshot. "He's magnificent this morning. How did you do it? I couldn't have managed with less than a transfer."

Valleroy didn't have a chance to reply. Just then Brennar came in with a rack of wedding dresses from which Valleroy was to select the ones he wanted to sketch.

Later that afternoon, three of Imil's lovely girls came through escorting the three new candidates. Valleroy scarcely had time to wave, though he knew they passed behind him several times. When they left, he got the vague impression they were headed for a tour of the fields.

Shortly after that, the Sectuib's flying squad swept into the studio clearing the way and making ready for the galloping administrator, who followed right on their heels.

"Sectuib Nashmar," said Valleroy, rising from his last sketch.

"Naztehr. I've been looking through your work. Beautiful!"

"Thank you."

"I wonder if we could prevail upon you for a special favor?"

"I am at your service, Sectuib."

"The Tarinalar Collection. If we could have just one real sketch from that . . . say the Martesa . . ."

"Well, I suppose so. Why not? It's your time, isn't it?"

Nashmar beamed, making his dark skin and shockingly blond hair all the more striking. "No other artist could possibly do the Martesa! I'll see that you get a copy of the catalog and full credit in print." He raised his voice, "Renita, pose the Martesa. Neztehr Hugh is going to do the Martesa for the cover!"

Valleroy struggled not to groan as the girls in the studio squealed with exquisite joy. He just couldn't see anything so exciting about another outlandish costume, but he resolved to do the best he could.

The ensuing bustle made the mad rush of the last few days seem like a leisurely vacation. Streams of lighting technicians with their lenses and mirrors, mountains of backdrop material, flushed models, half-clothed, dashing about as if preparing for a royal visit . . . all these boiled around Valleroy as he stood mutely in the center of the main salon while they turned one of the studios into an imperial coronation scene.

When Valleroy was finally allowed to enter, Nashmar

was posing two new models on the heavily draped dias. Not only were the models new to Valleroy, but both were men. One of them reclined on a cushioned couch that was oddly contoured to accommodate the one seated beside him. Nashmar was supervising the joining of their hands, tentacles twined in the transfer position.

As Valleroy approached, Nashmar was saying, "Are you certain you can hold the gradient steady, Zinter?"

"I'd better be able to if I'm going to Zeor!"

"If you get tired, take a break."

"Yes, Sectuib. But Enam will tire before I do."

Nashmar turned to the reclining figure . . . hardly more than a boy really. "Enam, don't over-reach yourself."

"Yes, Sectuib," he replied without taking his eyes from Zinter's.

"Naztehr Hugh, what do you think?" asked Nashmar taking Valleroy aside.

"A work of art, Sectuib. I'll do my very best with it."

"Be sure you get the lateral position exactly right. This will be the first cover we've ever used depicting a Sime-Sime transfer, and it must be technically accurate."

"Do you think it wise, Sectuib," asked Valleroy hesitantly, "to show such an act on the cover when the content of the catalog is so different?"

"Zeor's brand of conservativism can be practiced by lesser Householdings, you know. People respect Imil as *the* leading fashion house, but they've learned to forget *what* we are. It's time to remind them. And you are the artist to do it. Your work speaks on a deeper level than any mere photograph, a level deep enough to express our message as only a Companion could understand it."

Valleroy swallowed hard. He was no Companion. But Nashmar didn't give him a chance to temporize. "I don't mean to insult you, Naztehr, but it is my duty to remind you that you are above mid-field with respect to Enam. Although Zinter is unusually adept, he is young and well beneath your level of accomplishment while Enam is struggling with disjunction. Of course, Enam could never injure a Companion . . ."

"Of course not," agreed Valleroy weakly. "It's just that you wouldn't want me to disturb him unduly."

"I knew you'd understand." Nashmar laid a reassuring hand on Valleroy's shoulder. "Zeor's reputation is safe with you."

Nashmar swept out of the room, his entourage trailing.

Seating himself at the drafting board, Valleroy found all his customary materials neatly laid out. The table was positioned to view the scene from the perfect angle. And, he had to admit that the two models had been well chosen. Not only were the classical, angular planes of their faces perfect for their costumes, but their body masses were balanced with a subtle line harmony that made Valleroy's heart sing. The loose robes they wore had been arranged to accentuate that harmony.

The artist in Valleroy came to grips with the problem. It was the most stimulating challenge he'd been handed in Imil. It drew forth his need to express himself as had the portrait of Hrel and Klyd.

He positioned the figures on his page, carefully measuring and balancing the perspective; a touch of color here and a shadow there; a carefully placed highlight; a gossamer blurring at the edges gradually converging on an almost painfully sharp focus around those twined tentacles.

He drew the robes with photograhic accuracy, emphasizing how they were designed for freedom while lending grace and a certain elegance to the act being performed. At last, he came to the detail work on the tentacles. Taking a sketch pad, he approached the pair for a closer view.

The empty tentacle sheath's formed striated lines from elbow to wrist. The loose skin of the empty sheaths revealed a slight bulge that appeared to be a gland about halfway down. From the wrist openings, the channel's tentacles extended to meet the Sime's. Valleroy noted carefully just how much smaller were the moist, pink-gray laterals compared to the strong, dry-skinned dorsals and ventrals.

In his mind, he could see the lines resolved into a force-diagram as delicately balanced as, it was intricate. The dorsal and ventral handling tenacles gripped and immobilized, protecting the exposed laterals from sudden disengagement. Valleroy could appreciate how vulnerable a Sime must feel with those nerve-rich laterals unsheathed. He could see it in the almost imperceptible

109

trembling of the soft pink flesh. And yet, these organs were the most deadly survival equipment possessed by any species on the face of the earth.

Therein lay a contrast that sent Valleroy back to his board in a fever of insight. The very source if the Sime's strength was his greatest weakness. That was the message those twined tentacles had to convey!

He worked with a rising excitement. Every few moments, he rose to circle the models, peering, measuring, and studying. Heedless of the destruction he wrought, he clambered over the backdrop to get a new angle and rushed back to his board to add the precise nuance he'd discovered. He did this over and over again, unaware of the passage of time, oblivious to the fatigue of the models, unmindful of his own exhaustion.

At length, almost satisfied he'd achieved all that could be done, he climbed wearily over the tangled drapes to check those exposed laterals one last time.

Without warning, Klyd's voice called from the studio door, "Hugh!"

Startled, Valleroy jerked erect. His foot caught in a fold of drapery tugging him off balance. He stumbled, arms flailing!

With surrealistic slowness, he plowed into the model. A moist lateral grazed his face leaving a tingling trail across his forehead. Then his head struck the edge of the contoured couch. He blacked out momentarily. When his vision cleared, he was lying on his back, Zinter's legs were sailing over his head, and Enam's face was zooming toward him twisted by a feral grimace!

Sime tentacles lashed about his wrists, steely bands biting deep into his flesh with a peculiar intensity he'd never felt before. The moist laterals slithered around his arms, sensitizing his skin in hot streaks. Just as he realized this was the attack of a killer, another pair of Sime arms intervened!

The attacker was lifted away bodily. Valleroy shook his throbbing head once more to clear his vision. It was Klyd who had rescued him. Zinter lay in a dazed heap as if thrown there by Enam. Now, Klyd stood facing Enam, engaging his tentacles in a secure, protective hold. "I will serve you gladly, Enam, but I must reserve my Companion to myself. Without him, I cannot function."

Struggling feebly against the channel's hold, Enam

110

gritted, "Without the kill, *I* cannot function! I cannot *live!*"

"You can't kill a Companion. Surely you know that by now."

"Let me at him. I'll show you . . ."

"I can't do that."

Sullen resentment burned out of dark eyes. "You keep all the Gens to yourselves! Without them, I'd rather be dead!"

"If Zelerod is correct, we all will be dead very soon."

"I must kill." Enam had surrendered to a deeper instinct, one that could not be repressed.

"You must *not*. Believe me, Enam, you would obtain little more satisfaction from attacking a trained Companion than from attacking me. A Companion doesn't panic in transfer; you can't harm him; and such a transfer can't give you the egobliss of the Choice Kill."

"I *had* him, Sectuib. I know it!"

"Fantasy, Naztehr," Klyd asserted firmly. "Pure . . . wish-fulfillment fantasy."

"Better than nothing."

"You're not in need. But you are high-intil. It will probably break before your next transfer. Wait another three weeks and then come tell me that."

"You won't be here."

"Sectuib Nashmar will be able to provide as complete a satisfaction as you will ever require. If that is not so, Enam, come to Zeor."

"You really believe . . ."

"It will be so. For you as for all the rest. Make that final decision to disjunct. Afterwards, if you still want to, you can always leave. But don't attempt a kill within these walls. You owe us that much."

Zinter was on his feet now, rubbing the growing lump on the back of his head. "Enam, I'd be glad to escort you . . . if you want to go to the infirmary. We have tranquilizers and other methods of helping you get through the worst of it."

Fists clenched, head bent, Enam followed the young channel out while Klyd helped Valleroy to his feet. "Hugh," whispered the channel while examining Valleroy's injuries, "a message just came from Zeor . . . from Hrel. Andle's agent in Imil is Enam. Hrel thinks he's been ordered to get you. If he'd killed you, or even just injured . . ."

"They'd know I wasn't a trained Companion . . . but Zeor knows that already."

"Zeor believes you are talented enough to become a Companion. Otherwise, I'd have had no excuse to give you this," he said, fingering the Zeor crest ring that Valleroy wore.

"But I'm *not* talented . . ."

"I had to vouch for you before Zeor in order to bring you here. I've placed my reputation in jeopardy for your mission. It's a matter of public record that you and I have achieved selur nager. What possible motive, other than collaboration, could I have to lie about that?"

"I see."

"Your incompetence under Enam's attack could have given Andle all the evidence he requires to expose me."

"You've placed too much faith in me. Enam might have succeeded."

"But he didn't when he had all the time he required. That proves I'm right about you."

At that moment, Nashmar burst into the room. "Klyd, what's going on . . . ?" His eye fell on the sketch Valleroy had just finished. He froze, gaping. "Naztehr, this is . . . is . . . there are no words. It is pure glory. It is *truth*."

Klyd moved down to see what so affected the Sectuib of Imil. Immediately, he was caught in the same spell. When he shook himself free of it, he said, "What did I tell you, Nashmar?"

Nashmar nodded, speechless.

Klyd looked directly into Valleroy's eyes with a double significance. "A very rare, very special, very . . . precious talent."

"Thank you, Sectuib Farris. Thank you, Sectuib Nashmar." He'd learned recently that "Sectuib" had no plural.

"Nashmar," said Klyd briskly, "we would like a word with you in your office . . . privately."

"Certainly." He motioned to one of the men who had crowded into the room behind him. "Take this sketch down to Amran's shop . . . and be *careful* with it." Then he led the procession out of the salon and through the halls of Imil.

Valleroy was a little shocked to find the Sectuib's office windows black with night. The studio had no outside windows. Time had ceased to exist while he worked. It was the very thing Stacy had warned him not

112

to allow on this assignment, but this was the third lapse he'd suffered while his assignment stagnated.

Klyd settled into Nashmar's desk chair and turned to face the Head of the Houesholding. "What do you know of Enam?"

"He's an enthusiastic young man, perhaps a bit overly fond of the women, but the juncted are often like that you know. He has many redeeming qualities. Why?"

"He attacked my Companion."

Valleroy saw the lean channel of Imil tense as if attacked himself. Nashmar whispered, "When?"

"Just before you got there. I intervened in time to talk him into the infirmary. He's high-intil."

"A bit early. He's only been with us . . ."

"Figures. I had the same trouble with Hrel."

"Hrel?"

"He had an incredibly long, agonizing time of it. But he made it."

"I don't understand."

So Klyd told him the whole story, leaving out only Valleroy's part and the exact reason Feleho had been investigating the Choice Auction. He ended, "So you see, Andle is up to something in Iburan. I think it is justifiable to assume that whatever he's doing, it means disaster for the Tecton."

"You think he knows you are following Feleho's trail personally?"

"I'm certain of it. His agent was waiting for us at Halfway House, but Hugh's quick thinking prevented him from making trouble."

Blankly, Valleroy said, "It did?"

"Certainly. You knocked all the fight out of those people by quoting the law at them. Otherwise that drummer with the sample cases would have started a riot. He's one of Andle's chief rabble-rousers."

Valleroy gulped, suddenly dry-mouthed.

A little quirk of a smile tilted Nashmar's cheeks. "A Gen reading the law at a crowd of juncts! I wish I'd seen *that!*"

"I didn't see it either, but it *was* something to hear."

"And then," said Nashmar, suddenly thoughtful, "Lutrel turns up at the auction with a swarm of Andle's retainers."

"Followed by Enam. Granted, Hugh actually stumbled and fell on him after teasing him unmercifully for God only knows how long . . ."

"Teasing . . . !" sputtered Valleroy indignantly.

"I know," placated Klyd, "how you get when you work, and I don't blame you for it. But you must admit you weren't considering what your field-gradient looked like from Enam's point of view. . . ."

Valleroy had to concede that. He wouldn't have known *how* to consider it even if he'd thought of it.

"And neither were you calculating the selyur on Zinter."

"True. I wasn't calculating."

"So in many ways, it was your fault—"

"Klyd," Nashmar interrupted, "don't. The masterpiece he created would have been worth making a spy start the disjunct sequence over."

A little stiffly, Klyd chuckled. "Yes, put that way, it doesn't sound so bad."

"And the Zeor genius saved the day, as usual. What have you learned of Andle's newest scheme?"

"Nothing."

"Nothing? An awful risk you've been taking coming out here for nothing."

"A man can't live in confinement all his life."

"But a channel . . ."

Squirming uncomfortably, Klyd said, "Please, Nashmar, I have to listen to enough of that from Grandfather."

"Well, at least let me provide you with an escort home."

"That won't be necessary."

"The East Thodian Road is far more dangerous than the way you came . . . Runzi Raiders in the hills, and unlicensed bands in the valley!"

"I'm fully aware of that. We'll ride alone."

Nashmar shook his head in a way that told Valleroy that Klyd was playing it in character, so he held his peace. A real Companion of Zeor would support that brazen pride which seemed so much a part of the Farris House-holding.

"All right, Klyd, it's your neck and your Householding. But next month, when I send Zinter to you, it will be under heavy guard."

"Fair enough. After he joins Zeor, he'll learn to ride like a man."

114

"Like a channel you mean. Don't you dare send him out without a Companion!"

For answer, Klyd only gestured toward Valleroy.

"All right. Tell me, does Imil owe you selyn?"

"No. Enam didn't draw. He wasn't in hard need, and I think he just used that excuse to get at Hugh. Even high-intil, he could have used Zinter more effectively . . . if he'd wanted to."

"It's hard to see why he didn't."

"He might have been trying to discredit me by injuring Hugh—"

"Then he's a fool! A Companion of Zeor?"

"Or he might have merely been instructed to put Hugh low-field out of phase with me."

"Oh, Denrau could provide."

"We're not *at* Zeor yet. Besides, Hugh and I have a . . . commitment."

"I see. But how could Enam . . . or Andle . . . have known that?"

"Hrel could have reported it."

"But he's changed sides now."

"Only recently."

"Think it will last?"

"Yes, I do. Nashmar, do you realize what this means? If you can pull Enam through . . . and bring *him* over to our side . . ."

"That we can absorb any spy Andle sends? It means we'll win. But how can I bring Enam over without losing one of my own people like you did?"

Klyd leaned his elbows on the chair arms, twining tentacles thoughtfully. "I don't think it will be that costly. Disjunction is its own end . . . once it is achieved. His own body's new freedom will argue for us. His own mind's new clarity will show him our side of it. I think Hrel marks the turning in this war, Nashmar. Victory beckons."

"Now I know where Hugh gets his talent. Zeor has a poet for Sectuib! I wish I had your vision, Klyd."

"I wish only to assure that my grandchildren will never know a junct, never witness the agony of disjuction, and never fear for their safety among Simes."

Nashmar smiled. "I'll second that."

"Then on that happy note of agreement, let us part," said Klyd, rising.

"Just be sure to invite us to the birthday celebration."

"The invitations are probably at the engravers already."

"Designed by Naztehr Hugh, no doubt."

"I wouldn't know. My wife wouldn't let me see them."

"You mean," said Nashmar, escorting Klyd to the door, "that you didn't have time to look though she chased around after you all day. A woman in that condition. You ought to be ashamed."

"Nonsense. Zeor is much better organized than your primitive steading."

"Aha! What you mean is that you avoided her ambush!"

For a moment, Valleroy thought the two channels were serious . . . but then he saw the crinkle lines around their eyes and relaxed. He'd sleep well that night . . . his last night in Imil.

CHAPTER SEVEN

Visions

THE NEXT MORNING SAW THEM ON THE TRAIL FOR home enjoying the fragrant Indian summer breezes. The air seemed alive, renewed from summer's dryness by the fall rains. Every intoxicating breath increased Valleroy's languid content.

They rode at a steady but unhurried pace, sharing the desire to store this moment against the fast approaching winter. To their left, a ridge of mountains running parallel to their road seemed to stretch long fingers toward them like a giant claw gripping the earth. The valleys between the ridges seemed rocky, forbidding gullies. Here and there some scar of Ancient handiwork could be seen. But for the most part there was nothing but stark cracked rock softened only by a wisp of fog.

To their right the neat patchwork of farms on the rolling flatland was crossed obliquely by an occasional farm road. It was a morning to enjoy being alive and free, a morning that conjured the happiest memories of childhood and the wildest exhilarations of youth.

Despite his serene contentment and the richness of the feeling of going home, Valleroy remained acutely aware of how this morning must feel to Aisha . . . if she still lived. Imprisoned. She wasn't the type to cower at the prospect of dying. But there were limits even to her courage.

Courage? Yes, Valleroy thought, he'd always admired her for that versatile courage she seemed unaware of having. He remembered the first time he'd seen it in action.

It had been a day very much like this one—sunny, mild, and almost too beautiful. They'd been hardly more than children then, sneaking off for a day alone, exploring some formidable ruins of the Ancients. It had been, Valleroy remembered, the last time they'd ever discussed Simes.

The ruins were nothing more than a huge brooding mound of rubble pierced by an occasional upright skeleton that refused to crumble. But to that air of the inviolate decay of senescent dignity, there was added the haunting terror of the Sime Berserker.

It was there, to that grotesque, treacherous, cave-riddled jungle that changeover victims came to escape being killed during their few vulnerable hours. Not many of them survived, but those who did had created legends of terror that clung to the twisted blocks of artificial stone like a visible pall.

Valleroy liked the place because people refused to go there. It was like his own private property . . . a unique sensation for him. He knew that he alone possessed the key to safe entry . . . the starred-cross. For several hours, he and Aisha poked though the outskirts of the forbidden area. Little by little they strayed deeper into the broken ground. On impulse, he invited her to come and see the secret temple he'd built to his own inner spirit . . . his secret hideaway.

They scrambled over crumbling stone mounded with scraggly vines, tufts of grass, and an occasional bush. It had rained recently, leaving fresh puddles and newly cut gullies to bar his usual paths. He chose his footing with ostentatious ease, acutely aware of the impression he was making on her.

She followed, darting furtive glances toward every

117

tiny sound of scurrying rodent or fleeing bird. He picked a trail a few yards ahead of her, his head high. He moved with all the confident pride of an owner in his private garden. So it was she who found the body.

Her choked gasp brought him back to her in three bounding leaps. To one side of their path and beneath them, a large rain water lake filled a depression that had been quarried for building material. The water was mirror smooth under the blue sky. Near the center of the lake floated a body, face down, arms extended as if groping for something just out of reach.

Even from where they stood they could see the bulging ridges that had just been developing along the length of the forearms. They knew they saw the fluid-filled tentacle sheaths swollen to the painful tension that preceded the breakout of the tentacles. This almost Sime had died just before changeover was complete, just before the wrist openings were broken open to release the tentacles that would take selyn.

"Don't worry, Aisha. She's dead. She can't hurt anyone now."

Aisha had given one excruciating shudder, glancing at the surrounding ruins. She had known the danger before she agreed to come. She didn't ask to go back now.

For a few minutes, Valleroy walked beside her, holding her hand. But then the climbing became difficult once more, and they broke into single file. She was a good climber, never wasting a motion nor seeming to tire. She was the only girl Valleroy had ever liked to go places with.

Finally, they arrived at Valleroy's private retreat. It was more than a cave really, lit only by a few broken pieces of mirror set to reflect the outside light. On a sunny day like that one, it was bright and cheerful within.

He held aside the mat of vines he'd cultivated to hide the entrance and motioned her inside.

Her gasp of appreciation was payment enough. She circled the room once, moving from rough-hewn easel he'd built into one corner, past the sketches he'd liked enough to save, to his rock collection spread on a tattered but painfully clean blanket. Her amazed reverence told him she knew the value of what she saw . . . knew it and treasured it as much as he did.

She paused, transfixed by one of his drawings. It was himself fancied as an adult Sime, standing on a

118

wind-blown hilltop, one tentacled arm raised as if straining to touch a passing cloud. Quietly, he slipped onto the bench before his easel and sketched her as she would look as a Sime.

It had been the first time he had ever committed to paper the form of her loveliness. He drew her as she stood there before him . . . grave, sensitive, open, undemanding, uncondemning.

When she turned to him, she said wonderingly, "You aren't afraid . . . of changeover . . . are you?"

For answer, he handed her what he'd drawn. She looked at it quietly for several minutes, her eyes straying occasionally to the upflung Sime arm in the other drawing. "Maybe you're right, Hugh. Maybe it wouldn't make a difference . . . for those who survive."

"We're both over sixteen now. Changeover isn't likely for either of us any more."

She turned to the picture of the windswept hilltop. "Are you disappointed?"

Here, in this place, secure from prying ears and the censure of his fellows, Valleroy dared answer, "I don't know."

"You'll probably never know."

"Will you report me?"

"No." She took his hand and ran her fingers along his muscular forearm, pausing at the raw-boned wrist, and then tracing a line down the too delicate, overly fine-boned fingers. For the first time in his life, Valleroy wasn't embarrassed by those hands. "Hugh . . . maybe . . . you should have been Sime . . . maybe you will be . . . it's happened to seventeen-year-olds, they say."

"Not often."

"But maybe it could . . . do you still hope?"

"I don't think I ever hoped."

"But you've never hoped not."

"I'm not sure."

"If you don't . . . become . . . what are you going to do with the rest of your life? Paint?"

"No, I don't think so."

"Why?"

He couldn't answer that. He tried, but his eye kept going to the windswept hill. It wasn't a well-done painting . . . the proportions were off . . . he'd tried too hard to graft his peculiar hands onto a too large wrist . . . the tentacles weren't right either. But he'd never felt any need to do the painting over with his more mature skill.

She nodded. "Because painting is too personal? Because you're afraid they'd see this in everything you did?"

"Maybe. Or maybe because artists usually starve. I've had enough of that to last a lifetime. I think I'll go into something that pays high with an early retirement. The Army, maybe . . . or the Federal Police Field Teams. When I've earned my retirement pension, I can spend the rest of my life painting. I won't have to show them to anyone . . . if I don't want to."

Now, Valleroy sat astride his horse, riding calmly beside a Sime through Sime territory. He was here to earn his retirement pension by rescuing Aisha . . . and all he'd done so far was earn a living by drawing. He thought he ought to feel guilty for enjoying himself so much while Aisha was in such danger. But there had been nothing he could do about finding her. Nothing.

Klyd had spent much of the four days at Imil screening their recently purchased Gens, gathering rumors, and discreetly probing for information. But he hadn't come up with a single concrete lead.

Valleroy felt it was now up to him to take matters into his own hands, but he was helplessly trapped in a strange society. So he rode beside the channel alternately enjoying the day and suffocating with frustration.

At noon, when they settled down in a shady grove to eat lunch, Valleroy said, "To hear Nashmar talk, you'd think the road would be swarming with unlicensed raiders looking for stray Gens, but we haven't seen a soul."

Klyd laughed, swigging at his canteen. "Well, the day is only half gone. Most unlicensed raiders are harvesting the fields now. Later on, they'll be heading home tired and looking for some fun."

"They consider channels excellent sport, too, I hear."

Klyd nodded. "This time of year they'd be looking for Gens, though."

"Why particularly now?"

"There's a brisk black-market trade. Large fields have to be harvested before the weather ruins them. It's cheaper to do the work under augmentation than to hire other Simes. But augmentation consumes selyn

120

at enormous rates . . . it can double the ordinary Sime's kill rate. There's another factor. The ordinary Sime relishes augmentation. His pen ration doesn't allow him to function at full efficiency very often. It's not quite like entran . . . but perhaps it is similar. He'll go to the black market if he can afford it. If not, he may go prospecting on his own. I've heard of captives taken in the spring being fed all summer, saved for the harvest."

"Sadists!"

Klyd shook his head. "One of the roots of Zeor's superiority is that I budget each of my Simes a regular schedule of graduated degrees of augmentation. It's more than a pleasure, Hugh, it's a necessity."

"How can Zeor afford it?"

"We have the best channels. We get a higher selyn yield from each general class donor. Our Companions are the best."

"Can raiders tell the difference between an ordinary Householding Gen and a Companion?"

"No, but Companions don't generally travel alone."

"With the licensed raiders working the area, pickings must be sparse."

"Sometimes, if an unlicensed band gets frustrated enough, they'll go after anyone . . . even a Householding itself. Several years ago, Zeor was almost wiped out in such an attack."

"Isn't there a law against that?"

"Certainly. If any attackers survived, they'd have been severely reprimanded and heavily fined. Of course, *we* wouldn't have received any of the fines to cover damages."

"Oh." Valleroy frowned. "But you've recovered."

"Not really. Grandfather never healed properly. I lost my first wife and two children. My brother was killed. My sister died in childbirth because of her wounds. No, Zeor never really recovered. That's one reason we require Zinter."

Valleroy absorbed that in silence. "I guess you were serious . . . about preparing the invitations so early. Yenava's child will be the hope of Zeor's future."

"Actually, the invitations haven't been done yet. Grandfather refused to approve the design Yenava chose. She got disgusted and decided to send them with blank fronts. But it will be *quite* a party."

They ate their lunch in silence until Valleroy said, "I'm beginning to think Aisha must be dead."

"Just when I've become convinced she's still alive?"

"Why do you think so?"

"Andle's up to something. I can feel it in my bones."

"Sime's intuition?"

"There *is* such a thing, you know. He's planning something dirty this time. I've seen evidence showing he was behind that raid on Zeor. I don't think he'll try that again . . . but I don't think he intends to fail this time. It's my business to see he doesn't get away with it!"

"How will you do that?"

"I don't know. But I'll think of something. Let's get going. I'm close enough to need to be looking forward to Denrau's company."

Slinging his canteen over his saddle, Valleroy vaulted up onto his horse and set off at a canter. Denrau was a real Companion. Somehow, that thought was depressing. He drew up beside the channel and offered, "When we get home, I'll design the invitations . . . if you want me to."

Klyd reined in sharply. For a moment, he searched Valleroy's eyes. When he spoke, his tone was softer. "Hugh, I did not mention Denrau to slight you. You have done your job well, but Denrau is specially trained to serve."

"I know." Valleroy squirmed under those arresting eyes, certain he wasn't jealous of Denrau.

"If you decide to qualify, you'll be welcome. But Grandfather is right. Even if you do serve, I'd require Denrau to be there too."

"It's nothing like that . . ."

Klyd set off again, slowly. "We'll be honored if you'll design the invitations."

Valleroy rode through the afternoon concocting and discarding various possible designs in a desperate effort to keep his mind off Aisha. He still hadn't chosen a design when, near sunset, Klyd pulled off the road into an orchard that appeared to have been abandoned by the Ancients even before the Sime Wars.

Dismounting, Klyd said, "Zeor is about a twelve-hour ride from here, and this is the last decent camp spot on the road."

Valleroy looked around the clearing. A lazy stream

122

meandered along one side while an Ancient stone cabin with a new roof occupied the other. A woodpile leaned against the cabin under a shed. A well-used ax hung near a scarred stump. "Looks inhabited," said Valleroy dubiously.

"Not a soul within five miles of here. The station is maintained for travelers by the Department of Roads." Klyd led his horse under the woodshed's roof.

Valleroy followed to discover a row of stalls sheltered from wind and rain by a fragmentary stone wall flung out from the corner of the building like a flying buttress. Tracing the faint markings left in the ground around the old relic, Valleroy said, "This looks like pre-War remains rebuilt."

"It is. We do a lot of reconstruction. Householding Frihill specializes in archeological research and makes quite a nice profit from it."

Scooping grain into the horse's trough, Valleroy grunted. "Are they the ones who rediscovered photography?"

"Yes. Simultaneously with several other researchers. It wasn't so much rediscovered as reinvented . . . but we've still got a lot to learn about it. The ancients did miracles with chemistry."

The modern Simes do miracles with chemistry too, thought Valleroy. But he said nothing. No use emphasizing the weaknesses of Gen technology. He worked on in silence.

With the horses thoroughly cared for, they paused a moment to watch the sunset over the valley. It was one of those fiery autumn blazes that turned every line of gray cloud into a symphony of bright color . . . the perfect end to a perfect day. They watched together until the rim of the sun dipped below the horizon, relinquishing the sky to the first stars. Only the swift drop in temperature reminded them that summer didn't stretch ahead indefinitely.

After a while, they carried wood inside and laid their fire on the magnificent stone hearth. To Valleroy's eyes, it seemed as if the tiny cabin had been constructed around a fireplace designed for a room bigger than Zeor's cafeteria. Soon the fire made the room a snug haven against the night's chill. A savory rice concoction that Imil's kitchens had packed for them filled the air with mouth-watering aroma.

123

Klyd divided the one-dish meal while Valleroy brought the toasted nutbread to the table. "I'm tempted," said Klyd, "to trade Zinter for Imil's head cook."

Valleroy glanced sharply at the wiry, dark-haired Sime. "You serious?"

"No, but I wish I were. This *is* delicious."

Valleroy laughed and dug into the heaping portion with gusto. It was definitely one of the best meals he'd ever eaten. It tasted like creamed peas in orange sauce but with something crunchy like apples and tangy like cloves but salty-sweet. "Tell you what," said Valleroy, "maybe we can buy the recipe with a portrait or something?"

"Now that sounds like a possibility. I'll put a negotiating team on it the minute we get home."

They ate with trail-honed appetites, not pausing to make conversation. Then, dumping the bowls into a pail of water, they moved outside to sit on the wooden porch and munch crisp apples. The huge, burnished moon was just rising to spill its soft brilliance into the night. Against the background of crickets and the softly murmuring brook, an occasional coyote howl rose to challenge the supremacy of the moon. Valleroy filled his lungs with the exquisite fragrance of freshly harvested fields and sighed deeply. It was an enchanted night standing outside of time.

"You know," said Klyd, "I've never been so *happy*."

"I was just about to say the same thing. Somehow, even though Aisha is still missing, and Stacy is probably circulating 'Wanted for Desertion' handbills with my picture on them . . . I *feel* happy."

Flinging his apple core into the orchard, Klyd said, "I think I know why I'm happy. It's a temporary condition. It won't last and it *shouldn't* . . . but"—he paused, glancing dubiously at Valleroy—"you won't tell on me?"

"My lips are sealed forever! What's the secret of happiness?"

"Schedules. Or rather the lack of them. For the last eight days, I've slept without interruptions, eaten without emergency calls, and I haven't been required to *be* anywhere to *do* anything by the clock."

In English, Valleroy said. "We call that a vacation. Do it every year."

"Vacation." Klyd savored the word, copying the Gen

124

intonation. Then he supplied the equivalent in Simelan. "Now I know why so many disputes break out over the assignments."

"You mean you don't take vacations?"

"Not since changeover. There haven't been enough channels in Zeor to do all the work."

"You ought to start a massive training program to get more people into the profession."

"Channels are born, not merely trained. And they are very rare."

"Well, then a vigorous recruitment program is what you need. One designed to attract more channels than nonchannels."

"Most channels don't even know they are channels unless they disjunct very shortly after maturation. Disjunction is much harder for a channel than for an ordinary Sime."

"Are channels really all that different?"

"Oh, yes. Anatomically and psychologically. A separate mutation. Some say a more perfect one since if all Simes were channels, Zelerod's Doom wouldn't be descending upon us."

"I've never understood that. Why the apocalyptic vision?"

"Think a moment . . . a junct takes between twelve and thirteen kills a year. Every year of his adult life. A hundred years ago, that averaged only twenty years. Most Simes died during changeover from pathological complications. Today, we have an eighty per cent survival rate and the Sime life expectancy has increased. The ordinary Sime may live to be sixty or seventy. Do you know how old Grandfather is?"

"No."

"A hundred and five years. And all that time, he's never killed. That's more than one thousand Gens that he hasn't killed."

"Now I see what you mean." Valleroy thought a moment, lining up the factors in his head. Each one served to increase the number of Gens killed per year. "What will Simes do when all the Gens are gone?"

"Die." The channel whispered the word quietly into the night. Valleroy could feel the shivering fear in that single word. The crickets' chattering rose to a crescendo and then fell into a momentary silence like the guests at a party embarrasesd by some too-frank remark.

It made Valleroy hold his breath as if afraid the crickets were reacting to that sentence of doom . . . as if mere insects knew and understood. Then they picked up their chirping song, and Valleroy sighed the bizarre impression away. "Then the Tecton ought to be recruiting . . . high-powered professional campaign . . . mass psychology . . . the works."

Stretching his long legs out and half reclining on the steps, Klyd inspected the stars. "Not only is that illegal in-Territory, but it's also unheard of. Gen society has retained a high level of accomplishment in areas that are total blanks here. We have photography, fertility drugs, some rudimentary electronics, and a certain expertise in chemistry. You have industries based on mass production, mathematical sociology, and assorted fundamental attitudes totally lacking with us."

"A perfect situation for an alliance?"

"A situation demanding an alliance. There's no choice. It's only a question of whether the race will survive long enough for it to begin."

Valleroy pitched his apple core in a soaring arc toward the moon. "With the channels to stand between the ordinary Sime and the Gen, we just might have a chance."

"But only the barest beginning of a chance," Klyd gathered his legs and turned toward the Gen, an earnest excitement written in every line of his taut body. "The Sime-Gen Union will be based, at first, on trust in the channels. But eventually, *all* Gens will be trained as Companions. There will be no need for any Gens to fear any Sime. Channels will become just *people* then . . . not slaves to a talent we never asked to inherit." He gestured. "Look at the stars and tell me what you see."

"Thousands of dots."

"In the old books, it says they are suns . . . many of them just like ours and probably with planets very much like ours. Maybe even people like us, who knows? The Ancients had only just begun to explore when the mutations began."

"Explore the sky?" Valleroy couldn't quite believe it, but the powerful vision that Klyd held seemed terribly important in that quiet evening.

"Hugh, they actually walked on the moon and on Mars! They sent probes farther than that." Klyd took Valleroy's hand, gripping his large-boned wrist to show

126

the contrast between the bare simplicity of the Gen arm and the complex harmony of the Sime contours. "Look at our hands and tell me they don't belong together! Reunited, mankind will go to the stars . . . and beyond . . . There's no limit to what we can do when we stop killing each other and learn to *use* each other's strengths and weaknesses."

Beside the Sime hand, Valleroy's own fingers seemed more like Gen fingers than they ever had before. With an effort, he pulled his eyes away from the Sime tentacles and looked at the moon. His mother had told him stories about walking on the moon. He'd always thought they were only fairy tales. Now, suddenly, the grandeur of the vision brought tears to his eyes. His voice was a husky whisper as he said, "Yesss . . . together we *could* do it." He felt as if he'd pledged his life to a cause far greater than his own existence . . . and it was a wondrously good feeling.

CHAPTER EIGHT

Flight

BUT IN THE HARSH REALITY OF MORNING, THE IDEALIStic vision faded into a childish fantasy ranking next to secret blood brotherhoods and code messages left in hollow tree trunks . . . and secret temples built among Ancient ruins.

The pragmatic fact was that, for Valleroy, there'd be no future at all unless he found Aisha. He no longer wanted to live if he couldn't paint—and he couldn't paint if he had to work for a living. Aisha was the key to both land of his own and a decent retirement income. His stay at Zeor had changed his outlook. He was no longer certain he wanted her to be a part of that life . . . unless she could come to see the Simes as he did, to understand Zelerod's Doom. . . .

Gradually, he became aware of awakening. He felt himself lying on the cot across from a dim window. The thoughts faded back into dreams as he opened his eyes.

Dawn was seeping through the cracks in the shutters . . . a gloomy, gray dawn with the sharp bite of winter once more in the air. Beside him, Klyd suddenly erupted into motion, rolling to his feet.

In three quick strides, the channel dashed to the window, throwing it open as if expecting to see hordes of attacking raiders surrounding the tiny shelter.

Worried, Valleroy joined him. They peered out at the lowering black clouds and a deserted landscape. Far out across the valley, there was a barely discernible movement. Valleroy said, "What's that . . . ?"

"We're cut off," snapped Klyd. "Let's get out of here . . . quickly!"

Without waiting for agreement, the Sime snatched up their few belongings and fled as if escaping a deadly trap. Valleroy took a moment to gulp some icy water from a pitcher. Then he pounded after Klyd, rounding the building and skidding to a stop at the tackle bar.

They saddled up with grim speed, Klyd finishing first and turning to help Valleroy. Moments later, they were racing east, away from Zeor and into the mountains.

Flattening himself behind the sorrel's long neck, Valleroy tried to protect his face from the icy wind. Between slitted eyelids, he managed to keep the channel in view despite the other's faster mount.

They flashed eastward through the early dawn as if pursued by nightmare monsters. Their horses blew frosty steam clouds into the sudden winter's promise of snow. It wasn't long before the horses were lathered into gray-white ghosts nearly lost among wisps of ground fog.

When the animals could go no farther, Klyd reined in. He leaped down and stripped canteen and bedroll from the saddle. "Hurry. We might make it yet."

"Wait a minute!" said Valleroy, loosening his saddlebags. "Whatever we're running from, we're running in the wrong direction! Zeor's back . . ."

"I *know* that! But so's an entire Runzi contingent."

"Between us and Zeor?"

"Right. Hurry! I'll help you make a backpack out of that, here . . ." The channel took the lashings of the bedroll and secured the bundle across Valleroy's shoulders. "You'll need both hands to climb. We'll send the horses back to Imil. If they make it, this ought to tell the story." Using the crest of his ring, he scratched a pattern of lines into the saddle of each mount. Then,

128

pointing them toward the north, he gave each weary animal a slap on the rump, starting them off in the general direction of Imil. "Let's go."

Valleroy's will to argue was paralyzed by a growing horror at being chased afoot through the Sime Territory mountains during a blizzard. The prospect was overshadowed only by the terror of being a helpless captive of killer Simes. He followed Klyd up the hillside.

They had dismounted onto rocky ground. Now they climbed almost straight up a jumbled pile of boulders at the bottom of one of the numberless ridges that stretched out from the range of foothills ahead of them.

Valleroy held his own for the first few hundred yards, but then the superior endurance of the Sime became apparent. Gradually, he lost ground. However, one glance out across the valley lent new strength to trembling knees.

There was indeed a line of dust motes forming a cordon between them and Zeor . . . riding straight across the checkerboard fields and seemingly aimed right at them!

Together, they scrambled over weather-beaten boulders, slipping in loose gravel, yet striving to leave no sign of their passage. Minute by minute, the clouds banked lower into a black, ominous mass relieved by an occasional glimpse of white. It was going to be quite a storm!

Raising his collar, Valleroy fixed his eyes on Klyd's boots and concentrated on climbing. The quilted jacket of the Zeor livery that had seemed too light to be worth wearing now provided a surprising amount of protection. He was too tired to question this new miracle, though. His legs were still weak from his long stay in bed. It was all he could do to keep moving.

By noon it was snowing so hard they could no longer see the top of the ridge they were climbing. The large wet flakes swirled downward, melting on contact. Exhausted, Valleroy let the channel haul him up one more precipitous rock face, and then collapsed against a boulder. "I've *got* to rest."

Klyd placed one foot on a rock and peered upward along their path. "We must find shelter before it becomes too slippery to climb."

But Valleroy had other things on his benumbed mind. "How did you know they were coming?"

"The Runzi?"

"Yes. And how did you know they were Runzi?"

"Selyn-field potential. A raider team has a distinctive pattern. Who other than Runzi would be beating across the fields in a frigid, prestorm dawn, blocking our way to Zeor?"

"Good question," said Valleroy. "But they were miles away! How come you . . . ?"

"I would have noticed them sooner, but I've gotten into a bad habit of sleeping too soundly. My sensitivity is high, even for a channel. They'll be surprised we're not in the trap." He paused, thoughtful.

"Klyd, isn't it illegal to attack a couple of peaceful citizens about their lawful business?"

"Who would file charges against Runzi if no House-holder were around to witness? And if a Householder did file against Runzi, whose word would be relied upon?"

"That's the way it is?"

"That's the way it is." Klyd made no effort to mask his sullen bitterness. "If charges were brought, Runzi might lose their license. But we'd still be dead."

"And Andle would simply put together another band to work for him?"

"Using mostly the same bunch, too. Licenses aren't cheap, but Andle isn't poor."

Valleroy rose onto his aching legs before stiffness could set in. "I can see Simes aren't so different from Gens after all."

Klyd held his hand out to catch a snowflake. "Simes don't particularly like being buried alive in snowdrifts. Do you?"

"Not at all."

"Then let's find a nice warm cave to sit this one out in."

"I'll go for that. There must be plenty around here."

"Also plenty of grizzly and wildcat too."

"I know. They raid the ranchers in Gen Territory, and then they come up here where we can't get at them."

With a grunt, Klyd led the way across the face of the slope they'd been climbing, but heading east into the mountains, away from Zeor. Twice, Valleroy's fatigue caused him to misjudge a step, but each time Klyd's strong hand was there to steady him. The first flurries had abated by the time they found their shelter, high up the side of a jagged cliff that had been partially crumbled by some long-gone glacier.

It wasn't much of a cave, only about twenty feet deep and barely high enough to stand. But with a fire going and a stock of wood laid in along with some edible roots and berries, it seemed like home.

Outside, the wind began to howl in earnest by the time they'd dragged in some pine boughs to serve as bedding. Shortly after that, a pelting hailstorm broke across the mouth of the cave forming a dark curtain.

"Nobody could be following us now," said Valleroy.

"No, but they'll be waiting. It's not really winter yet. The storm won't last long."

"The melting snow will erase our trail."

"They'll find us if we don't keep moving."

"Where can we go?"

"Back to Zeor, of course. We'll circle east, cross this ridge at Treadlow Pass, and then move southwest across the next valley, over the next ridge, and from there . . . straight home."

Picturing the countryside in his mind, Vallleroy said, "You make it sound so *easy* . . ."

"We can make it. Because we have to."

"Aren't there any alternatives?"

"Surrender to the Runzi. Or head in-Territory . . . back toward Imil. We could make that in a few weeks of hard traveling. We'd have to circle high into the mountains, though. I wouldn't care to try it with winter closing down so soon."

"How long to Zeor?"

"By myself, I could probably do it in less than two weeks . . . if nothing went wrong."

Absorbing this, Valleroy sat down near the fire. He wasn't accustomed to being the weaker and slower traveler in any group. It rankled.

Outside, the wind whistled over the roar of driving hail. It was black as midnight though it was scarcely sunset. The smoke stung his eyes as he fed another small stick into the fire.

Snapping one of the longer branches, Valleroy scratched a crude map in the dust. We're here." He bored a hole on the spot. "Hanrahan Pass is over here. You say there's a passage through *here?*"

"Treadlow. About here." Klyd took the stick and marked a point farther east than Valleroy had indicated.

"And," said Valleroy, "from there you want to cross the next valley and this ridge of hills?'

131

"Right. That will put us in the river valley not far from the Gen Territory border. Then we'll circle west around the end of the Runzi cordon."

"Suppose they block us all the way to the river?"

"We'll slip through somehow. They won't expect us there."

"I could find Hanrahan by myself," Valleroy speculated. "With luck, I'd be on the Gen side before they realized we'd parted company . . . and you could be home-free."

That earned Valleroy the strangest look he'd ever gotten from the channel. "Klyd, they'd never guess you'd be traveling at your own speed, not mine. I'll report to Stacy and meet you at the rendezvous again . . ." He trailed off uncertainly. "What's wrong?"

Wordlessly, Klyd stood up and went to the night-veiled cave entrance, leaning one hand against the stone wall. He seemed to be searching the roaring storm for something unguessable.

Valleroy followed to stand beside him and peer into the storm. "Klyd, don't you see? They'll never suspect because it would be so far outside the Householding pattern of . . ."

"They might suspect, if they've found out who you are."

"But they haven't . . . there's no way."

"They've suspected me of conspiracy to commit treason so many times, they're convinced it *must* be true."

"But they don't have a shred of proof."

"*You* are living, breathing proof. We don't know what Hrel reported, but you can be sure that if Andle actually has Aisha, and if he knows who she is . . . he knows who and what you are."

"But Enam failed to kill me, so there is no proof."

"If Andle gets you, Aisha, and one of those sketches you made of her plus a sample of your work from Imil . . . a Sime court can add just as expertly as a Gen court."

Suddenly shivering, Valleroy said, "Feleho had one of my sketches?"

"He did."

"You don't think I could make it by myself?"

"To Gen Territory? You probably could, though it would be risky. The main Runzi camp is rumored to be between here and Hanrahan."

"But most of them will be combing the lowlands for us. If you and I just show up at Zeor and don't say anything about all this . . . they won't be able to say anything either. Then we can start over. . . ."

"Is that what you want to try for?"

Something in the Sime's flat tone stopped Valleroy in mid-thought. He considered carefully. "Well, I don't see what else we can do."

Abruptly, Klyd turned and caught Valleroy's hand and held it up to the firelight. The Zeor crest on Valleroy's finger scattered light patterns onto the walls of the cave. Abruptly, Klyd released the Gen hand and moved back into the warmth of the cave. He settled down near the fire, stirring it with intense, jerky movements.

Valleroy examined the delicately boned Farris countenance . . . so typical of that particularly skilled family of channels . . . lit from below by the orange flame. The dark eyes were hidden in deep shadow while the cheeks seemed bruises pinched tight about the sensitive Farris lips. It was the face of a disappointed man furious at himself for having expected something unreasonable.

Suddenly, it dawned on Valleroy what he'd forgotten. Need! Klyd didn't have more than . . . he counted swiftly . . . five days, maybe a week at the most before he'd be in need!

Gingerly, Valleroy moved to sit across the fire from the Sime. His thoughtlessness had hurt the man deeply. For some reason, that mattered to Valleroy. It mattered very much. He whispered, "Unto Zeor, forever. I guess I meant that."

Klyd looked up enigmatically. "You guess?"

"No. I *know* I did. I won't leave you if you think I can do any good by staying. But I'm not a trained Companion. I think I could manage to donate to Zeor through you . . . but I couldn't serve your need. In the last few days, I've come to respect the Companions very much. But I'm not one of them."

"No. You're not. Not yet. Given a little time and a little luck . . . maybe you won't have to be until you're ready."

"I doubt if I could ever be ready!"

"You will. You have the talent."

"It seems I have many talents, not the least of which is causing trouble."

Klyd digested that for several minutes.

133

The tongues of yellow-orange flame licked persistently at the log that formed the heart of the fire. If, thought Valleroy, he had to stay with Klyd, slowing him down, neither of them would ever see Zeor again. All because he'd insisted on bulling his way into the search for Aisha!

"You need not feel responsible," said Klyd. "I agreed to bring you in-Territory, knowing the risks better than you did."

"The channels aren't the only people who accept responsibility for their own actions, you know." That earned him another of those sharp looks followed by a disapproving frown.

"Klyd, I wish you'd stop reading my emotions!"

"I wish you'd stop creating uncomfortable ones!"

They glared at each other belligerently while the hailstones smashed into the mountainside. The fire crackled between them, shooting a cascade of sparks that made both jump back in surprise. As suddenly as it had arisen, the mutual anger broke into laughter, ebbing into chuckles.

"I'm sorry," said Valleroy, "I can't very well help . . . how I *feel*!"

"And I am more sensitive than usual to the nager of your emotions."

"You feel need already?"

"No. The anticipation of need . . . a ghost of the reality. But you are the only Gen within miles. And we have established . . . a closeness. I have no defenses against you."

Valleroy dropped his eyes, embarrassed. It seemed somehow incongruous for the quick, competent, powerful man across from him to have weaknesses. "I . . . guess we'd better get some sleep."

"With luck, we may be able to get an early start tomorrow morning." Klyd spread his bedroll over a heap of pine needles well away from the fire. Valleroy did the same.

There was no need to keep a watch. Nothing could move in that driving rain/snow/ice mixture. Curled up with his back to the fire, Valleroy concentrated on going to sleep.

That was a mistake, he thought, about an hour later. Sleep flees before concentration. The scent of the pine needles had reminded him of Aisha and the hopes he'd had for their life together. His mind conjured up visions of the little house they'd have, a small ranch, a steady income . . . just enough so that he could devote himself to the real *art* that comes from the soul.

It was an old dream, which he found himself questioning piece by piece. He wasn't sure he wanted Aisha unless she'd grown as much as he had. And he wasn't sure he wanted just that small ranch. He still wanted to paint . . . but not just for himself. The dream seemed shallow, without content, or meaning, or purpose. But he couldn't see what was missing.

Heaving a sigh, he rolled over. The quilted jacket wasn't enough against the cold that filtered in around the fire. He was shivering.

"Hugh?"

"I thought you were asleep."

"I told you, I've given up sleeping. It's a dangerous habit. But you require your rest." The channel moved to bend over Valleroy, touching Gen hands and face. "You're freezing!"

"I'm all right."

"Come over here next to me. We'll pool our warmth under both blankets."

"No, really . . ."

"*Naztehr.*" Klyd's voice crackled with the impatience of one accustomed to being obeyed.

"Coming, Sectuib." Valleroy knew it was irrational, but he was extremely reluctant to make that move. Nevertheless, he couldn't deny that his teeth were chattering. When they'd piled both blankets on top of them, he was almost comfortable.

But then he found Klyd'd tentacles seeking his skin, gently caressing his neck. He couldn't help stiffening against that touch.

"Relax. This will only take a moment, and then you'll feel warmer."

"What are you doing!"

"I will only help you tap the resources of your own body. Then you will sleep."

Valleroy tried to do as he was told, but the moist laterals left tingling trails on his skin. He almost screamed.

"Easy, Hugh. I'm not attempting transfer." Klyd went on talking in that infinitely persuasive tone that soaked into Valleroy's mind, loosening all the knotted fears.

135

"Now, I'm going to put you to sleep. When you wake up, it will be dawn."

Valleroy lay quietly as the Simes tentacles gripped his arms and the unyielding, impersonal lips touched his mouth in the kiss that was not a kiss.

It seemed as if he only blinked his eyes and the pale gloom of a sodden day was etching Klyd's silhouette against the cave entrance.

The instant Valleroy realized it was morning, the Sime turned. "You're finally awake. I've been debating whether we should try to move out this morning. It looks as if it's going to snow some more."

"We wouldn't want to get caught out in it." Valleroy pushed the blankets aside and went to join in the weather inspection. To the west, as far as they could see, black clouds massed as if for an attack on some giant mountain stronghold. To the east, a tattered piece of blue sky floated red-rimmed by the sunrise over the mountain peaks. Rocks and trees were encased in sparkling clear sheaths of ice. Sticky blobs of snow spattered the windward side of every surface.

Valleroy shook his head. "We have to have sun to melt this ice before we can climb."

As they watched, a dense curtain of snowflakes drove in from the west, blotting out the scenery. Frigid gusts invaded their cave, sending them both scurrying for the fire.

"We'll just have to wait," Valleroy said, rationing out the few tubers and berries left. That, together with the broth powder they carried, would last another day. But it would be a hungry day.

Valleroy shoved that thought out of his mind. He'd been eating well lately. Several days fasting wouldn't hurt him. "Come on and eat, Klyd. Nothing else to do."

"No. Save it. You may require it later."

"You have to eat."

"The Sime body operates on selyn, not calories. You require calories, not selyn."

Valleroy sipped his hot broth. He knew Simes ate only to replace body-building materials, but still he felt guilty. "Zeor must be wondering where we are. We might be rescued."

"No. Runzi controls the valley. It's up to us to get home. But we can't do it today, so I'm going to sleep."

"I thought you'd given up sleeping as a bad habit."

136

"Menar sleep, it reduces the basal selyn-consumption rate. With luck, it may stave off full need for a few extra hours. That might make all the difference."

"Is that safe, in this cold?"

"No. If I go too deep, I might never wake."

"I suppose a real Companion would know how to guard against that?"

"Since you're high-field now, you should have no problem waking me. Any intimate contact will bring me around if I don't come out of it at dawn tomorrow. Meanwhile, just keep the fire going." He went to the mouth of the cave to search the sky once again, but the snow was thick and heavy, showing no sign of stopping.

Valleroy shelled a nut. He didn't like the idea. Before he had time to frame any objection, Klyd had resumed his place under the blankets, instantly asleep. Valleroy resigned himself to being cold, lonely, and hungry. It wasn't the first time he's spent a miserable day . . . and he hoped it wouldn't be the last. He sighed and stretched out his legs.

All in all, he'd been lucky. Growing up in Gen Territory, he didn't have to worry if he'd mature into a relatively helpless Gen—and since his mother and father were both Gens, that had been the highest probability.

He tried to imagine what a childhood would be like on the Sime side of the border. To children who had seen the kill many times, who had seen the madness of need and the overwhelming strength of the Sime, becoming Gen would be the worst possible horror they could imagine. Their neighbors, their parents, their sisters and brothers, their schoolmates, all would suddenly consider them a Choice Kill.

The uncertainty, the insecurity would be as black a cloud to them as it was to the child in Gen Territory. Only on the Gen side of the border, one feared the changeover into a Sime adult—hunted, despised, hated by relatives and friends. How many adolescents finding themselves helpless in the grip of changeover had sought to hide from their parents and, failing, had been beaten to death by those who had once professed love for them.

And how much of a parent's love was warped by the fear that this child might change over and attack them while they slept? It was a wonder, thought Valleroy, that there were any sane adults on either side of the border!

But maybe that was the crux of the problem. Andle's

137

Simes had grown up in dread of becoming Gen. They accepted without question that the natural Sime instinct was for the kill—and that his instinct was even more powerful than parental love. If it was so powerful, then it must be moral. They *had* to rationalize Gens into a sub-human category in order to be able to kill. They weren't quite sane on that subject.

On the other hand, Gens had to convince themselves that Simes were the evil spawn of the devil sent to destroy the integrity of the unmutated form of the Ancients. The Gen's mission in life was to keep the race pure. That way, killing Simes was all right because Simes weren't really people, just totally vile beings who looked like people when they were children. Gens weren't quite sane on *that* subject.

Valleroy poked a new stick into the fire and watched the soot collect on the roof. He'd never realized until now just how different his own childhood had been. His mother had loved him—unreservedly, wholeheartedly, without the slightest qualification. And he loved and trusted her because he knew she'd have loved him just as much as a Sime or as a Gen. Many times she'd rehearsed with him what he had to do if he found himself in changeover. She'd taken him over the trail to the border and told him how to find the green pennants of the pens. "You can take with you nothing but my love for you. But you must not forget to take that."

She hadn't lived long enough to find out which way his life would go. But she hadn't really cared that much. He was her son, one way or the other. After his father had died, her attitude permeated his childhood homelife. It had been the same feeling he'd found anew at Zeor. Acceptance as a person, not a body.

For a brief moment, he remembered Yenava's science class in the school garden. They had nothing to fear, she'd said, one way or the other. It had been later that same day when a young Gen recently adopted from outside the Householdings had confided to Valleroy the secret of the Companions' ability. From infancy, they know that as Sime or Gen they have a secure place in the adult world. Perhaps that was the quality that Klyd had sensed in him during that moment among the greenhouses.

But it took more than childhood security to make a Companion, thought Valleroy. It took training and edu-

138

cation that he'd never have. For example, it was widely accepted among Simes that *both* Simes and Gens were mutants . . . neither one being closer to the Ancients.

The juncts used this to prove that Gens weren't human. But Valleroy felt that the truth was seen only by the Householdings. He recalled the way Klyd had gripped his hand. "Look and tell me they don't *belong* together!" It took a Sime *and* a Gen to be the equivalent of an Ancient.

Maybe.

Another thought struck him. Perhaps Zelerod's Doom would be a blessing, a way of leaving only Simes who could live with Gens and Gens who could live with Simes . . . channels and Companions. The Householdings were obstructing evolution. But then, thought Valleroy, the avoidance of human misery had always obstructed evolution. It would just take longer to get wherever they were going. Valleroy was in no hurry.

He stirred the fire, and toured the cave restlessly.

Gens *looked* exactly like the Ancients. How could it ever be proved whether the Ancients produced selyn? By the time the Simes had begun to record history, there weren't any Ancients left alive. So all the Simes had was a vague tradition that in the time of chaos there were a few people who looked like Gens but who didn't have any selyn field potential. Adults who were as selyn-neutral as children . . .

But this was only a Sime tradition. The notion had never penetrated 'Gen Territory. It would never be accepted by Gens except as crude propaganda meant to undermine the sacredness of the Ancients. That was a sacredness Valleroy had been taught to respect. Now he found that respect turning into revulsion for modern Gen beliefs.

If Andle and his self-righteous followers were the villains among the Simes, then the Church of the Purity was the villian among the Gens. Both were pretenting the union that was the only chance for racial survival.

Despite the wind-driven snow that skirled about the cave entrance, Valleroy could see the stars as Klyd had pointed them out. Once again he felt a new dedication to the Householder's ideal of a Sime-Gen Union. It was a goal more important than any single person's life.

Suddenly, it seemed to Valleroy that until this moment he'd been a child scrambling for the larger piece of candy. From his newfound pinnacle of maturity, he wondered what it was that had been driving him all these years. What did his art really matter, if Zelerod's Doom was inevitable? What could he do with his talent that would be of any significance forty years from now?

That question echoed and re-echoed in his brain as the silent snow slanted downward in anechoic profusion. He fed another log to the fire and stood up to stretch. His body was as numb with the cold as his mind was numb with the shock of realization that everything he'd ever wanted was incredibly petty. But he had nothing to fill the sudden vacuum except Klyd's idealism. It was a burning reality for the channel, but it remained abstract to Valleroy.

Chilled to the bone, he crawled under the blankets next to the Sime. Klyd didn't even stir, and before very long Valleroy fell into a fitful slumber interspersed with hours of listless daydreaming. The thick snow curtain kept danger at bay while the heavy waiting blunted the urgency that might soon condemn them both to death . . . or worse.

CHAPTER NINE

Shrine of the Starred-Cross

THE CRISP BLUE DAWN TURNED THE WIND-MOLDED snowfield to scintillating dazzle piercing Valleroys eyes, skewering his thoughts on shafts of pain. But the brilliance didn't seem to bother the channel, who trudged the snowdrifts ahead with dogged determination.

As long as they stayed on the lee side of the boulders that lined the slopes, they avoided the worst of the ice, and the snow provided traction of sorts. Klyd had insisted they take time to dry out their socks over the fire before starting. Valleroy had understood how much will power that delay had cost the channel. Now he was grateful. The sun was high in the sky, and the day was

140

warming up pleasantly, but the ground was still cold enough to frostbite.

Valleroy could hardly wait to top the ridge and descend into the sunshine that bathed the valley ahead of them. But he was no longer so eager for that warmth that he forgot caution. When they finally reached the foot of Treadlow Pass and were about to start through it, he called out, "Klyd, wait a minute!"

The Sime stopped, eyes fixed on the pass, which sloped gently upward before them. Scrambling over one last obstacle, Valleroy stamped snow from his feet and bent to retie his pants leg around his boot. "You said this is the only pass across this ridge. Stands to reason they'd be watching for us here. Let's scout around before floundering into a trap."

"There's nobody here. The Runzi detachment that flushed us out of the way station probably returned to Valzor to wait out the storm. It will take them almost a day to get back from there and start searching."

"You're sure there's nobody around?"

"Absolutely. But that doesn't mean we should abandon caution."

Valleroy nodded. They'd heard the hunting screams of puma during the night. And a broken leg would be the end of them both. They might be alone, but they were still in danger and far from home.

They waded into the pass using long branches to test the footing. The snow flowed ahead of them like smoothly undulating sand dunes. If only they'd had skis or snowshoes they could have flown through the pass instead of plodded!

Grimly, Valleroy concentrated on finding solid footing. About halfway through the pass, he did discover a ridge that jutted up under the snow. It provided a fair walking surface compared to wallowing knee-deep in wet snow, so they took to it single file.

At long last, they came out into the sunshine. It was like waking from a nightmare. There was still enough warmth left in the late autumn sun to melt the snow, leaving ragged patches of rock and grass showing on the hillside that fell away at their feet. Even though it was late afternoon, the air was still warming up. Valleroy was sure most of the snow would be gone by morning.

They paused only long enough to catch their breath

and then continued down the treacherous slope. There was no path, but it was much easier picking their way *down* visible rock rather than *up* melting snowdrifts. Valleroy was wet to the skin and so cold it hurt, but his spirits soared. Even the raw patch of skin where his frozen pants leg had rubbed all day didn't seem to hurt so much any more. They were going to make it, one way or another!

Near the bottom of the hill, Klyd turned to look back. "What are you so happy about?"

Grinning, Valleroy closed the gap to stand beside the channel. Shadows were lengthening into twilight already. "I think that's the worst morning I ever . . . Klyd, look!"

Following the Gen's finger, Klyd spotted the apple tree with its load of rosy ripe apples. "Come on!" called Valleroy, sprinting. But even with his head start, Valleroy arrived only just in time to watch Klyd swarm up the tree trunk and shake it mightily. The ripe fruit showered down in a thundering cascade.

Valleroy caught one that seemed least bird-pecked and bit into it. It was sour and frostbitten, but still the best apple he'd ever tasted. Before long, Klyd had joined him, seated amid heaps of fruit and selecting the best to pile onto his blanket. "We'll dine tonight on nature's bounteous gifts!"

Valleroy laughed. "Sectuib Nashmar was right. Zeor has a poet for Sectuib!"

"This poet is slightly frostbitten at the moment. Do you suppose you could perform one more miracle and find us some dry firewood?"

Suddenly grave, Valleroy measured the angle of the descending sun and then surveyed the hillside. At first sight, it had looked so invitingly dry, but he could now see that every patch of soil was sodden from the melting snow. "Let's find a cave. Maybe there'll be some leaves or something inside."

"Maybe there won't be a cave."

"This is the same sort of rock as on the other side of the ridge . . . and look over there. Holes. One of those must be deep enough. . . ."

Quizzically, the channel said, "I asked for a miracle. I better be careful, what I ask for next. Give me a hand with this blanket."

Together they knotted the corners together to form a crude sling, which they carried on a branch between them. The caves that Valleroy had spotted were several hundred yards west of them and a bit higher up the slope.

That last quarter of a mile uphill seemed much longer than the morning's climb. Valleroy found he ached in every muscle and, when he tried to put his strength into the climb, his limbs trembled with fatigue. At last, Klyd's firm hand helped him up the last rock slide, where he sprawled on the flat ledge in a dwindling patch of sunlight.

If it hadn't been for the channel, Valleroy knew he'd just fall asleep right there and freeze happily to death during the night. But he couldn't give up while Klyd refused to show the slightest sign of fatigue. Gritting his teeth, he humped to his feet. They needed firewood and dry clothes.

Depositing their apples inside the cave, Klyd said, "We're in real luck. No recent occupants to dispute our claim and even some dead leaves for kindling. You make us a fireplace, and I'll prospect for wood."

"No," Valleroy shook his head doggedly. "You'll be in need soon. Save your strength. I'll go."

Cocking his head in politely suppressed amusement, Klyd leaned against a boulder while Valleroy took a few wobbly steps toward a nearby thicket. His trembling legs gave out. He pitched headlong over a fallen log. Before his head hit the ground, the channel was there breaking his fall. "Now *that*, Naztehr, cost more selyn than merely fetching the wood myself. In order to move that fast, I had to augment to a selyn consumption rate nearly seven times basal."

Angered, Valleroy sat with his elbows on his knees. "Well, you didn't have to augment to save me! I'm not exactly the world's worst tumbler, you know!"

"We can't afford injuries. Your safety is as important to me as my own. Now, will you go see what you can do for a fireplace? Next time, you might go head over heels down the mountain and never be heard from again!"

Stung, Valleroy retorted, "I suppose you couldn't fall?"

"Simes have a better sense of balance and a more reliable kinesthetic sense than Gens."

"I suppose you're not tired either?"

"No, I'm not tired in the same way you are. I am

143

fatigued, yes, and need approaches rapidly now. But I have not been exerting myself beyond normal limits as you have. And I'm not affected so severely by the cold . . . yet."

Valleroy framed a sarcastic commentary, but checked himself in mid-breath. They both would freeze if they didn't get dry. No sense arguing. "Yes, Sectuib."

"That's better." The Sime headed down the slope to a promising cluster of scrub oaks, apparently unaware that Valleroy resented being told what to do.

Valleroy climbed to his feet and brushed off the clinging mud. He'd almost broken his fool neck, and he was madder at himself than at Klyd's smug, supercilious attitude. After all, he rationalized, the channel had led a very sheltered life. He expected obedience as his rightful due. Valleroy resolved to teach him a lesson . . . some other time. He vented his anger in dragging a pine bough up to the cave. He used it to sweep all the dead leaves into a heap in the corner leaving a nice, safe rock surface for their fire. Then he stripped all the needles from the bough and wedged it across the top of the cave forming a very neat, impromptu clothesline.

By the time Klyd got back with his first armload of firewood, the tiny alcove was beginning to look like a camp. While Valleroy selected the driest pieces of wood, Klyd brought a second armload. Then they bent to the chore of getting a blaze going. It took five of their remaining matches, but within the hour they had a cheery fire warming their retreat.

It was only then that Valleroy began to shiver. Teeth chattering, he said, "I could use something hot to drink! Suppose we could bake some of those apples?"

Smiling lopsidedly, Klyd said, "I'd never have thought of that. But it's a good idea. I'll get some leaves to wrap them in. Meanwhile, get out of those clothes before you catch pneumonia."

While the channel made one last foray out into the gathering dusk, Valleroy fought the instinct that told him wet clothes were warmer than no clothes. Teeth chattering, he managed to strip off his jacket and shirt and hang them over the clothes bar. Then, wrapped in his blanket, which was damp only in spots, he peeled off pants and socks. It wasn't long before he stopped shivering.

"Hugh, guess what I found!"

144

Valleroy looked up to find the channel approaching the fire, arms loaded. He guessed facetiously, "A pot of steaming coffee?"

"Almost. How about some mushroom soup?"

"You've got to be kidding."

"Well, a little the worse for the snow, but still mushrooms."

"I hope you know which are edible and which kinds are poisonous."

Mildly offended, Klyd said, "I served an exacting apprenticeship in Zeor's pharmacy. Do you think I'd poison you?"

"Maybe by accident. I'll be honest. I wouldn't know a mushroom from a toadstool."

"Trust me?"

"If you trust you, yes, I guess so. What have we got to lose, anyway?"

Stripping off his wet clothing, Klyd wrapped himself in his blanket and then bent to sort his mushrooms. "Some of these are good for Gens, some are good for Simes. I've got enough to make each of us a pot of soup. I wonder how it would taste with some apples added?"

"To me, it doesn't sound very appetizing."

"That's a Gen for you. No imagination."

Valleroy reared back in indignation, but before he could launch a protest, Klyd laughed. "The Sime taste is as different from the Gen taste as the Sime metabolism is from the Gen metobolism. The Householding kitchens strive to please all and rarely please anybody. That's why Wednesday night is always a party night."

Valleroy thought hard. Wednesday. "Oh, yes!" He snapped his fingers. "I remember. On Wednesday, the Simes eat at the first shift, and the Gens eat at the second. You mean the menu is different?"

"Right. Some of my favorite dishes would send you to the hospital within the hour. Take this little item, for example." He held up the mushroom. "It's a mutant that seems to have appeared at about the same time the first Simes were being born. A good third of the kitchen gardens at Zeor are planted in vegtables that are essential in the Sime diet, but pure poison to Gens. Their existence makes a good argument for the theory that the Simes were an artifically induced mutation that got out of hand."

145

"I didn't know that."

"Of course, one can make an equally strong case for the theory of spontaneous mutation in reaction to the increasing environmental pollution of an overpopulated world. The books of the Ancients provide a great mountain of data that is reliable right up to the appearance of the first Simes. After that, all that can be learned is that nobody could figure out, *officially*, where the mutation came from. So we just don't know."

"What happens if you don't get these poisonous vegetables in your diet?"

"Enormously shortened lifespan."

"So cultivation and culinary art also contribute to Zelerod's Doom?"

"You are so right, Naztehr. Have some soup. I think the apples are ready."

They slept that night huddled together under both blankets, skin to skin, leaving their clothes on the rod to dry. Valleroy woke during the night. Unable to get back to sleep, he watched the sharp shadows cast by the waning moon as it arced across the cave entrance. He was keenly aware of the warm body beside him.

Thinking back to that first night out of Zeor, he remembered how stiffly he'd lain beside the Sime. His awareness of Klyd was different now. The channel was a man dedicated to a job he'd inherited, not chosen. The job had a grip on his soul stronger than the steely tentacles of an attacking Sime. If it hadn't been for their first encounter, Valleroy would truly believe Klyd physiologically incapable of harming a Gen.

It was only now that Valleroy was able to realize how traumatic an experience inflicting that injury had been for Klyd. Comparing some of the remarks he'd heard about Klyd's behavior right afterwards with things he'd learned at Imil, a picture began forming in Valleroy's mind.

Lying there watching the shadows of drifting clouds, Valleroy assembled that picture as he would one of Stacy's composite drawings. It was an image of a man whose responsibilities were larger than his abilities. A man whose primary asset was an invincible self-confidence. A man whose self-confidence had been shattered by one miscalculation on a cold rainy night . . . a night haunted by need.

Slowly, as Valleroy had recovered from that injury,

146

so had Klyd. Since only a Companion could overcontrol a channel in transfer, Klyd had to convince himself that Valleroy's talent as a Companion had allowed him to wrench control of the selyn flow away from the channel. In response to Klyd's rationalization, Valleroy thought, he had indeed developed some rudimentary skills, especially the sort of quiet confidence that allowed him to share a blanket with a Sime almost in need. He wondered what his mother would have thought of that. His hand sought the starred-cross that still hung around his neck beneath his undershirt, and he fell asleep wondering.

With the first dawn light, they packed up the remaining apples and struck out across the valley floor. Klyd warned of a concentration of Sime riders off to the west, but calculated that they'd be safely up the far ridge before the horsemen got close enough to spot a field-gradient. As a channel, Klyd could control the "show gradient" nager to a certain extent. He hoped it would be enough to get them past the end of the cordon.

Valleroy found himself still weak from the previous day's exertion. Spending two weeks in bed and two more as an invalid hadn't kept him in condition for cross-country marathons. But he was no longer ill, so as the day progressed he was able to draw upon inner resources for strength. A few more days at this, a decent meal or two, and he'd be back in shape.

It was the meals that were worrying him most. Klyd kept insisting that approaching need had already destroyed his appetite, but Valleroy felt that even a Sime body would benefit from a few solid calories. He wanted to stop and set some rabbit snares, but he knew that Klyd would be so revolted at the thought of eating animal tissue that he'd probably just go on alone.

Denrau was the channel's goal now, and on his twenty-sixth day since his last transfer, Klyd was in no mood to pause for any reason. Valleroy understood that well enough. He didn't even complain when they reached the other side of the valley and Klyd started up without slackening pace.

Silently, Valleroy tried to follow the trail the channel picked among the tumble of boulders. He could see they were trending toward a deep cut in the ridge that appeared to be a pass of sorts. If the weather held, they might make the crest before nightfall. He began searching for likely looking cave areas but had found none by the time he noticed that Klyd had drawn ahead out of sight.

Concentrating on his climbing, Valleroy strove to close that widening gap. He caught occasional glimpses of the Sime, always farther ahead, scampering effortlessly up the treacherous slope, apparently making no concessions to Valleroy's slower pace. Almost wondering if he'd been abandoned, Valleroy picked his own trail toward the cleft in the mountainous ridge.

Then his self-pity turned to anger, and he stepped up his pace recklessly. From the top of this ridge, he expected to see both Hanrahan Pass and the river. He could be in Gen Territory and safe by noon tomorrow if Klyd decided not to wait for him. After all, he'd suggested that himself, and it still seemed like a reasonable course.

Thus sunk deeply into his own thoughts, Valleroy failed to notice the lithe shadow that softened the outline of one towering boulder. As he passed beneath, that shadow detached itself and plunged downward with a blood-curdling animal scream!

Whirling, Valleroy caught one glimpse of gaping cat jaws, needle fangs, and wet red tongue. The fetid breath of the animal filled his nostrils. He thrust his hands out to fend off the attack. Wicked claws slashed at his jacket. He threw the animal off. It landed hard against some sharp stones. It was stunned for a moment, but not giving up.

Valleroy cursed the Zeor ruling that decreed members travel unarmed. Pride was fine, but there were limits. Circling the crouched cat, Valleroy grabbed a fist-sized stone from the ground. It would have to be a good throw. He wouldn't get another chance. But as he hefted the missile, he felt his arm trembling uncontrollably. Yesterday's fatigue was compounded by today's exertions. Gritting his teeth, Valleroy continued to circle uphill. If he fell backwards, he didn't want to roll all the way down. The fall might not *quite* kill him.

He watched the cat gather for the spring. The lean muscles were clearly outlined under the tawny skin. Bracing his foot against a firm rock, Valleroy hurled his weapon with all his strength.

But in that instant, the cat sprang into the air! The missile whizzed past through empty space. Valleroy took the impact of the predator's weight on his arms, heedless of the sharp claws. For a moment, he had a grip on its neck, but his hands slipped. The cat squirmed loose, leaving Valleroy sprawled helpless against the slope of the mountainside. He expected those dripping jaws to close on his throat any second!

But it didn't happen. Gasping, Valleroy rolled over. He gathered his feet under him, looking uphill. There, silhouetted against the late afternoon sky, stood Klyd.

As the cat seemed to sense his presence, Klyd threw a fist-sized rock at the animal's head. The rock grazed its skull, opening a long gash between the ears. Screaming its rage, the cat leaped at the Sime!

Valleroy saw fingers and tentacles curve firmly about the cat's neck. He heard the blunt snap of breaking vertebrae that finished the animal. But the cat's body carried enough momentum to throw Klyd back several steps. His footing gave way and he fell backwards, the cat on top of him. The cats death spasms raked its claws across Klyd's torso, its hind legs braced against Klyd's thighs, ripping deep. Valleroy heard a dull thud when Klyd's head hit something solid!

Before the two limp forms had stopped moving, Valleroy was at the channel's side. He put all his remaining strength into heaving the furry body aside. Hardly daring to breathe, he inspected those precious lateral tentacles. He sobbed a prayer of thanks. The only damage was on the upper arms and the thighs. They were deep, bloody gashes, but considering the Sime immunity to most infections, they ought not to be too serious.

The head injury was another problem. Valleroy was no doctor, but he knew enough to be worried. He'd no idea what concussion could do to the channel's nervous system.

With trembling fingers, he tore strips off his shirt and bound the wounds tightly. A Sime could control bleeding by will power, but this Sime was totally unconscious. Night was approaching. They had to have a warm shelter.

Decisively, Valleroy finished his first aid and stood up. Klyd heaved the cat's body far enough downhill so that scavengers wouldn't bother Klyd. Now, he had to scout for shelter.

Valleroy labored toward the pass that had been their goal. He was on the northern slope of the ridge, the deepest part of the afternoon shadow. He dared not go too far in search of shelter. Somehow, he'd have to transport Klyd's unconscious body. And he was already too weak to haul himself along! One bad fall could be the death of them both . . . it was a long way down.

Pausing to catch his breath, Valleroy scanned the eastern part of the mountainside. If there were no cave, at least some sort of pocket or recess must be near. Then he saw it!

Not half a mile from them and only a few hundred yards up the slope . . . nestled snugly among the boulders and almost hidden from view by a screen of evergreens and shrubs . . . the regular shape of a building was just discernible in the gathering dusk.

Marking the spot carefully, Valleroy scrambled back to pick up the channel. By leaving the backpacks, he managed to straighten up with his burden slung across his shoulders. Klyd was a tall man, but sparely built. He wasn't as heavy as he looked. Still, it was all Valleroy could manage to make that climb along the sloping ground.

He took his bearings, narrowed down his thoughts to the step he had to make next, and drove himself by pure determination. Before he'd gone a hundred yards, his left ankle was shot with pain and his right thigh shook uncontrollably. He shifted his burden, gritted his teeth, and went on unaware of the sweat standing out on his face in the freezing wind. He knew that moving a concussion victim was bad, but he also knew that low blood pressure from shock could be fatal if the patient is not kept warm.

What he didn't know about moving an unconscious Sime didn't bother him . . . yet.

One step. Then another. And one more. Gasp the freezing air into parched throat. Another trembling step. And another. One more. He was alone on this mountainside. If either of them was to survive, it would have to be by Valleroy's own efforts. Unaided.

He fastened his thoughts on Zeor. A Companion was responsible for the well-being of his channel. Zeor was a Householding with pride, and he was a Companion in Zeor—at least as far as the outside world was concerned he was a Companion in Zeor. And he'd promised Grandfather that he'd take care of Klyd. Hugh Valleroy kept his promises just as well as any Farris who'd ever lived. He'd keep this one if it killed him.

He repeated that over and over as he stumbled toward safety. Twice he fell, twice he picked himself up. Twice he shouldered his burden and stumbled on.

And at long last, he fell lengthwise over the threshold of the refuge. For long, agonized minutes, he lay oblivious to his success. But then he raised himself on trembling arms and looked around.

The heap of dark clothing on the floor in front of him resolved itself into Klyd's unconscious form, alive and still bleeding. Beyond that lay a tiny cabin, hardly larger than one of Zeor's washrooms. But there was a fireplace laid with dry wood. A striker hung from a chain beside it. Before trying to see the rest of the dark room, Valleroy crawled over to the fireplace and used that striker to squeeze hot sparks onto the waiting tinder. Too tired to use the bellows, he breathed gently on the tongue of flame until it seemed able to live alone.

The warmth of it revived him enough so he could get to his feet. He dragged Klyd onto a pallet of straw covered with clean blankets that lay ready in the corner. There were no windows in the miniature cabin. He didn't see the candles on the mantelpiece, so he set to work on Klyd's bandages as best he could in the dimness.

Rummaging in one of the chests set near one wall, he found some bandaging cloth wrapped with the Sime sterility symbol. There was even a tube of healing ointment. Certain that he was stealing somebody's property. Valleroy cleaned and bandaged the wounds. His head was swimming with fatigue now that the cabin was warm, but he couldn't allow himself to rest.

Systematically, he explored the contents of the chests until he came to a basket of grain. Buckwheat, it looked like. And salt, too. He measured some water into the kettle over the fire and poured in some of the grain. Then he turned and staggered back out into the chill night. He *had* to get their packs.

The thought of food waiting for him would lure him back. But if he ate first, he'd fall asleep in his tracks. It wasn't so bad this time, with only his own weight to drag, but it was bad enough.

The waning moon lit the way clearly, but the temperature continued to fall. On the way back, he wrapped himself in his blanket, using Klyd's for the apples and their rudimentary camping equipment. He fell several times, and yards from the cabin he fell one final time.

Only the aroma of the cooked buckwheat brought him to his feet again. He made it to the safety of the warm haven too tired to worry about the Sime who probably owned the place and would return momentarily.

He never remembered eating that pot of cereal or bedding down next to the injured channel. But he must have done both, for when he woke late the next morning the pot was empty and he wasn't very hungry. He lay for long minutes trying to dive back into dreamless sleep. But thought of Klyd brought him fully awake.

Examining the bandages, he found the wounds almost half healed. But the channel still seemed unconscious. His skin was icy cold despite the warm bedding.

Clutching his blanket about him, Valleroy built up the fire with the driest, hottest burning wood he could find. If the smoke attracted the Runzi, then so be it, he thought. Klyd *had* to have warmth. But on the other hand, he thought, if they were going to be discovered, they'd have been discovered already.

He made himself another pot of buckwheat and ate hungrily, still trying to figure out what sort of place this was. The only light was from the fire and a few chinks in the stonework. But by that, he found the candles and lit them.

Only then did he see the writing inscribed on a recessed section of wall framed by an arch. He took the candle to it to see better.

It took no linguistic talent to recognize the symbol at the top of the plaque . . . this was a Shrine of the Starred-Cross! Below that symbol were instructions indicating the safest path to the Gen Territory border. Then came a series of requests for users of the way station. Leave dry wood on the hearth, and water in the crocks. Write on the plaque the date of usage and whether Simes might have spotted that usage.

Toward the bottom came the admonition to trust in the starred-cross. One such talisman hung from a nail beneath the plaque. It was the same as the one he now wore—the one that had seen his mother safely out of Sime Territory. This was a way station of the children's underground.

Fishing his talisman out of his shirt, Valleroy kissed it joyfully. How lucky they had been to find this place!

CHAPTER TEN

Messenger

KLYD MOANED, TOSSING FEVERISHLY, AS IF TRYING TO twist away from some unnameable horror. Not knowing what to do, Valleroy kneeled beside the pallet and tried to keep the Sime from hurting himself with the violence of his thrashing. As the minutes wore on, Klyd became more and more delirious, alternately screaming for Denrau and begging urgently for help.

In an anguish of indecision, berating himself for his own ignorance, Valleroy fought his unconscious friend until he had to retreat to avoid the wildly searching laterals, which now were coated with the ronaplin secretion, a sure sign that the channel was in need.

Helpless, Valleroy stood aside watching his patient wrestling with unseen demons. He'd carried this man across a mountainside, and to do it, he'd promised himself he'd save him or die trying. Now it appeared as if the channel would kill himself in delirium.

Right now, Klyd was in need, and Valleroy was highfield. Such a combination would end in transfer, and Valleroy knew it. He thought he might nerve himself to try it if Klyd were conscious and somewhat able to control himself. But only a highly skilled Companion would dare do anything with a channel in this condition. Yet he had to do *something*.

Suddenly, Klyd let out a wide-eyed scream of undiluted terror. He clutched at the straw pallet as if he were falling off the world. Valleroy threw himself on top of the thrashing Sime. He grabbed Klyd's arms above the tentacle sheath openings. He could feel the swollen ronaplin glands under the lateral sheaths. His grip was surely causing incredible pain. But perhaps pain would bring Klyd to his senses. He hung on as the thin body was wracked with spasm after spasm. With the Sime strength driving muscle against muscle, surely the very bones of Klyd's body would crack under the strain.

153

Valleroy sobbed, "Klyd, wake up. It's me, *Hugh*, not Denrau! Wake up so we can go to Denrau. He's home, in Zeor . . . waiting for you. Klyd wake up! Oh, for God's sake, wake up!"

Valleroy never knew how long the ordeal went on. Slowly, the channel's screams subsided. His thrashing quieted until only an occasional moan of pain filled the cabin. Valleroy released his grip and sprang back out of reach, praying fervently that he hadn't hurt Klyd.

Instantly, Klyd's eyes opened, focused and sane. He froze, motionless. Then he let out a ragged sigh and melted into the straw bedding, limp with an unutterable fatigue. "You idiot Gen! Don't you know better than to move an unconscious Sime!"

It was like a slap in the face to Valleroy. "Why you ungrateful . . ." He choked on raw indignation, all thought of the channel's welfare banished by a growing rage.

Klyd flinched under the savage wave of emotion as if physically assaulted. *"Naztehr . . ."*

"Don't 'naztehr' me, you fugitive from a freak show! If you can't . . ."

"Quiet!" Klyd said it softly, but that single word carried all the weight of unquestioned authority that had rested upon the Farris family for generations. "That's better. I apologize. No matter how intelligent a person may be, he could never deduce the effect of moving an unconscious Sime. Now you've seen it, you'll never make that mistake again."

Somewhat mollified, Valleroy calmed down enough to see Klyd's point of view. It had been a pretty gruesome experience. If it was caused merely by his being moved, Klyd had every right . . . "I'm sorry, Sectuib, if I did wrong. But the next time you tackle a wildcat, kindly instruct me in the rudiments of Sime first aid before allowing yourself to become injured. I *thought* I was saving your life by getting you inside here where it is warm. Concussion and subfreezing weather don't make for blooming health among Gens."

Valleroy had tried to speak politely but it came out sounding belligerently sarcastic. Klyd, however, seemed to take it as it was meant. "I'd rather freeze to death than undergo psycho-spatial disorientation. I'm going to have nightmares for months!"

"Psycho- . . . what?"

"We have a sense that is lacking in the Gen. It is not usually obtrusive, but when disrupted . . ." He shuddered. "We always know exactly where we are. It seems to be connected with some fundamental uniqueness of every point in the universe. Right now, I'm aware of my position on the Earth. I'm aware of the spinning of the planet on its axis. I'm aware of the motion around the Sun. I can even sense, vaguely, the motion of the Sun around the galaxy. I suppose there must be some subliminal awareness of the motion of the galaxy through space. But when unconscious, I'm not aware of my motion relative to the Earth's surface. When awareness returns, the conscious mind is convinced that the old position was the correct one, while the unconscious mind senses the new position. The confusion is . . . horrible!"

"I'm sorry. I guess a Companion would know all about that."

Klyd assented with a weary blink. "And there are ways to make the awakening easier, if necessary." He massaged his forearms. "Remind me to teach you that trick after you qualify."

Valleroy frowned. "You're in need."

"Not quite. But . . ."

"But what?"

He fingered the deep gashes on his upper arms and thighs. "Healing these has cost enough selyn to keep me functioning for two days. And disorientation is . . . also expensive."

"You mean you are dangerously low-field, yet not in need? Isn't that paradoxical?"

"Channels are different, Hugh. The need cycle appears to have little connection with the available selyn reserves for a channel. It's almost as if need were a vestigial holdover from the pure Sime mutation. I could be high-field and go berserk with need. Or I could be close to death by attrition and not experience half the agony of the ordinary Sime in disjunction. Right now, I must acquire selyn to sustain my metabolic functions. I don't absolutely require transfer. I can accomplish through a fundamental internal shunt. . . ."

"My Simelan isn't up to understanding that. Can you tell me in English?"

"No. English doesn't have the vocabulary to discuss Sime experiences. But what I must know is the same in both languages. Will you help me?"

Valleroy couldn't answer. Last night, he'd been willing to give his life for this man. Not two minutes after awakening, safe and warm, the patient had turned on him. Oh, he'd apologized and explained. But Valleroy wasn't able to go from worried concern to resentment, to realization that his efforts to help had done more harm than good, and then back to willing helper . . . all in a matter of minutes. His emotions churned uncontrollably.

"Hugh, I *do* understand what you did for me last night. Are you going to let that go to waste? If so, you'd better get out of here right now and bar the door from the outside. I haven't got much time, and I can't be responsible for my actions toward the end."

"Oh, hell, I'll do whatever I can. I've never run out on a team partner yet. Stacy would fire me. Besides, we haven't found Aisha yet. I require you to help with that."

"Come here, then, and sit down."

"I don't know what to do."

"It's only a bit more demanding than the simple entran outfunction that you mastered at Imil."

"All right. But you'll have to teach me."

"Come."

Apprehensively, Valleroy moved closer.

"Sit here." The channel indicated the side of the straw pallet. Valleroy took a deep breath of resignation and assumed the position.

Klyd propped himself up against the wall, obviously drawing upon ironclad self-control to deliver a memorized classroom lecture in a dryly impersonal tone. But his voice shook occasionally.

"The channel is a secondary mutation that differs radically from the basic Sime mutation. One important difference is the dual selyn-storage system. The ordinary Sime can only draw, store, and utilize selyn to sustain his own body functions. The channel, too, has this basic selyn transport system. But in addition, the channel has a separate system that is used to gather selyn from Gen donors and to dispense it to Simes.

"This secondary system has a much larger storage capacity. It is a Householding custom that all channels carry about three-quarters capacity. I have about half that right now. It would be sufficient, but it's inaccessible to my personal use. If I die, it all goes to waste."

"The fundamental internal shunt is the process of

156

transferring selyn from the secondary system to the primary system. To do that, the deproda must be balanced exactly."

"Now wait a minute. I'm lost. What exactly is . . . dep- . . . whatever you said?"

"Deproda. You can think of it in terms of an electrical analogy. It's not exact, but it will do. By increasing the resistance across certain circuit elements, current can be shunted into other elements. You don't have to understand it to do it, any more than you have to understand quantum theory to flip a light switch."

Valleroy, like most Gens, knew nothing at all about electricity. Fingering the starred-cross, he said, "All right. What's resistance and where do I get it?"

"*You* are a resistance. Your entire nerve system is usually one colossal resistance. That's why a swift transfer damages your cells."

Valleroy thought that over. "By putting . . . me . . . across . . . you can shift selyn from inaccessible storage to useful storage?"

"Exactly."

"All right. Now what?"

Rolling his head toward Valleroy, the channel opened his eyes. "The first requirement is an absolute emotional steadiness. The slightest flicker of apprehension could trigger reflexes I couldn't possibly control."

Valleroy's hand went again to the starred-cross. "Absolute emotional steadiness is humanly impossible. There has to be a margin—"

"*Hugh!*" The channel's hand darted out and snatched the medallion out of Valleroy's fingers. "Where did you *get* this?"

Valleroy gasped, pulling back instinctively.

The surge of adrenaline that flashed through the Gen's body hit the oversensitized empathic nerve in the Sime and sent a convulsive shudder through his body. "*HUGH, DON'T MOVE!*"

Valleroy froze in position, watching with growing horror as sweat beaded on Klyd's forehead and rolled off his chin. Handling tentacles extended to reinforce his grip, Klyd hung onto the talisman. Muscular spasms washed over the channel, forcing harsh little groans out of him. It lasted for several minutes, long enough for Valleroy to become more concerned for Klyd than for the secret of the starred-cross.

At length, the Sime fell back, panting. Valleroy wiped Klyd's face with a corner of the blanket. "I did something wrong again."

"When I said steadiness, I meant steadiness."

"I wasn't afraid, only startled. My mother told me never to show this to a Sime. I guess she didn't mean channels, though."

"Your mother? Your mother was born in-Territory?"

Valleroy took a deep breath. "She escaped."

"Do you believe in the power of the starred-cross?"

"Well, I. . . ."

"It's important, Hugh. It could make all the difference. Give me truth. The truth of the soul."

"I don't know. I think I do. Now more than ever. If faith in a talisman removes fear, then faith protects."

"So it is. Do you know where she got the medallion?"

"She never said, but I suppose in a way station just like this one."

For the first time, Klyd took an interest in his surroundings. "This . . . is . . . oh, no! Hugh, if you know any prayers, say them passionately!"

"It's warm here. There's food. It's dry. I checked the chimney and it vents through a dispersal system that's not likely to be spotted—"

"But the Runzi keep watch on these places. Most of them are probably off beating the bushes for us, but they might check here again any moment."

"Is there anyone near?"

"Not very. NOW CALM DOWN!" You're hurting me. I'm not able to retain control against you."

"Yes, Sectuib."

"That's better. I'll qualify you yet."

Not too happy with that prospect, Valleroy said, "Yes, Sectuib. But if it requires my absolute emotional control you may die trying."

"Lesson number one,' said Klyd doggedly, "is that in any transfer situation, the Gen always has the upper hand. There are moments when the Sime is totally helpless. By the application of a rudimentary knowledge, the Gen can cause pain or fatal injury."

"Doesn't sound like the sort of thing most Simes would want any Gen to know. I know some Gens who would gladly use it to wipe out all Simes."

"Which is why the Tecton and the Companions are so hated. The Companions is actually the complete master

158

of any Sime. It is the Companion's *knowledge* that gives him the necessary degree of emotional control. One doesn't fear what one can destroy. I fear your fear—and the only way for me to control your fear is to surrender the situation to you . . . completely."

"If we ever get back to Zeor, remind me to have your translate that."

"The translation is very simple. Give me your hand."

Valleroy extended his left hand. Klyd placed the Gen fingers around his wrist. Then he moved the sensitive, artist's fingers upward, applying pressure gently to the lateral sheaths. "You'll feel the ronaplin gland here. Just above it and right beneath the lateral sheath, there is a point where the major transport nerve is exposed . . . huuu!" Klyd's indrawn breath marked the spot as Valleroy's fingers tightened gently.

"At that point, Hugh, and on the corresponding points along the other laterals, a slight pressure can kill. The normal transfer grip exposes these nodes to the Gen. It can't be avoided. But usually the Gen's instinct causes him to pull back and away, trying to escape the inescapable. Pressure on any one of those nodes can immobilize or kill any Sime when his laterals are extended. Pressure on the sheathed lateral can fatally cripple. It doesn't take great strength. The laterals are very delicate."

"I must have hurt you badly trying to restrain you."

"It's still painful, but I can manage the shunt. It won't take very long."

"All right. Let's try it before I lose my nerve."

Shifting his grip so that Valleroy's right hand joined the channel's right arm, Klyd took the Gen's left hand in his left. Closing his eyes for a moment of concentration, he whispered, "You hold my life in your hands. Literally. One slip and Zeor loses a Sectuib before the heir is even born. I don't mind admitting that idea frightens me. I don't quite trust you."

"I don't quite blame you."

"I wouldn't normally ask this of a Companion who hasn't qualified. But there isn't anyone else to ask. Can you do it?"

"Yes, Sectuib."

"Good. Now, slowly move in closer. All four laterals are now in contact. You must initiate the fifth contact.

Any point will do, but my control is greatest through a lip-lip contact."

Prudently, but not prudishly, Valleroy pressed his lips against the Sime's. Those sensitive, Farris lips were smooth, dry, and hotter than any Gen's because the Sime body temperature is much higher. But there was absolutely no similarity with the kiss of a woman. As he waited for some signal from the channel that it was over, Valleroy wondered about that. Every time he'd touched or been touched by a Sime, there had been not the slightest tinge of any sort of sexual overtone. Here was a totally separate body function. A complete new life process to add to the traditional biologist's list. And, like the other vital life processes, it took priority over reproduction. In the case of selyn transfer, the libido was completely short-circuited—very much as adrenaline suspends digestion.

Yes, thought Valleroy, Klyd was probably being honest when he claimed that approaching need spoiled his appetite for food and for women. But if Nature followed her usual pattern, the post-transfer Sime would be quite eager for both food and sex. He felt he finally understood something profound about the Simes, and it warmed him comfortably.

The channel moved, retracting his tentacles, systematically dismantling the contact. Valleroy didn't dare move. Klyd sat, head bowed as if in concentration. When he finally did speak, his voice was gravelly with enforced relaxation. "Hugh, need is only hours off now. I can go on for a couple of days, perhaps. We might be able to steal some horses and make it to Zeor. But we might not. You have . . . selur nager . . . that differentiates the Companions from other Gens. I wish I could call on your service if it becomes necessary."

"I said I won't leave you, if you think I can do any good by staying. I owe it to Zeor."

Slowly raising his head, Klyd searched Valleroy's eyes. "I promised I'd never hurt you again. If I wait too long, I might break that promise. Entran functions and shunts are one thing, serving need is entirely different. There aren't many Gens who have the capacity to deliver selyn at the rate I must demand."

"You're trying to scare me."

"No, warn. Remember what it felt like when I hurt you?"

"I'll never forget."

"I was being very gently then. Your fear upset me. You interfered with my control as only a Companion could. I miscalculated . . . not that I've had much practice at burning people . . . but I had a field-gradient driving that transfer at about one-one-hundredth the rate I'd normally use to satisfy need. The day after tomorrow, I won't be normal."

"Meaning, you might hurt me?"

"I wouldn't attempt to qualify a Companion under such circumstances."

"Are you suggesting that we get it over with to-morrow?"

"No, not while there's hope. We're a long way from home. There's no Householding infirmary closer than Zeor."

"For me, you mean."

"If necessary."

"All you might require would be a spade."

"*Hugh!* I've never killed and I never will. You've got to believe that. You've got to make it such a part of yourself that you can't possibly fear me. The worst that could happen would be that I'd break my promise to you. But we'd both survive it. You've tasted the sensations of rapid draw. If you could nerve yourself not to react to it—not to fight or retreat from that feeling—then you would be safe, and the sensation would *not* be unpleasant."

"It's as simple as that."

"It's not simple. I *know*. I felt what you felt that time. But, Hugh, you were hurt because for a fraction of a second, you wrenched control away from me . . . *and you did not know what to do with it.*" He reached out to finger the starred-cross that dangled from Valleroy's neck. "Something in your ancestry has given you a natural aptitude for this work. One day, channels will fight over the priviliege of your service. I believe you could serve me this time . . . if you want to. That's the important part. Wanting. Selyur nager and selur nager must be absolutely complementary. We almost had it a few minutes ago. I could have qualified you then . . . painlessly."

"Why didn't you?" Valleroy wondered just how much

Klyd really wanted to qualify another Companion in Zeor . . . especially one who might be as talented as Denrau. He remembered Householding Frihill. "There just isn't room for two really great Companions in one Householding."

"It wasn't in the bargain," said Klyd. "Besides, Grandfather wouldn't approve."

"It would have solved most of our problems."

"Maybe. Maybe not. You might not have been able to hold together long enough since you weren't expecting it. But you handled the shunt satisfactorily. I feel well enough to travel."

"Then let's go. It's not quite noon yet." Valleroy gathered his legs under him. The Sime rose with one of those incredibly graceful motions that always excited the artist in Valleroy.

"Naztehr, from now on, you must try not to touch me without preparation."

"Yes, Sectuib."

"Now, let's see what kind of day it is outside. Maybe we can put some distance behind us."

They both turned toward the door then; suddenly Klyd tensed. "There's a Sime"—he pivoted like a hunting dog —"*there*, about four hundred yards! He's not moving."

"That would be near the top of this ridge. Does he know we're here?"

"Might. Would be extreme range for an ordinary Sime, and these places are always well insulated . . . but . . . he might. There's nobody else . . . correction, there *is* a concentration of Simes and Gens! Far though. Maybe in the next valley. You're such high-field, I could hardly discern . . ."

"Never mind. We'll have to scout. How are your legs?"

"Sore, but adequate. The scratches are almost healed."

Hastily, they shrugged into their coats. Valleroy began gathering their bedrolls and riding cloaks.

"Leave them. We'll come back for them. Let's get out of this trap, and get some maneuvering room. That Sime might be Runzi."

"What do we do if he is?"

"Let me handle it." The channel led the way out into bright sunlight. "You go that away. Don't get closer than that twisted out-cropping up there. Your field will distract his attention while I close in from the other side."

"Maybe he's watching us now?"

Klyd squinted toward the crest of the ridge directly above the way station. "No. He's watching what's going on down in the valley."

"I can't see anybody." The sun stood at a southerly noon angle that etched the rocks black against the pale blue sky.

"I can barely make out what appears to be the back of his head," said Klyd. "It's just at the center of the selyn field. From the emotional nager, I infer he's watching a battle but feels safe and a bit frustrated. I'll have to get closer to see if he's wearing a Runzi uniform. Unless he's a Householder, he's a danger to us."

"Let's go." Once again,. Valleroy wished fervently for a decent weapon . . . if not a rifle, at least a single-shot, homemade muzzle-loader! But he didn't even have a knife. He scrambled up toward the outcropping Klyd had indicated.

Before he'd gone ten yards, he lost sight of his partner. The channel proved phenomenally agile despite his wounds. Valleroy wondered if he was augmenting. That was one trick that he'd come to envy during the last few weeks. By increasing selyn consumption rate, any Sime could perform feats of speed, strength, and endurance that seemed beyond human limits. But he wondered if Klyd could afford it.

Hauling himself up one last pile of boulders, Valleroy squirmed into position among the wind-carved convolutions of the outcropping. By squinting against the sun, he could barely make out a profile . . . the head and shoulders of a crouched figure, hands cupped around eyes, peering down into the far valley.

As a cloud drifted across the sun relieving the glare, Valleroy caught a glimpse of color. Bright red. The Runzi uniform was red like that. Valleroy wondered what Klyd would do next.

He didn't have long to wait. As if sensing that somebody was watching him, the distant Raider turned toward Valleroy's position and then moved behind a twisted bush seeking cover. But that left his flank exposed to Klyd, and the channel wasn't slow in seizing the advantage.

With the swiftness of a racing cougar, Klyd flashed out of nowhere diving for the unsuspecting Sime. In the instant before contact, the victim whirled as if alerted

163

by Valleroy's distant reaction. Then the pair of Simes rolled down out of Valleroy's sight.

Recklessly, Valleroy scrambled down off his pinnacle. Leaping from rock to rock, he made his way toward the battle. Loose gravel showered down the hillside in his wake, but his footing held firm. He arrived just in time to see Klyd step lithely aside to avoid a stiletto charge. Klyd finished his opponent with a neck-severing chop of his hand.

Dead in midair, the Raider's body thudded limply to the ground, jerked a few times, and was still. Valleroy watched the tension drain out of the channel's stance, leaving him stoop-shouldered and obviously exhausted. Now Valleroy was certain Klyd had been augmenting heavily.

Careful not to be seen by those in the next valley, the Gen picked his way toward the two Simes. "Klyd . . . is he . . ."

"Dead? Yes."

"Runzi?"

"Undoubtedly. He used a tenth-degree augmentation on me. Do you know anybody else who could afford that?"

"I wouldn't know a tenth-degree augmentation from a selur nager. But did you have to kill him? He might have known something about Aisha."

Indignantly, Klyd rounded on the Gen. "Hugh, do you know what he'd have done to me?" Bending, he scooped up the long stiletto, which gleamed wickedly in his hand. "Today is the thirteenth day in the Death Count of Feleho Ambrov Zeor. And the first installment on his Death Price has been paid by Sectuib of Householding Zeor."

Valleroy bowed his head. The icy control in Klyd's voice was more passionate than any ferocity could have been. "Unto Zeor, forever. Would that the next installment be paid by my hand." He raised his eyes. He didn't know in just what form that petition would be granted. Had he known, he might not have made it.

Silently, Klyd nodded.

"I just wish," said Valleroy, regarding the body, "we could have questioned him first."

"He was junct . . . and approaching need. I could never have kept him away from you. And I wouldn't have enjoyed trying. The sadistic streak of the junct is missing in the channel. Can you imagine what kind of mixture of masochist and sadist a Sime must be to threaten another Sime with one of *these?*" He brandished the slim weapon.

"When it comes to sadism, the licensed raiders must be the worst of the lot."

"And of all the licensed raiders, the Runzi have the reputation of being the most sadistic. They consider channels lesser creatures then Gens. A Gen is merely an animal to be used. A channel is a pervert who seduces other into perversion. If they capture one, they make an object lesson out of him. Not in public, of course, but word spreads."

"Cheerful thought," said Valleroy, unwilling to ask what they did with Companions they captured. They couldn't sell them to the Choice Auction since Companions didn't make satisfactory kills. "I wonder what this fellow was doing up here? Are there any more around?"

"No. But something is going on down there. Let's have a look."

They climbed up to the vantage point the Raider had been using and inched into prone position on the cold stone. Valleroy remembered to allow plenty of distance between him and his partner. Then he cupped his hands around his eyes and peered into the hazy valley.

"So!" hissed Klyd. "That's why the Runzi detachment that was chasing us never caught up. They were called to defend the border!"

Way off to his left, the foothills rose precipitously, broken only by the artificial cleft of the Ancient's road and Hanrahan Pass. Valleroy could see parts of the glittering ribbon that was the river, the border with Gen Territory. It descended from the mountains and meandered across the plain toward Valzor and Zeor. Below them spread the fertile valley floor that had been ceded to the Simes when the border was fixed. It was the best pasture land in the area, but the Simes didn't run cattle and wouldn't plant so close to the border. Its main usage in recent years had been as a battle ground for border skirmishes. That seemed to be what was going on at the moment.

Valleroy could just make out the rifles carried by the Gen forces. He wasn't the world's greatest military tactician, but even he could see that the Gens had ridden into an ambush and were being massacred. Rifles were little use against a well-co-ordinated Sime infighting team, or individual Sime whip-masters.

As he watched, three separate Gen riders were un-horsed by groups of Simes. The system seemed to be to confuse the soldier's mount while one Sime vaulted up behind the victim and disarmed him. Then a third Sime slipped a complex harness over the Gen's head. With the help of a fourth, they had the Gen immobilized, blind-folded, and on the ground within seconds . . . not even bruising the merchandise. Two of the attackers would lead the helpless captive away while the others combined with new partners to attack a new victim. A well-rehearsed ballet.

The strategy worked repeatedly despite the Gen's best efforts to remain in formation. Puzzled, Valleroy said, "I never realized that Gen troops were so stupid."

"They're not stupid, Hugh, they're frightened. From the cradle to the grave, they are taught that Simes are devils with superhuman powers. Surely you've heard all the superstitious nonsense they believe?"

"Never made too much impression on me."

"From the way you reacted at our first meeting, I'd say you'd received the full measure of anti-Sime indoc-trination."

"But I got over that."

"It only takes a small measure of that kind of fear to shatter any military maneuver. The Raider's strategy is to pick off one or two of the point men first . . . even though it may cost many casualties. They kill the first few captives in plain view, leaving the bodies with the burn bruises for all to see. One look and Gen formations fall apart in panic."

"Diabolical."

"No, just good business. Remember, raiding is a high-risk profession demanding extensive periods of aug-mentation. Runzi is smart enough to use men in hard need as an advance spearpoint. The reward is immedi-ately the most exquisite type of kill known to a junct . . . or death. The policy weeds out the weaklings from the Runzi ranks. And there is nothing so terrifying to a Gen as the attack of a Sime in hard need."

"We can't just sit here and watch all those soldiers taken captive!"

"There's absolutely nothing we can do about it. That's one of the harsh realities of the Householder's existence. That Raider I executed was enjoying this show. But he was also frustrated. We still don't know why he was up here and not down there."

"Maybe he was sent to watch the way station?"

"Then why wasn't he watching it?"

"Maybe he was. He'd require help to handle you, but all his help was engaged in that battle, so he was frustrated."

"If he knew we were in that building, why wasn't he aware that we'd left it? No, I believe the building's insulation held even against your field."

"Could be. But it's still possible he was watching us and just got interested in the battle."

"As I said, Runzi's methods weed out the irresponsible and the weaklings. If he knew we were there, he would have called in help immediately or been denied his next transfer on time. But suppose . . ." Klyd stopped as if struck by a new idea. Then he began worming his way back from the edge and searching the ground about him.

"What are you looking for?"

"Message tube . . . *here!*" What he fished out of a nearby crevice was a tube about a foot long and four inches in diameter. The outside was carved in an intricate design and painted in shades of red. The ends were sealed by blank caps of metal.

"He *was* a messenger on detached duty! Now, to get this open," said Klyd, "without destroying the contents. There's probably more in here than you could have learned by questioning him."

Valleroy examined the cylinder curiously. He could see no way to open it. "If we had a saw, we could slice it in half."

"No. It would burst into flame the minute the air entered."

"Neat. Stacy would pay a fortune to learn that one."

"Simple chemistry. There are things we'd pay a fortune to learn from Stacy. Aisha may be the key to a future where such exchanges become common. And this case may be the key to Aisha."

"How do the Raiders open it, then?"

"There's a tricky combination. Secret, of course, and always different." Klyd seated himself on a rock and probed the carvings with all eight handling tentacles and all ten fingers.

Valleroy crawled back up to watch the battle. It was

nearly over by now. The shattered Gen squad had re-grouped and was racing toward the river in full retreat. At least some of them had got away alive, thought Valleroy. A thrill of grim triumph rose in him as he counted the red cloaks on the field. The Runzi tactic wasn't a hundred per cent effective against trained sharpshooters. Maybe next time it would be the Simes who'd blunder into an ambush. But that would require better rifles than the Gens now had. The Simes could sense the selyn field of the Gens in hiding—unless they were beyond extreme rifle range.

Klyd called, "What are you so sadistically gleeful about?"

Valleroy told him and finished, "You weren't very sorry for murdering that Raider, so don't be so smug."

"It was an execution in self-defense. But I didn't enjoy it. Death is never gentle and never quite painless. Need sensitizes."

"You mean you . . ."

"Died with him. Yes, you could put it that way."

With a sigh, Valleroy went to stand over the corpse. "He doesn't deserve it, but I think we ought to bury him."

"He does deserve our respect. He became a slave to an instinct greater than any man should have to face alone. The results of that are not his fault."

"Klyd!" Valleroy was amazed. "He'd have done to you just like they did to Feleho!"

"Yes. And he had to die. It is good that he is dead. I am honored to be the instrument of that death. But still I can respect him and the battle he fought. That is a difference between Sime and Gen."

Valleroy shook his head, baffled.

The channel studied that bafflement for a moment and then rose. "My ancestors would have died in poverty and misery long before the first channel was born if it hadn't been for the Raiders and the pens. The juncts established our civilization. That's not something we al-low ourselves to forget. I was born out of the deaths of others. I can't blame those who still kill merely because there aren't yet enough channels for everyone."

"So what are we going to do with him?"

"Leave him here. Runzi will be sending parties out to collect the dead. Somebody will check on the cabin soon. They'll take care of him. Come on."

Klyd started off down the side of the hill, and Valleroy followed. "Where are we going?"

"Back to the cabin. We can't go home until that battlefield is cleared, and I think I have this cylinder's combination figured out."

Valleroy followed in silence. It seemed that every time he thought he had Klyd figured out, some new facet of his personality came to the surface to confuse things. Revenge was something that Valleroy understood. He wanted his share of it, too. Pride was innate, in him despite his humble upbringing. Loyalty, dedication, ideals. All seemed comprehensively enough, until Sectuib Klyd Farris got through twisting them into the Sime mold. But after a while that bizarre Sime point of view became quite comfortably familiar. He made a mental note to read some Sime philosophers if his Simelan ever became good enough.

Back in the snug building, Klyd set about opening the dispatch case using a hot poker from the hearth to score one of the lines of the pattern that went all the way around the cylinder in a graceful S curve. Then he took the cylinder in hand and applied pressure at eighteen points simultaneously, a trick no Gen could master.

The cylinder fell neatly into two halves, which Klyd laid out on the table. Within, several documents were clipped to the cylinder wall. Very gingerly, the Sime removed them. He shoved the cylinder aside and spread out the papers, scanning quickly. Two were in code, but the third was a handwritten letter.

Looking over the channel's shoulder, Valleroy said, "Read it aloud. I can't read handwriting very well."

"It's from Andle. To the man in charge of the main Runzi encampment, Tellalian. It's . . . about Aisha, I think. How do you spell her last name?"

"R-A-U-F. What would that be in Simelan?"

"I think this must be her, then. Seems a reasonable transliteration."

"What does it *say*?"

The channel read silently for several moments, while Valleroy strained to decipher the spidery scrawl of Andle's handwriting. At length Klyd said, "You're not going to like this, Naztehr."

"I don't like not knowing either."

"They have her. They apparently know who she is and what she can do. She's refused to help them despite

169

the entire repertoire of Runzi persuasions. She must be quite a person!" He paused, bracing himself against Valleroy's emotions. "Andle has ordered her reserved for his personal need."

"He'll kill her? When?"

"I've no idea."

"We've got to get to her. Where are they keeping her?"

"At their main camp, somewhere near here."

"The messenger must have been heading there. He could have told us where—"

"Never. Even truth drugs don't work on the Runzi. They have hypnotic conditioning against revealing the camp's location."

Truth drugs, thought Valleroy! Some of the stories about Simes were true then! "We'll have to search for the camp. You must know these mountains pretty well. Where would the most likely place be?"

"You can study a map when we get home."

"Home? Oh . . . damn."

"You want to go now? I'll release you from all ties to Zeor."

"Release me? You mean, 'Get out and don't set foot in my house again!' "

"I didn't say that."

"But that's what you meant. A Companion is nothing unless he's trustworthy."

Klyd didn't answer and somehow that hurt Valleroy more than an angry ultimatum would have. He yelled, "All right! Have it your way. We'll go to Zeor first. The worst that can happen is that she'll be killed. At least that won't hasten Zelerod's Doom any more than the death of any other Gen." He leaned over and pounded the table so that the halves of the cylinder danced a tattoo. "Not that you care!"

Chin propped on clasped hands, Klyd endured the tirade with closed eyes. "You're hurting me, Naztehr. It's cold in here. Why don't you build up the fire."

"I ought to clear out and follow those Raiders who captured all my people this afternoon, not that you care about their fate."

"I doubt if they are taking the captives to the Runzi camp. Considering that they are all trained soldiers, it would be foolish to attempt to detain them so near the border, or to reveal to them the location of the camp.

No, the Ferolis Choice Auction would be the more probable destination. It's far enough in-Territory that escape would be of no avail. The security at Ferolis exceeds that at Iburan. And the price will be higher there."

"You ... cold ... unfeeling ... *snake!*"

Klyd continued, eyes still closed, tone level. "As soon as I get back to Zeor, I'll have a watch put on Andle. We'll know when he approaches need, and we can follow him. The Householdings aren't totally without influence in the halls of the mighty. If we can prove that Andle used his position to set up the Runzi to supply him with personally chosen Gens, we can destroy him once and for all."

"And Zeor's prestige will triple. But what about Aisha? What if he's headed there right now?"

"I can't hold you here against your will. I don't want you here ... against your will."

Valleroy hit the table again. "Damn!"

"Naztehr, will you please do your emotional agonizing outside? This is beginning to irritate me."

Valleroy's frustration exploded into a red rage at the impassive Sime. He grabbed Klyd's shirt front and half lifted him out of the chair, trying to provoke some sort of reaction ... *any* sort.

What he got was more than he'd bargained for. Steely tentacles closed on his wrists. The spare Sime body became all muscle under his hands. Valleroy's full strength couldn't hold against the Sime. He suddenly found himself pinned against the wall breathing the warmth of the Sime's breath. "Naztehr, it is *you* who have no *feeling!* Or is it that you so hate what I stand for that you want to force me to attack you in the kill mode? You could do it, you know. A Companion has that power. But if you do, you'd better be ready!"

Klyd released him then, and Valleroy felt like a discarded rag doll left to collapse. Turning his back, Klyd strode to the fire and began to add wood. He asked conversationally, "I don't know about you, but I feel hungry."

"I thought need suppressed appetite."

"I lost a lot of blood. The body demands replacement material."

Still fighting the wildly cashing emotions within him, Valleroy was unable to answer. He wanted to apologize for his behavior, and he wanted to pick up and leave. He could understand that Klyd was desperately trying to act normal, but he almost wished Klyd had attacked and gotten it over with.

The channel turned, a ruefully perceptive grin cocking his lips . . . those terribly expressive Farris lips. "Naztehr, what's for lunch? It's almost dinnertime."

That did it. "You haven't had any breakfast yet. I'm sorry, Sectuib. I'll put the kettle on."

"Good. I wouldn't want you to leave on an empty stomach."

"Do you still want me to leave?"

"Not if you can learn to behave yourself."

"This cracked buckwheat makes a nice cereal with the apples."

"Why haven't you told her how much you love her?"

"How did you . . . ?"

"Know you're afraid of losing her? Gen psychology is one of my specialties. I wasn't very professional a few minutes ago."

"That's what happens when you get personally involved with a patient!"

"I'd like to make up for it. I'd like to save her for you. But I can't right now."

"You know," said Valleroy, sitting down opposite his partner, "I wasn't very professional either. I forgot about Yenava. She's just as good a reason to go to Zeor as Aisha is to go to the Runzi camp. I'd never be able to do anything if I did find that camp . . . not by myself. So we'll head for Zeor soon as we eat."

"No. We'll sleep over here. The valley will be flooded with Runzi tonight. They should be gone by morning, though. We could still make it by sundown tomorrow with luck."

"But every hour we stay here means Andle . . ."

"We can't travel by night, even with three quarters of a moon. Also, Andle doesn't know that we know his plans for Aisha. I want to reseal the dispatch case and leave it by the messenger's body. Knowledge is often the decisive advantage in a contest of wills."

With his own will divided against itself, Valleroy was unable to answer that. He used a dull table knife to gouge out pieces of apple and drop them into the porridge. He was hungry and weak from days of short rations. Tomorrow wouldn't be much better.

It took Klyd several hours to close the cylinder so that

it looked as if it hadn't been opened. There was a delicate trick with the heat-sealing substance that caused it to regain its former decorative pattern. Valleroy marveled at the steady-handed patience that Klyd could summon at will. The man worked like a watchmaker without a care in the world while Valleroy paced, cataloging all the pressures converging on them from different directions.

After a few hours of this, Valleroy flung himself onto his blanket. As much as he wanted to be off and running after Aisha, he knew that Klyd was right.

But being right didn't make it any easier to take. He fell asleep and dreamed fitfully of Aisha's execution.

CHAPTER ELEVEN

Capture

VALLEROY KNEW IT WAS A DREAM. YET IT WAS ALSO real.

Aisha stood before him draped in filmy white, collar and chain a glowing red against an infinite night. Her dark hair flowed back into a rising cloud around her fear-blanched face as if she floated in water. Without his volition, his own arms reached toward her. He saw his arms as if for the first time . . . tentacled!

He felt a tangible, pulsating aura around her, drawing him in. He knew it would kill her, but he had to consume that aura. His fingers touched her arms. His tentacles ached for contact. But as they touched . . .

Flick. He was himself . . . watching Klyd kill Aisha.

Flick. No, it was Enam killing Aisha, wide-eyed and vividly terrifying. She was struggling to control her fear . . . and losing.

He ran, struggling against a leaden fatigue . . . to save Aisha . . . losing her because of his body's weakness. He refused to stop. He refused to give up, no matter how much effort it took to gain an inch.

He saw tentacles wound about her arms. He struggled,

chest aching, face twisted into a painful grimace, though what he'd do if he reached her, he didn't know.

Flick. Again it was he, himself killing Aisha. He couldn't stop it. He could only watch himself do it.

Suddenly the Gen arms under his tentacles writhed. They became Sime arms, tentacles lashing out to join his own. Their mutual grip drew them closer. Her face loomed larger and larger, flushed and smiling now. He knew that smile. It wasn't invitation . . . it was triumph. Their lips met.

He twisted free and sat up, throat constricted about a scream that couldn't get loose. His arms ached all the way up to his jaws with the effort to extend tentacles he didn't have. He shook himself, gasping, and lay back. He pulled the blanket back up to his chin.

It took him some time to orient to the real world, relegating the nightmare to its place. He chided himself for the lingering sense of horror. Nightmares are what you get, he thought, for wanting something too much . . . and not being sure exactly what it is that you want.

He pulled his arms under the blanket and rubbed the aching muscles. Realizing he was imitating one of Klyds unconscious mannerisms, running his fingers along forearms reveling in the pure sensation, Valleroy forced his hands to his sides.

He didn't remember covering himself before falling asleep. Klyd must have done it for him, thought Valleroy. He tried to visualize the Sime in the act. It helped to dispel the aftertaste of the nightmare.

Propping himself on one elbow, Valleroy saw that the cylinder lay whole again on the table. The channel's face seemed deeply lined in the ruddy light from the fire embers. As he watched, Klyd tossed from side to side as if trying to escape from something. He moaned incoherently, breathing in shallow gasps. He began calling feverishly for Denrau just as he had when he first awakened to the torture of disorientation.

Alarmed, Valleroy caught one of the Sime's hands. "Sectuib! Klyd, wake up! It's just a bad dream. Wake up! You're safe . . . here." He said it over and over in both languages until the tossing subsided and the channel's eyes opened.

"Naztehr"—drawing a ragged breath, Klyd repossessed his hand—"*Hugh*. For a moment I thought Denrau . . ."

He sighed deeply, fully awake now. "Thank you. I should know better than to sleep."

"Can I get you something? Drink of water? Something to eat?"

"No. Thank you."

"Maybe I should build up the fire . . ."

"Hugh!" The channel sat up rigidly alert.

"What . . . ?"

Casting back and forth as if homing on some unheard signal, Klyd muttered, "Must be a Gen. Recently established. Badly frightened and exhausted." He finally settled on a direction, downhill from the cabin. "Headed this way, but slightly east of us. He'll miss the cabin. Let's go."

"Where?"

Klyd flicked aside his blanket and pulled on his boots in one fluid motion. "To get him. Can't let him wander down into that valley full of Runzi."

Not sure exactly why the channel was determined to risk their lives for one lost Gen, Valleroy followed him out the door. Whatever Klyd's reason, Valleroy agreed with the necessity.

But the recent snowfall had left patches of ice in spots. Even the bright moon didn't reveal them all. By the time they'd spotted the desperate fugitive, Valleroy had collected a new assortment of bruises. He was very glad they'd decided not to travel by night.

They crouched down behind a rock and watched. The tiny figure scambling up toward them slid two paces back for every forward pace. But undaunted or desperate, he continued to struggle inch by inch up the slippery ice and gravel slope. The darkness kept the fugitive from seeing the easier path just a few hundred yards west.

Klyd said, "If he spots me, he'll probably try to run. That could be fatal on such gravel. And his fear would be like a beacon to the Runzi."

"Right. What do we do?"

"I'll give you their recognition password. You go down and meet him. Bring him to the cabin, but be sure you prepare him well for the sight of me."

"How come you know the recognition signal?"

"Never mind. Address him as Thrino. But get him calmed down at all costs. His field is not so high, but the fear he's already broadcasting is still too conspicuous."

"Anybody following him?"

"Not within my range."

That range was considerable, so Valleroy said, "Let's go."

Klyd cupped his hands around his mouth and gave out the most perfect imitation of an owl hooting that the Gen had ever heard. He repeated the call three times, and then three times again in a pattern just a bit too regular to be quite natural.

The scrambling figure stopped to listen. "All right, Naztehr," said Klyd. "Go."

As Valleroy stood up displaying his silhouette, Klyd moved back, using every scrap of cover to make his exit unseen. Valleroy picked his way methodically down toward the waiting figure, calling softly, "Thrino, you've missed the shelter. I'll guide you in. This way."

Nearing the dark figure, Valleroy gestured westward toward the better footing. The figure made no move to approach. Valleroy bared his arms and held them out in the moon light. "I mean you no harm." He dared to approach a little closer. The other didn't move, but it was the stillness of a frightened animal ready to bound away at the slightest threat.

Valleroy tried to imitate Klyd's reassuring manner. "Come to the shelter. It's warm. There's food. It's safe there."

"How did you find me?"

Valleroy was close enough now that he saw the rocks held by those youthful fists . . . arms tensed and ready. The fugitive's voice was a half-whisper, but high like a child's. "You were making a lot of noise in that loose gravel," said Valleroy. "The footing is better over here."

"Who are you? What are you doing here?"

For answer, Valleroy fished out the starred-cross and dangled it in the moonlight. "Ever see this before?"

The answer was a gasp of recognition and a relaxation of the vise-like grip on the throwing rocks.

Valleroy coaxed, "There's one like this waiting for you in the shelter. Come."

Slowly, the child began to work over toward Valleroy, dropping the primitive weapons behind. Valleroy pulled his jacket sleeves down and shivered. He was sorry he'd left his cloak behind.

"Who are you?" The child's voice trembled faintly.

"My name is Hugh Valleroy. What's yours?"

"I have no name. I'm a Gen."

"I'm a Gen, too. But I have a name. Several in fact."

Closer now, the child examined Valleroy's clothes with interest. Suddenly, he spat, "*Householder!* Pervert!" He jerked away, running back toward his original path.

Valleroy spun around and leaped in front of the child, catching him by the shoulders. They struggled silently for several moments until the hood of the child's cloak fell back loosening a flood of rippling black hair that fell over her face. "You're a girl!" blurted Valleroy.

"And you're a filthy pervert! Let go of me!"

"I will not. You're trying to get me killed by the Runzi that are down in the next valley and I don't like that. Even perverts resent being murdered!"

At the word "Runzi" the girl froze. "How do you know?"

"My partner and I watched them yesterday. They're gathering their dead. We figure they'll be gone in the morning so we can get home."

"Home?"

"Zeor."

Coldly passionate now, the girl said, "Get your hands off me."

Valleroy let her go. She started away, trudging down the hill.

"I'm sure," called Valleroy, "there must be Simes following you."

She stopped and turned, obviously caught in a dilemma.

"It's warm in the shelter. There's food. My partner says we ought to be safe there until morning."

"Your partner?"

"Sectuib Klyd Farris, Head of Householding Zeor. He doesn't eat little girls."

"I'm not a little girl any more. I'm a Gen."

Valleroy could hear the self-hatred in that repeated admission. It was a horrible emotion to see on the delicate lips of a young girl just flowering with womanhood. He said, "And I'm Sectuib Farris's Companion. He's in need, yes, but I guarantee he won't touch you. Your fear can hurt him, though, and maybe kill us all by leading the Runzi to us."

"Perverts! I hope they do catch you!"

"But you're here, too. Come. We have a warm shelter to offer. Share it with us. I promise we won't try to convert you."

177

The cold and the lonely flight through darkness had taken their toll on the young fugitive Gen. Lip trembling with suppressed tears, she stood silently. "Come," said Valleroy one last time and led the way.

After a moment, he heard a furtive scrambling behind him. Soon they came out on firmer ground and climbed toward the almost invisible shelter. She began to hang farther and farther back until Valleroy was forced to go back after her. "Klyd's really nice when you get to know him. Even when he's in need, he's very considerate. He's never killed and he never will."

She hung back staring at the cabin fixedly. Valleroy took her by the elbow urging her onward. "He's waiting for us. Don't be afraid."

Reluctantly, she moved under his hand. Valleroy led the way through the door and into the brighter light where Klyd had built up the fire and put some grain on to boil. The channel turned from the hearth. Still sitting on his heels, he said, "Welcome to the Shrine of the Starred-Cross . . . and to safety."

Leaning against the closed door, the girl made no move. Valleroy watched her eyes appraise Klyd's dexterous handling tentacles. Klyd used them as he had when Valleroy had seen them for the first time, unselfconsciously, firmly, naturally. To Valleroy, they seemed the embodiment of all the grace and beauty the human soul could contain. His own arms seemed incomplete. Obviously, the girl didn't feel that way at all. She was terrified.

Klyd spoke as if welcoming a guest to Zeor. "Naztehr, you can hang up her coat while I put her meal on the table. Thrino, I regret I have little to offer except what we found here. We, too, are fugitives from Runzi."

"And I hope they catch you!"

"But not while you are with us. You are still lowfield. You must have been warned quickly. You will escape."

"To die savage in the wilderness."

"To die your own death in your own way. If it is so hopeless, why do you run?"

She sagged limply against the door. "I don't know! I don't know or *care* any more!" Averting her face, she let the tears of weariness flow unchecked, but without sobbing.

Valleroy moved to take her shoulders. She came into

178

his arms like a lost child deserted to die alone. He let her cry a few minutes. Then he shook her gently. "You *do* have a future to live for. Look into yourself! Are you any less a real person now than last week? You're a Gen. Is it really true that Gens are mere animals? Do you feel any different? If you don't feel any different, do you think any other Gen feels any different . . . any less a human being? And if Gens really are the same, what makes you think they don't have just as much of a going civilization out there?" He waved his hand vaguely toward the border.

Really confused now, she lifted her tear-stained face to look into his eyes. What she found there, Valleroy never knew, but it stemmed the flood of tears. After that it didn't take long for her to clean out the bowl of grain and apples. The warm food and the cheerful fire worked on her weary body. Within moments, she was alseep under Klyd's blanket, leaving the two men in muttered conference over steaming bowls of a predawn breakfast.

"We've got to get out of here."

"Yes, Sectuib. It will be dawn soon."

"No. Now. She *was* followed."

Valleroy sprang to his feet. "Where . . . ?"

"Sit down. They're still pretty far away. But the Runzi will probably spot them shortly if they have scouts out. As soon as the Runzi realize that only a chase could bring out nightriders, they are bound to check here. We must not be here when they do."

"But what about her?"

"Naztehr. We can't take her with us." The grim resolve in the channel's voice was the coldest death sentence Valleroy had ever heard.

"You lied to her! You knew she wouldn't be safe here!"

"Unto Zeor, forever. Sometimes the things one must do for Zeor are not pleasant."

"I won't leave her here to be slaughtered!" Valleroy half rose to his feet, but Klyd's right hand shot out to grip his arm. "Nazethr. Wake her and we die too. Now at least she raises no beacon of fear to guide them. Finish your meal. We must go."

"You cold-blooded . . ."

"*Naztehr.* Anger carries well in these deserted hills!"

Valleroy gulped hard and settled back into his

chair. The wisdom of Klyd's proposal was undeniable. But Valleroy knew that his own mother had been just such a child once.

"Eat. The sooner we are gone, the better chance she has to survive. Together, we form a conspicuous deformity in the selyn field."

"I've lost my appetite. Let's go before I lose my dinner."

Softening, Klyd said, "She *does* have a chance, you know. They might not spot her if she's alone and has faith in the starred-cross."

"You're lying to *me*, now."

"No. Just hoping. A perverse human habit that attacks Simes and even channels sometimes."

They gathered up their things, but left Klyd's blanket covering the child. Before stepping out the door, Valleroy moved the starred-cross from the shrine's wall into the girl's hands.

Then, grimly, he followed the channel out into the predawn dark. Moving over familiar ground, they deposited the closed cylinder in the niche where they'd found it. They continued along the top of the ridge, westward toward Zeor. There was still a chance they might avoid the Runzi and make it down into the valley.

But it was a slim chance and growing slimmer. The channel flitted from shadow to shadow as if he had merely to think of a place and *be* there without touching ground in between. Valleroy was hard put to keep in the position Klyd had calculated would bring their combined field resultant into an inconspicuous level with that of the Runzi. But Valleroy tried to keep up. In the process, he acquired a wrenched ankle that made him swear luridly.

The channel didn't even drop back to investigate the mishap. Nor did he slacken pace to accommodate Valleroy's limping process. The Gen had to keep reminding himself that need drove his partner now. Only a stalking predator intent on his goal could move through the night with such ease. By keeping his attention on the goal ahead, Klyd was trying to avoid qualifying Valleroy on the spot.

And Valleroy had never been less certain of his ability to qualify. He'd spoken boldly to the girl, calling himself Companion and had felt proud at that moment. But with every passing hour, he'd become more and more aware of the signs of Klyd's need growing beyond his control; the fact, flickering eyes always darting restlessly, measuring distances, hyperaware of everything; the laterals trembling almost visible throbbing of the ronaplin gland. Even the Sime's voice revealed a tension that hadn't been there hours earlier.

As Valleroy watched this transformation come over the channel, he began to doubt once more whether he'd be able to face the test if it came. Here, again, was the man he'd met that long-ago night in the rain. Since the second time he'd seen the channel, Klyd had become a different creature. Calm, strong, self-assured, dedicated, but never demanding. He could be arrogant and insufferably authoritarian, but never grasping, greedy, or thoughtlessly callous. But now, thought Valleroy, Klyd had become once again that hyperactive predator intent on nothing outside of personal survival. This time, the transformation would continue even farther.

Absorbed in his own thoughts, Valleroy stumbled along peering at the ground just in front of his feet. So it was a double shock when he walked into an outstretched arm. He jumped back, stumbled, and sprawled against a fallen tree trunk. "Hugh! What's the matter with you?"

"You scared me!"

"Quiet now. The hills are crawling with Runzi."

"I don't see anybody."

"Gens!" snorted Klyd. "All alike. Blind, deaf, and dumb."

"Save the insults. Just con us out of this."

"From here we go down. Watch your step."

"That's what I was doing!"

"If you value your life, stay in position!"

"Yes, Sectuib. But you'll have to go slower. I twisted my ankle. I think it's swelling."

"We'll take care of it when we get home. For now, ignore it."

Valleroy just grunted and started off in the channel's wake. He tried to forgive his partner. It must be easy for a Sime to forget that Gens can't ignore injuries. He gritted his teeth and concentrated on keeping up. A misstep might mean a long fall.

But it wasn't the Gen who took the fall. Klyd stepped onto a jutting rock table and prepared to lower himself over the edge. Just as he was squatting on the rim, the whole rock table tilted, uprooting its deeply implanted

181

end! Instantly the Sime leaped sideways out of the path of the falling and sliding rocks, but he wasn't quite fast enough. The rubble carried him head over heels nearly fifty yards downhill where he came up against a lone, gnarled tree trunk. The cascade of rock continued down the hill. In its wake, slipping and sliding, came Valleroy.

Catching a overhanging branch, Valleroy danced to a precarious halt beside the Sime. He bent to examine his partner. The first flush of dawn was chasing the stars. It cast a vague gray light over the world. The ugly red gash on Klyd's head looked even more ghastly by that light, but for Valleroy the first area of concern was the laterals.

He kneeled to draw back Klyd's sleeves. There was an angry welt rising across the right hand dorsal sheaths, but apparently all four laterals were unharmed. Just as Valleroy ran a lightly probing finger along the fourth lateral, Klyd came awake all at once. He grabbed Valleroy in the transfer position but without the right dorsals. After the briefest instant, far too brief to allow Valleroy to react, the Sime withdrew and forcibly relaxed his body. "Your field is up and climbing steeply. You knew I had to augment to avoid being crushed by rocks . . . *why* did you have to touch me like that!"

"Well, it brought you back to consciousness, didn't it?"

Sullenly, the channel propped himself against the tree trunk. "May as well not have bothered. We might have made it to the valley before dawn. They were withdrawing eastward. We *might* have made it."

"Can you travel? That cut on your head . . ."

"Is nothing. But it's too late. They've spotted us."

Valleroy's heart pounded a little faster as the realization of failure washed over him like black ice water. In the growing light, he could see little flickers of motion converging on them from every direction. The hillside was alive with the enemy!

"We'll run for it," said Valleroy. "Let me help you up."

"Don't touch me! If I could depend on you, I'd draw now and make them wait a month to watch me die. But your attitude toward me has changed in the last few hours. Attempting transfer in haste like this, I might hurt you."

Dry-throated, Valleroy gauged the tightening circle of

the Runzi. There was no escape. "Sectuib. If you can bring my field down low enough, it will grant me another month of life, too. A lot can happen in a month."

"They won't touch you as long as they believe you are immune to the kill. If one of them tries to take you, just remember that none of them are channels. Their draw is slow and shallow compared to mine . . . and you *are* capable of serving me. I'd require time to qualify you now . . ." He broke off, looking over Valleroy's shoulder. "We don't have any more time."

The Gen turned, heart thudding madly, to find three Simes holding stilettos and observing them silently. Klyd rose to his feet, brushing the dirt off the proud Zeor colors. Glancing over his shoulder, Valleroy caught the hawklike intensity in the channel's eyes. Here was the whole House of Zeor prepared to go down fighting.

Then the channel did a strange thing. Standing just behind Valleroy and to his left, Klyd rested his right hand on the Gen's right shoulder, extending the nearest lateral to brush Valleroy's neck. With his left hand, the Sime gripped Valleroy's left hand, extending his laterals in the same position he'd used to accomplish the internal shunt.

For an instant, Valleroy thought he was being asked to serve despite the emergency. He was nerving himself to give it a try when he saw the Raiders' reaction. Klyd's need and Valleroy's intent to serve were tangible to the Simes. They'd heard of such things, but the reality was still a compelling strange, luridly daring, repellently fascinating attraction.

Knowing now that Klyd had clamped down a rigid control that allowed him to make contact without surrending to instinct, Valleroy was able to dampen down the last vestige of apprehension. He played his part with calm assurance that captivated each Raider as he arrived at the scene. Beginning to enjoy holding his audience, Valleroy conjured a genuine concern for Klyd's feelings. He tried to project the impression that he *wanted* to serve.

Evidently, he succeeded too well. Simultaneously, Klyd whispered. "Ease off. You're tempting me." And the latest arrival who appeared to be the leader said, "All right, perverts! Step apart."

Klyd answered calmly, "A channel and his Companion do not separate."

"You try for a transfer and you'll wish that rock slide had buried you both right here. Move."

"I'm tempted to call your bluff," said Klyd levelly. "You wouldn't dare try to break up a transfer. Who would be the worse pervert then?"

"Even afterwards you'd be no match for all of us. But to avoid bloodshed, I'll give you my word that you'll get your transfer. Now just step apart so we can search you."

The ring of Simes surrounding them tightened until it seemed to Valleroy like a wall bristling with wicked steel blades. Loosening his grip, Klyd whispered in English, "I've given you the best credentials I could. Now, you're on your own." Disengaging gingerly, Klyd moved aside and stood to be searched.

Valleroy struggled to retain his concentration on serving Klyd. It was the only way he could endure the probing and poking of the Simes. They confiscated every loose item on his person except the starred-cross, which they didn't seem to notice. Valleroy was thankful for the layers of warm clothing that protected it and for the Sime's reluctance to expose merchandise to the cold. The talisman was all he had left now, and it was little enough against the heavy manacles, collars, and ankle chains in which they were marched back to the local Runzi rallying point.

The sun finally cleared the horizon, but the sky remained filmed with a slate-gray haze that dissipated all the warmth. The chains were searing cold against Valleroy's skin. Where the cruel barbs dug in, they were torture. The collar made him walk erect with his eyes fixed on the horizon. It took two Simes, one on each side, to get him down off that hillside. But the comparatively level valley floor wasn't much easier walking. His ankle had begun to swell. The pain brought freezing tears to his left eye every time he took a step.

He kept telling himself over and over that the ankle didn't matter because he was going to die anyway, and very soon too. He didn't believe the squad leader's promise to allow Klyd a transfer. But even if the Runzi had meant it, he'd worded it in such a way that it was doubtful if that transfer would be from a Companion. If the Runzi lived up to their reputation, they'd offer the channel a kill—probably some recent captive who'd never heard of channels. They'd wait to the last minute so that even a channel couldn't resist the Gen's fear. And then they'd gloat.

Somehow that humiliation of Klyd and of Zeor seemed more dreadful to Valleroy than his own fate. It never occurred to him that he might be taken all the way to the main encampment.

CHAPTER TWELVE

Captivity

THE NEXT THREE DAYS WERE A NIGHTMARE FOR BOTH Klyd and Valleroy. For the most part, the time passed in a blur of meaningless impressions for Valleroy. But several events did stand out with a stark clarity that haunted the Gen ever afterward.

When they had arrived at the rendezvous, the squad leader had turned them over to his superior, who was in charge of the entire burial operation. There was no spit and polish to this army, Valleroy noted, but the discipline was stiffer than he'd ever seen anywhere.

No sooner had they arrived than they were given hot food and drink, better than they'd had for days. Ignoring the heavy chains, Valleroy started to dig in but then noticed Klyd watching him. He looked around to find the other Simes also watching him. Experimentally, he moved his spoon over the plate, observing their reaction out of the corner of his eyes. It wasn't poisoned food, no. But a lot of it was for Simes only. He ate greedily, but only those things he recognized.

Almost before he finished his meal, another group of Runzi escorted a new captive into the camp. It was the young Gen girl who had taken refuge in the cabin with them. She was in a state of such hysterics that she didn't even recognize them. But it wasn't the screaming, struggling girl that shocked Valleroy. Nor was it the manner of her demise. It was Klyd's reaction to it all.

She was thrust into the arena between the other two captives. Her cloak and jacket were stripped away leaving her skin bare to the cold. Then the chief of the

Raiders came forward to examine her, evidently reading her field. Surveying his men, he singled out one obviously in need and thrust the two of them together . . . a pirate chieftain awarding the spoils.

Sick with fascination, Valleroy watched, but he also watched Klyd. The expression on the channel's face paralyzed him. Klyd was a detached scientist observing a demonstration. He was a physician observing a dissection. He was an actor watching a performance, judging its artistic effectiveness but totally immune to emotional involvement. There was no trace of a human being watching a murder.

It was all over in a few seconds. As the Sime approached, the girl's hysteria mounted to a peak. Valleroy could see bruises where she'd been beaten. He thought sourly that she'd probably been raped too. As the Sime grabbed her, eagerness written in every muscle, her eyes rolled up. Valleroy thought she'd fainted to cheat the Sime out of his fear-ration. But the junct did something to her head. She began to struggle again, wildly and desperately. In that instant, the predator struck. Her frantic motion kept him from making lip contact. He took his fifth point off her cheek. The result was the same. A moment of bone-snapping rigor followed by instant death.

The murderer casually scooped up the wilted heap of cloth and flesh, a tiny bundle, and walked off to the common battlefield grave pit that was just being closed.

The sight of him discarding that unimportant piece of litter was engraved painfully on Valleroy's memory forever. But the look on the channel's face was even worse. Klyd's expression wasn't something one could exact retribution for. It wasn't a betrayal for which a court could execute. It was a disillusionment that threw Valleroy's new-found ideals into chaos.

His mind churned, throwing up fragments of beauty that had just begun to have meaning for him. A Sime-Gen Union? Impossible. The Householdings joined together under a strengthened Tecton thwarting Zelerod's Doom? Why bother? A place of pride serving as a channel's Companion? Repulsive notion. He wanted to cry. He wanted to vomit. He wanted to slit his own throat.

Instead he walked. He walked chained behind a horse-drawn buckboard. A few feet behind him came another team of horses, another buckboard, and after that, Klyd, also in chains.

Valleroy's clothes became caked with dust. He was savagely glad that it covered Zeor's colors. He wanted to tear off that uniform and bury it. His stiffened ankle paralyzed his leg with pain. He was glad because it took his mind off the itch where he imagined the channel's eyes on his back.

He let himself sink into misery, seeking oblivion. He didn't even try to focus his eyes. When they stopped to eat, he just let the plate sit before him. Eventually, a Sime came to shove the food into his mouth. He chewed and swallowed because he didn't have the will to fight. He didn't care if they poisoned him.

They turned into a logging road that led upward into sweet-scented evergreen forests. The nights became colder, but the lone Gen was always given a place nearest the fire. He didn't even notice that there hadn't been any active sadism directed at him. And what they did to the channel didn't bother him.

On the third morning, they rounded a bend in the old road that Valleroy thought must be Ancient handiwork. They came out immediately into the main encampment of the Runzi Raiders. To their right and a little to the west of them Valleroy spotted Hanrahan Pass. There was a deep, majestic, evergreen-filled valley between them and the pass, but there was an old winding road that crossed the valley; it was barely visible as an intermittent scar among the dense foliage. To their left, in a large flat clearing at the foot of an enormous cliff, lay the camp.

It was the first time since the murder of the girl fugitive that Valleroy had clearly noticed anything. He focused his eyes with effort. They entered the camp under an archway with the Runzi symbols inscribed over it. Before them, two rows of temporary buildings stretched all the way back to the granite face. Obviously they were barracks. To their left, stables and an administration complex were also housed in temporary structures. To their right, row after row of close-packed cages stood ominously empty.

The entire camp looked deserted. As far as Valleroy could see, there were no Gens in the cages and very few horses in the stables. From one of the buildings a curl of fragrant smoke rose, marking the commissary. That was the only visible sign of life. Adding the contingent arriving with them, Valleroy estimated there couldn't be more than a hundred residents in a camp designed for eight times that many plus captives.

As they passed through the archway, two security guards counted them and recorded obscure data in crisp notebooks. It took only a few moments for the column to disband, every man knowing his job and doing it with swift efficiency. The two captives were handed over to fresh guards, who processes them into numbered cages as if they were sacks of potatoes for the larder. They were given not the slightest opportunity to attempt an escape.

Valleroy had to admit that they'd been treated better than Gens treated Sime prisoners. Since the Sime was the most dangerous animal on the face of the earth, Gens took great care to deplete the prisoner's · strength at every opportunity. The Sime prisoners were kept in bonds, which Valleroy now recognized as inhumanly painful, especially to the laterals. They were given nothing to eat or drink. And they were interrogated at close intervals until they died, sometimes of attrition but more often in some frantic escape attempt.

Gen captives had nothing that could threaten their captors. Nevertheless, the Simes never relaxed their vigilance. No wonder, thought Valleroy, there were no Gen captives returning to tell the story.

It was the mystery of no return that gave the Raider's pens their aura of supreme dread. The actuality wasn't really that bad. And in a way that made sense. These were professionals harvesting a valuable crop. They took care not to spoil their wares before they reached market.

The cages themselves were rectangular boxes divided into six equal compartments by a triple row of bars down the long axis and two triple rows across the short axis. The outside walls of the cages were double rows of bars, one row six inches inside the other and offset so that there was almost no space between bars.

The roofs and floors were solid metal. The whole unit was mounted on stubby legs fitted with rollers, and the whole unit looked like nothing so much as a circus wagon.

Placing a ladder at the head of one cage unit, the guards marched the captives up one at a time. The foremost guard used one of a bunch of jangling keys with numbered tags. Then he pulled open a trap door in the top of the cage. Two of the other guards lowered Valleroy

188

into the hole. Then they let go. He fell three feet onto cold metal plating where he lay stunned, his swollen ankle shooting hot pain all through his body.

By the time Valleroy recovered his senses, Klyd had been installed in the adjacent cage and all but the last guard had departed after rigging flexible transparent sheets around the sides of the cages. Shortly, vents in the floor began to blow hot air into the cages. Valleroy sat up, massaging his ankle and looking around.

The interior of the cage was bleak but clean. Dividing his compartment from the adjacent ones, the three staggered rows of bars almost provided privacy of a sort yet without the effect of solitary confinement. There was a full eight inches between the rows of bars. They were set so close together that only a child's wrist could fit between them. There was no way occupants of adjacent cages could combine resources for an escape.

"Hugh! Come here."

The Sime's hushed whisper grated on Valleroy's nerves. His impulse was to retreat to the farthest corner of his cage. But before he could move, Klyd asked, "Is this Aisha?"

That drew Valleroy to his feet in spite of himself. He'd forgotten she must be in the camp somewhere. He shuffled to the bars and found the channel peering into the cage to his right. By closing one eye and moving back and forth, Valleroy got a slim view of the cage that shared only one corner with his. However, it was enough. That creamy tan forehead, straight nose, and unmistakable eyebrow were distinctive. Their neighbor was indeed Aisha Rauf.

But she lay as if unconscious, a boneless heap on the bare floor. They'd finally found her, but it wouldn't do any good. "She's dead!" Valleroy blurted despite his reluctance to speak to the channel.

"No. She lives, but she seems to be drugged. When she wakes, she'll fear me, and the Raiders will gather to watch the spectacle of a channel's disgrace."

"She's too smart for that. You can't get at her, and you're a prisoner too. If that's what they're expecting, they're in for a disappointment."

"I'm not so sure. I'm only human. With you so close, yet beyond reach, I may break before dark."

"I may enjoy watching you die the way you enjoyed watching that poor child murdered."

189

"Nobody murdered that girl. She committed suicide."

"That's right. Worm out of it. Twist the words. I don't care what you *call* it. I saw the look on your face!"

"What did you see on my face?"

"Curiosity. Interest. A cold calculating spectator at a . . . a . . . *circus!*" All the disgust welled up anew, leaving Valleroy shaking with revulsion and self-pity.

" 'Curiosity,' 'interest,' 'calculation' . . . I'll admit to those. But 'cold' . . . no. Never. The difference between you and me is that I'm directing a war while you are a refugee from that war. Every general officer accepts that some of his troops must die if *all* are to achieve victory. However much he may want to, he can't try to save any given individual in preference to the cause. The refugee lives only for himself and must salvage the fragments of his own survival. Neither role is enviable." Unutterably weary, the channel slid to the floor, where he sat propped against the bars like a discarded toy.

Valleroy didn't say anything. Again his world was coming apart. He'd learned to trust Klyd. Then he'd learned to hate him. Now, he wondered it it wasn't himself he should hate. He'd been a soldier. He knew what a wartime command was all about. He said, "But she was just a kid . . ."

"She was a soldier in the biggest and longest war humanity has ever fought. And when it's over, she will be remembered in my family and suitably honored by all of us . . . forever. That I promise."

In spite of himself, Valleroy felt Klyd's idealistic vision gripping him anew. The worst of it was that it brought back the memory of what Klyd's death would mean to Zelerod's Doom; it brought back part of Valleroy's will to live.

"Hugh, don't you understand? I couldn't let her death go to waste. I had to learn as much as possible from it."

"Learn? What? That Simes kill Gens?"

"No. *Why* Simes 'kill' at all. If I knew what it is that so attracts the junct to the kill, perhaps I could learn to simulate that quality for him. Then it would be easier to get Simes to disjunct. Maybe, one day, we might learn the technique so well it would be more pleasant to go to a channel than to kill."

Visions again. Valleroy resisted that tug at his imagination. "It wouldn't matter. You'd still be condemned as perverts."

"Perverts are risqué. If perversion is also cheap, profitable, and emotionally satisfying to the majority of normal people, it spreads until *it* is the norm. Can't you imagine what this world would be like if the kill were considered perverted?"

"You could learn to do all that just by watching a kill?"

"It's an opportunity I don't get very often. I could have learned a lot more if I'd been allowed to monitor at close range. But I was in no condition to do that. I'm in worse condition now."

Looking at the channel with new eyes, Valleroy saw a gaunt, deeply lined face, eyes sunken in bruised wells of despair. "I didn't even notice what they've been doing to you."

Klyd shrugged. "They've been treating me pretty well. If they'd driven me to desperation on the trail, I might have done a lot of damage before they could kill me. But they made every conspicuous effort to demonstrate how well they cared for you. By promising repeatedly that I'd have you as soon as we arrived, they subdued that desperation. Standard technique."

"They promised *we'd* . . ."

"Oh, yes. But I didn't really believe. And I was right. Don't you see what they're going to do?"

"By putting us close, but not close enough to touch? My field must be driving you mad."

"It is." The distant gentleness of his voice underscored the intense emotion as no display of anguish could. "And they'll come to watch the spectacle."

"How long until . . . ?"

"I don't know. I'm already in hard need, but I have selyn reserves available for a few more days. I will lose control before death. Have you ever seen attrition?"

"Once or twice. When I was in the Army. Prisoners."

"Ordinary Simes. Horrible enough, but quick. This . . . will not be quick."

Valleroy didn't think the days of agony he'd witnessed had been quick. He'd been busted for shooting the second Sime they'd caught. "Maybe something will happen in our favor. We're about due for some good luck."

"Now who has succumbed to hope?"

Valleroy laughed but it came out too harsh. "Guilty, General, Sir. I'd like to rejoin my outfit, Sir."

In spite of the growing burden within him, Klyd

191

smiled. "You're a commissioned officer in this Army, Naztehr. The Companions are our elite corps and our secret weapon."

Valleroy felt his ears turn red at that easy acceptance. It seemed they'd always been willing to take him in, but he kept rejecting the thing he wanted most: to live for something beyond his own small life . . . something that mattered.

It wasn't long until the guard was changed and lunch appeared. Near the center of the outside wall of his cage, a section of the floor slid aside revealing a recessed compartment. Inside this he found a covered chamber pot smelling strongly of disinfectant and a wooden plate heaped with hot food. The cup and spoon were also wooden and slightly sour with disinfectant. But the food was good and the chamber pot was welcome.

When he'd finished, Valleroy placed the wooden implements back in the compartment and waited. No cage was escapeproof. He was determined to find the weak point in this one. It wasn't the bars. They were solidly implanted in the floor and ceiling and there was no sign of rust weakening the structure. Valleroy didn't know how they managed that trick, but it didn't seem important. If he couldn't break out, he'd have to think his way out.

That meant, noticing everything, no matter how trivial. One thing he'd noticed was that they'd given Klyd only broth and water. It wasn't starvation. They just didn't see any reason to feed a Sime in need. Neither did Klyd. He barely touched the water and didn't even sniff the broth. To Valleroy, that meant Klyd would be too weak to run if they could engineer an escape. They'd have to confiscate some horses.

Patience paid off later in the afternoon. He watched carefully as the guard was changed. The noon relief used a key that somehow closed the sliding section of floor and opened the side of the compartment from which he extracted the wooden implements. Now Valleroy knew how the device worked, but he was no nearer escape. Apparently, it was impossible for both doors to be open at the same time. This he could test by jamming his door open next time around. He resolved to try it.

He spent the rest of the afternoon studying the ceiling door and the transparent sheets—very like the stuff the kids had used for their hothouses. It was stored on rollers and pulled down like window shades. At the bottom, there was an air-strip opening that let fresh air in, and another one along the top. The warm air from the heating vents made the cages healthy enough if not comfortable.

The cell was large enough to allow exercise. There was no way to climb the bars. They were set too close to allow even a small person to get a leg around one, and they were polished so smooth, hands would slip. If a prisoner did manage to get to the ceiling, though, the trap door was still a good four feet away in the center of the cage.

There was also a guard stationed up on top of the cages. Any escapee would have to contend with him even on a foggy night. Selyn fields were as good as vision to a Sime. Klyd could deal with the guard when he was in good condition. But the channel had spent the whole day lying in the farthest corner of his cage, eyes open, but breathing with a forced regularity. It was an invisible, motionless battle he was fighting, but it was a crucial one in Valleroy's war. Escape would be useless to him if he couldn't deliver Klyd back to Zeor and Aisha back to Stacy.

Over dinner, Valleroy concluded that the only way he'd ever get out of the cage would be to induce the Raiders to *take* him out. It seemed to be a very clever idea at the moment it occurred to him, but when he tried to devise a way to implement it, he found there just wasn't any argument he could use that would convince them.

If he were sick, they'd probably just let him die. Companions were no good for the kill, and his death would probably create quite a spectacle in Klyd's cage . . . so they'd have nothing to lose by letting him die. He couldn't talk to the guards because he was only an animal or a pervert.

He was ticking off his inventory of prisoners' tricks for the fourth time when a piercing scream rent the air and sent him scurrying for the corner he shared with Aisha's cage. Despite having been in a semitrance all afternoon, Klyd was there first, clutching the bars and staring wide-eyed.

Valleroy watched in horrified fascination as the strong-minded courageous girl he'd loved so much cowered like a sick animal in the farthest corner of her cage. She was trembling in psychotic dread, saliva curling out of sagging mouth, eyes bulging. And she screamed her terror with every breath until her beautiful voice was a harsh whisper. Then she continued to scream as if by habit . . . mindlessly.

"Aisha!" called Valleroy over and over, but it had no effect except possibly to increase her fright. Unable to understand what had happened to her, Valleroy turned to the channel.

He found Klyd also shaking, beads of sweat tracing runnels down his deeply lined face. But the channel somehow managed to pull himself together enough to move toward Valleroy. "Come . . . over here." He led the way along their common wall until they crouched beside the outside bars. With visible trembling still wracking him, Klyd slumped to the floor. "That *fear*! Help me, Naztehr. Help me."

Valleroy tried to squeeze his hand between the bars, but it caught at the wrist, no more than touching he center row of bars. "I want to, Sectuib. But I can't reach you. I don't understand what's making her like this. I don't know how to stop it."

Klyd's shaking subsided under the influence of Valleroy's emotional nager, but the Gen's field was a torture of a different sort. Eyes closed, Klyd leaned his head on his knees and said, "They've drugged her. I've heard about this, but I never really believed anybody would do it. A drug-induced fear used to spice the kill. Fits Andle's personality."

Valleroy shook his head, stunned. "Every time I almost decide Simes are just people, I discover some new horror worse than any of the superstitions."

"This is new, even to me. I think they'd given her an overdose and had to tranquilize her while some of it wore off."

"Must be still overdosed. She's afraid of her own shadow. She'll die of heart failure."

As if on cue, a troop of guards marched up to the far side of the cage. Three of them climbed to the roof. A moment later, two of them had leaped down into Aisha's cage and clamped a breathing mask over her face. There was a purple-banded cylinder attached to the mask. Valleroy heard the hiss of escaping gas. Moments later Aisha subsided into unconsciousness.

Both guards turned and leaped up to the ceiling, catching the rim of the trap door. Each hauled himself out as effortlessly as if climbing a stair. Then the trap door clanged shut. The detail marched off with many backward glances toward Klyd. The only words Valleroy could find to describe the expression on their faces at that moment were "anticipatory leer." They were sadists preparing for a feast.

When they'd gone, Klyd wiped his face on his cloak and breathed a little easier.

"Sectuib, could you do that?"

"What?"

"Jump out of that cage."

"If the door wasn't locked from above, certainly. Scarcely requires augmentation. But they aren't going to unlock that door until I'm safely dead."

"If I get a chance, I'll unlock it."

The channel peered through the bars at the fragments of Valleroy's face that he could see. "And I thought *I* was delirious. You better get some sleep." He pulled himself to his feet and tottered carefully to the far corner, where he resumed his prone poistion.

Valleroy was thankful that his partner was still fighting. But there was no telling when he'd give up. To minimize the field-gradient between them, Valleroy took himself to the farthest corner of his cage and prepared to spend the night scheming. But he fell asleep to the montonous throbbing of his ankle.

CHAPTER THIRTEEN

Aisha's Kill

"HUGH! NAZTEHR, WAKE UP! HUGH!"

Valleroy rolled over, groaning and tried to pull the sheet higher over his head. But there was no sheet. That brought the flood of wakening memory. He sat up aching from the hard floor.

"Hugh?" It was Aisha's voice!

He gathered his feet under him and staggered toward the corner of the cell. She was standing, haggard but calm, in the center of her cell, and she was almost smiling. "I don't believe it's you. I must still be dreaming!"

"Aisha. It's no dream. We're here."

"I wish it were a dream. It was only me who'd die before. Now they'll get you too! They made me watch it . . . how they do it. It's horrible. I can't stand the thought of them doing that to you."

"Don't worry. My partner here saw to it I had my immunity shots before he brought me."

Her eyes traveled to where Klyd stood gripping the bars and watching her.

Valleroy said, "You two have met, haven't you?"

"I'd appreciate a formal introduction, Naztehr," said Klyd in his most cultured English.

Feeling a bizarre sense of propriety, Valleroy said, "Sectuib, this is Aisha Rauf, model and artist extraordinary. Aisha, this is Sectuib Klyd Farris of Householding Zeor. He's the finest channel within a hundred miles and I'm proud to be here as his Companion."

With a quizzical little smile playing about her mouth, Aisha said, "I'm pleased to meet you, sir, but I doubt if I'd shake hands under the best of circumstances."

"No need to be rude," chided Valleroy. "It's usually quite safe to shake hands with Klyd, though I wouldn't recommend it at the moment. He's a *channel*."

"A channel of what?"

"Selyn. He's one of those Simes that can take selyn from any Gen without killing and then channel it to Simes so they don't have to kill."

"I thought that was just a story."

"It's true. I've lived in his Householding for several weeks while we were looking for you. I ate with Simes, roomed with them, and worked beside them. I don't look very dead, do I?"

She inspected what she could see of Valleroy and then shifted her attention to Klyd. "He's kidding."

"Madame, my Companion speaks truth."

"Companion?" she echoed as if perceiving the unique intonation for the first time.

Valleroy explained the more obvious implication of that title. He finished, "So you see, they can't kill me the usual way. And they won't kill me until after . . ."

She picked up when Valleroy choked on the thought. "Until after Klyd dies? *Are* you dying?"

"Slowly."

196

"But even so, you wouldn't kill Hugh if you were put in the same cage?"

"Definitely not, but they wouldn't allow us contact."

"How cruel. I can understand the poor beasts killing us because they can't help it. But torturing their own kind with that same instinct . . . they ought to be exterminated!"

Klyd turned to Valleroy and spoke in Simelan, "You see? Typical reaction. Exterminate the Simes and solve the problem. Haven't the centuries taught the Gens anything about this?"

Valleroy nodded. "I see what you mean. The channels are really the only answer, and even the sensible Gens can't see it." Valleroy suddenly realized just how far he'd come from the night he'd entered Sime Territory feet first. Aisha spoke for her whole society, but Valleroy was no longer a part of it.

"Naztehr, this is the woman you love. Give her time to adjust. She may yet learn."

Aisha said, "Hugh, I didn't know you spoke their language so *well!*"

"I couldn't before I went hunting for you. You've led us a merry chase, you know.

"I've been right here the whole time."

"But," said Klyd, "we didn't know that. I lost one of my best men getting the lead that brought us here."

Suddenly, the thundering of horses hoofs broke the morning stillness. Lathered, blowing thin puffs of steam, the horses cantered under the archway and disappeared behind the buildings. A large, ornately decked party of riders . . . obviously someone in authority . . . "Who do you suppose . . .?" said Valleroy.

"Andle, no doubt," said Klyd.

"Who's he?"

As Klyd withdrew to a far corner, Valleroy explained Andle's part in the complex of events that had brought them all here. His heart lifted as he watched her assimilate the information. She wasn't beaten. She was defiant. He thought it was a very special woman indeed who could be heartened by the knowledge that she was a victim of a truly meaningful, gigantic war maneuver rather than of random chance.

From the outer bars, Klyd called, "Here they come!"

The sharp clatter of shod hoofs on bare stone echoed from the cliff face. Then a party of riders erupted from the passage between two barracks buildings. They were all well-dressed Simes, men accustomed to commanding others and proud to advertise that fact in their appearance.

The rider in the lead stood out conspicuously from his retinue.

He was of medium build, well into middle age, and seemed to come from the usual mixed racial descent. But there his similarity to his followers ended. He carried a short, dress version of the Sime whip, hardly more than a riding crop with a jeweled handle. His black boots were polished to an impossible mirror finish. His flamboyant white riding cloak draped his horses flanks with the smooth fold of the richest material. His impeccably tailored jacket was cut for fashion, not warmth. And his few items of jewelry were chosen with the ostentatious conservatism of the confidently wealthy.

But it was not the painful attention to grooming that labeled him. He would have been just as impressive clad only in muddy rags. It was the flash of eye, the tilt of brow, the confident arrogance of every smoothly coordinated movement that gave him an aura that could subjugate a reigning monarch. Here was the kind of leader who would attract followers intent on supporting only the winning side.

In that momentary pause before the visitors dismounted, Valleroy suddenly saw the entire conflict in a new light. On the one side, the Tecton founded on ideals and personal loyalty; on the other, the juncts banded together by personal greed. The Tecton was creating a society of interdependent units; the juncts' society was composed of mutually repelled units that would fly apart if the binding force were to falter.

That instant would be Andle's death. And, promised Valleroy silently, that would be the second installment in the Death Price of Feleho Ambrov Zeor!

The flash of inarticulate hatred that accompanied his vow attracted a momentary glance from the intended victim. Even so, when Andle had dismounted, he went directly to Klyd.

The grimace that twisted Andle's mouth bespoke a dire victory on the Sime's side. Even before one word had been said, Valleroy's heart chilled. His shifting emotional nager earned him another piercing glance that culminated in diabolical laughter. "Sectuib . . . Ambrov

198

. . . Zeor . . . your Companion is right!" And more laughter, so cultured yet so barbarically triumphant.

Valleroy thought even the laughter was as carefully calculated for impressiveness as was Andel's appearance. But even so, it wasn't Andle who dominated that scene. It was Klyd. Imprisoned though he was, obviously at the others nonexistent mercy, dirty, ragged, and torn with need, the channel's quiet dignity somehow made Andle seem overdressed . . . a buffoon too inept to clown in Zeor's kindergarten.

It was the oddest thing Valleroy had ever seen, that wordless confrontation. Later, thinking back on it, he decided it was the triumph of co-operation over competition. Klyd did not stand alone. Even isolated in a cage, he could draw upon the combined strength of the whole Tecton while Andle had only his own self-confidence to support him. At that time, though, Valleroy could see only how Klyd's imperceptible source of strength shattered the unity of Andle's retinue. And with that observation, Valleroy again found hope.

But not for long. The awkward laughter ceased, and the twisted face hardened. Only the lips moved, curling around each word sneeringly as Andle pronounced, "Zeor is DEAD!"

Valleroy guessed it wasn't those words that devastated Klyd. It was the emotional content behind them. Words could be bluff or boast. But the channel's expertise was in reading emotions. No ordinary Sime could deceive a channel.

"What do you mean?" The question was delivered tonelessly, but that itself indicated the intense control behind those words.

Now came the long awaited moment of total victory for Andle. He produced a newspaper, unrolled it, and held it up for Klyd to read the headline. It was a special edition of the *Tecton Weekly*. "Yesterday," read Valleroy, "Yenava Ambrov Zeor, wife of Sectuib Klyd Farris, died at Householding Zeor."

The rest was beyond his field of vision, but Andle supplied the news. "Yenava went into labor. There were complications. Because you weren't there, your grandfather tried to help her." He paused to observe the effect he was creating. "Your wife, son, and your grandfather are dead. You will follow shortly. Without leader, Zeor . . . is . . . *dead!*"

Klyd betrayed little outward sign of reaction, but there must have been some flicker of emotion that set Andle laughing again. But that laughter was a serious tactical blunder. Eyes narrowed, the channel shifted his weight ever so slightly and waited.

The solidarity of Andle's men, which had begun to coalesce once more, dissolved in an instant. The defeated prisoner still dominated the triumphant captor. It couldn't be, yet there it was, undeniable even to an emotion-deaf Gen.

The laughter died away more quickly this time, and into the silence Klyd said, "Zeor is not a person, it's an idea. Ideas cannot be killed by destroying the people who hold them. Unto Zeor, forever."

Realizing that his victim had claimed victory, Andle spat, *"Pervert!"*

At that, Klyd smiled gently, almost as if Andle had offered the traditional Zeor pledge. Speechless, Andle stormed toward Aisha, smacking riding crop against his thigh as he inspected his merchandise. Valleroy saw her retreat from the angry Sime. She hadn't understood a word that had been said, but most of the communication had been nonverbal and universally clear.

To cover her fear, Valleroy shouted, "You're the pervert, you coward! You're too gutless to take a Gen who isn't drug-crazed into fear"—Valleroy paused to space his words like poisoned darts—"because . . . *you* are terrified of what a Gen could do to you!"

Andle froze in the act of confronting Aisha, as if unable to confront his accuser.

Valleroy sneered contemptuously. "Or is it that you must have a Gen artificially stimulated in order to trigger your own sluggish reflexes . . . because you *really* want to go to a channel!"

"SHUT UP!"

"You leave her alone, do you hear me, Pervert," said Valleroy with chillingly dangerous control, "or I'll carve my initials on your laterals!"

Abruptly, the Sime abandoned Aisha and rounded on the Companion. "So! Our brave Companion wants the girl! And our conceited pervert wants his Companion. It might be interesting to put the girl in with the pervert and see what happens . . . in . . . say . . . another three days from now?"

Valleroy bluffed, "Klyd wouldn't hurt her. She'd serve him as well as I could."

"She probably would," said Andle grinning. "Just as well, and no better!"

At Valleroy's startled reaction, Andle snorted, "Oh, yes, we know all about you, Mr. Federal Policeman. And I am personally going to arrange a little test to see how much you've learned from the perverts!"

The politician strode back to his horse and mounted with a flourish. A moment later he was gone, taking even the roof guard with him as a gesture of utter contempt for the prisoners.

As soon as the Simes were out of sight, the three who had stood solidly united collapsed into solitary hopelessness, each for his own reason. Valleroy slid to the floor feeling stripped of his camouflage of invincibility, forgetting that Andle couldn't know *all* about his background and would never believe how much Valleroy actually had learned. Aisha merely added one more ignominious defeat to the long list she'd suffered here. And Klyd allowed himself at long last to react to the loss of the three who meant the most to him.

It was the sound of the channels grief that brought Valleroy out of his own misery. Quiet dry sobs of a brave man's defeat, it was nothing that even the closest friend should witness. Yet there was no avoiding the intrusion.

"Klyd, listen. He came here to break you . . . to smash Zeor's pride. Don't let a few words win his victory for him! Make him fight for it!"

The sobbing went on and on while Valleroy talked for what seemed like hours, saying the same thing over as many different ways as his Simelan vocabulary permitted. Then he said it all again in English, partly for Aisha's benefit and partly to say more exactly what he meant.

At last, he had nothing more to offer but, "He was wrong about me, Sectuib. I can serve . . . and I will serve well. You've said so yourself. You know it's true. Aisha has courage. Together you and I can teach her enough to cheat Andle of whatever thrills he expects."

Valleroy fell silent, and gradually Klyd's anguish came under control. Moments later, the channel turned his grimy drawn face toward them. "They too were soldiers who died in the war that we . . . must . . . stop. Their sacrifice will not be in vain."

Valleroy answered, "Unto Zeor, forever."

The channel's dark eyes revealed the slow agony that consumed him. But his voice was steady when he answered, "Unto Zeor, forever."

In English, Valleroy said, "Let's sit down. We have a lot of work to do today."

They gathered around the corner where their cages met. Klyd opened. "I don't see what we can do with nothing but words . . . but you evidently have some idea."

"Well, for a start," said Valleroy, "we can try to figure out how much time we have to prepare. Andle didn't appear to be in need, but then I'm not the expert on that. How about it, Sectuib?"

"I expect he'll hit ivren early tomorrow morning. If he follows the usual custom, he'll call for his kill before noon."

"So soon? That doesn't give us much time."

"What's your plan?"

"I don't really have a plan. But if this is a war, it seems to me we're on a suicide mission. We have to take as many of the enemy with us as we can."

"Enemy?" said Klyd, as if tasting the word. "No, the reason this war hasn't been resolved is that we're all actually on the same side. There are no enemies, and nobody is in the 'wrong.' "

"We don't have time for any Sime philosophy," said Valleroy, brushing that aside in unconscious imitation of a Sime gesture. "It seems to me our deaths can serve the cause best if we take Andle with us."

"That loathsome beast?" said Aisha. "I'll vote for that. But how?"

"I'm not sure. Depends on what he decides to do next. But I think your hand will be our only weapon. It's going to take courage, but your father always said you were stubborn, and stubbornness is a good substitute for courage."

"What if he drugs her?" asked Klyd wearily. "That fear-inducing compound shatters the mind. The victim doesn't remember much but nightmare."

"The victim," said Aisha, "remembers all too much! I think if they threaten me with that again, I'll die of fright on the spot."

"Here's another 'what if,'" said Valleroy. "Suppose he drugs her and puts her in there with you. What would happen?"

Klyd took time for a long, deep sigh before he answered. "Without the drug, I probably could manage to avoid killing her. Just barely. But with it, I doubt if I would have any control at all." He shuddered. "It would certainly please him to watch the pride of Zeor so stained. But I don't think he'd do it."

"Why not? I called him a coward. He wants to get me for that."

"If he made me kill Aisha, I'd still be alive. He requires me dead, preferably this month, in order to make the charge of high treason stick. If he can show that I died of attrition when my so-called Companion was taken by an ordinary Sime in the kill, the entire Tecton will come under official investigation. Our way of life would probably be outlawed. Then where would we go? Gen Territory?"

Shaking her head bewilderedly, Aisha said, "How is it that the Householdings were ever allowed to organize legally?"

"Before the channels, nobody thought of making such a law against us. After all, do Gens have a law forbidding them to breathe water instead of air?"

Aisha laughed. It was a delicate, bell-like sound that aroused memories for Valleroy. He'd forgotten how good her laugh made him feel. She said, "I see what you mean. All Simes kill, so why make a law against not killing? A good question."

"And by the time somebody thought of it, we had too many friends in high places."

"Couldn't those friends squash the treason charges?"

"Not any more. Our sympathy with the Gen Government is an open secret. Sentiment has been running very much against us for several years. Andle's faction has been waiting for a test case, and now they've got it. Even if they have to invent the evidence."

"And you can't fight it," said Valleroy, "because the manufactured evidence happens to be real."

"None of this is real for me," said Aisha, slumping back against the bars.

"It will be," answered Valleroy, "when he gets his tentacles on you. And that will be your moment to strike . . . for us, for Zeor, and for the whole human race."

203

"That sounds so melodramatic. How can a Gen do anything once a Sime gets hold of him? And how could *I* do anything that would save the world?"

"With Andle gone, his movement will collapse," said Valleroy, "at least for a while. That will give the Tecton time to consolidate. Public opinion is antichannel right now, but it's changing, isn't it, Klyd?"

"Slowly. Andle's death won't win peace. But his continued existence is all that holds his movement together. He's been careful to expunge every leader of ability from his organization. There's nobody to take his place. His death would stave off Zelerod's Doom for a few more years perhaps."

After they'd explained the Sime mathematician's forecast to her, Aisha said, "I see. Then I'll *have* to kill Andle. But I've never killed anybody before. I wouldn't know how. Do you have a knife or a gun hidden on you somewhere?"

"No," said Valleroy, pulling the starred-cross from the neck of his jacket. "All we have is this."

"It doesn't look very sharp. I could scratch his eyes out more efficiently with my fingers. Not that he'd give me the chance."

"No," said Valleroy. "The power of this lies in the faith you have in it."

"But I don't have faith . . . I'm not even sure I believe in God any more. I've prayed, oh how I've prayed!"

"Well," said Valleroy, fingering the talisman, "it worked, didn't it? You prayed, and here we are."

"With all due respect to the . . . uh . . . Sectuib . . . *some* rescue party!"

"Not rescue party," corrected Valleroy, "strike force. We're going to put Andle's whole operation on the scrap heap. Or rather *you* are."

"You haven't told me how yet."

Valleroy switched to Simelan. "Klyd, you pointed out that she reacted as a typical Gen . . . kill all the Simes and solve the problem. Is she too typical to be trusted with the secret of how to kill Simes?"

Pursing his lips in consideration, Klyd shifted his weight. Restively, he massaged his laterals in that peculiar mannerism that so disturbed Valleroy. "Aisha," said the channel slowly, "tell me what would happen if all the Simes now alive suddenly dropped dead."

She frowned in concentration, sensing there was more

to the question than showed on the surface. "Well, it would certainly take a long time to get all the bodies buried. There'd probably be plague from that."

"Hmmm," agreed Klyd. "And after that? Would the world be a better place to live?"

"Oh, no! Simes would continue to go through change-over. But there would be no adult Simes to teach them. They'd have no language, no culture, no technology . . . no way to live except killing and raiding and no *place* to live except the wilds. Before long, we'd be right back where we were eight hundred years ago. We'd have to start all over. And we might not be lucky enough to get channels the second time."

"What would you do if you could teach your Gen friends how to kill Simes?"

"You mean all at once, in a massacre?"

"No. One at a time."

"Well, I don't know. Take Ginnie Simms, for example. She's the kind of fanatic who'd jump at the chance to make all Simes drop dead at once. She'd never think about plague and future Simes. I don't think I'd tell her even to save her life. But Mildred is different. She thinks Simes are evil people, but she's content to let the Lord take care of them. The only trouble is, Mildred is a gossip. Tell her, and Ginnie will know by sundown." She thought a moment. "I can't imagine anybody I *would* trust . . . except . . . Hugh."

"Now," said Valleroy, "you understand why we hesitate to show you. And there's another factor. The method is even more cruel than what they're doing to Klyd. The victim suffers . . . terribly."

"And," put in Klyd, "if he happens to survive for a while, he develops what amounts to a phobia against taking selyn. I had the misfortune to attend the death vigil of such a victim. Can you visualize an armless man dying of thirst within reach of a water faucet?"

"Horrible. Most ordinary people wouldn't deserve it, but someone like Andle . . . I think I would like to do unto him as he's done unto others. Besides, when somebody is killing you, you don't worry about hitting back painlessly."

"If you'll promise you won't be unnecessarily cruel . . . even to Andle . . . I'll teach you what I can."

Aisha pondered that. "I wouldn't go out of my way

to torture even the likes of *him*. But I won't promise to be careful either."

It was Klyd's turn to consider carefully. Because of her high-field and his growing need, he couldn't read her anger accurately. He decided to gamble. "Naztehr," he said in Simelan, "I think she can be trusted."

"All right. You explain it to her, then I'll give her the starred-cross."

The three of them worked through the afternoon, pausing only for meals or when Raiders passed by to see if Klyd had broken down yet. The jeering taunts of the Simes served only to reinforce the captives' determination.

It was after dark when the sorely abused girl had fallen into exhausted slumber that Klyd said, "I'm beginning to hope she might be able to do it, if he doesn't drug her."

"I just don't think he'll drug her . . . not after the way I called him a coward for it right in front of his men."

"You did that perfectly, Naztehr. They knew what he'd been doing, but they never thought of such a novel explanation."

"You think I might be right about him?"

"Partially, perhaps. I've never known an ordinary Sime to develop a fixation on Sime-Sime transfer before disjunction. True, there might be some variant strain of Simes that might react that way . . . but I doubt it."

"It was just a shot in the dark."

"You *did* hit him where it hurt, Naztehr. Close, but not close enough to make him order your execution."

"I'm glad of *that!*"

"From what you've said, his followers may figure out the truth."

"Which is?"

"I have observed that channels who are junct often develop just such characteristics . . . a near inability to kill . . . after one exposure to a Companion."

"You think Andle is really a juncted channel?"

"It's possible that he isn't aware of it himself. But he'd never be able to function as a channel. He's been junct far too long. What worries me is what he'll do to you for exposing him like that."

"If Aisha is successful, he won't have a chance to do anything to me."

"And if she isn't? I've never known a Gen not to panic at first experience of a lateral contact."

Valleroy thought of the little nameless refugee girl the Raiders had killed before their eyes. She'd been brought up among Simes. She even had the starred-cross. Yet she had panicked. And he couldn't blame her. He'd panicked, too, the first time . . . and also when Enam had come at him. There was something about Simes that was just inherently terrifying.

"Well, if she doesn't make it," said Valleroy, "we'll just have to devise a new stratagem."

"It's Andle who'll be devising the stratagem. I'm afraid I won't be good for much by morning. You'll be more or less on your own."

"The cruelest thing he could do would be to have me killed right before your eyes. But suppose, just suppose, I survive it."

"That would be just about the worst eventuality. You would be alive, but unable to serve."

"No, not the worst. Because if I survive, it proves I'm a Companion. His treason case will be thrown out of court."

"Sorry, I'm not thinking clearly."

"That's all right. I understand. I just wish I could help."

"Your desire to help is comforting."

"But you require more than comfort."

"Yes."

Valleroy shook the bars of the cage, hissing through his teeth. "There's *got* to be a way!"

Klyd recoiled from that blast of frustration, massaging his laterals ruefully. The night lights of the camp showed Valleroy the ronaplin fluid oozing from the lateral offices. The swollen glands were visible lumps, stretching the skin halfway up the forearms. Valleroy said, "Need must be . . . painful."

"Oh," said Klyd, seeing Valleroy eyeing his tentacles, "it's not just the laterals, it's the whole body. Metabolic rate increases, sensitivity up fifty per cent, the entire system primed and yearning to function. The Sime is a predator by nature, and need is the hunting mode. Even the personality changes. We become insufferably aggressive, inconsiderate . . ."

"I hadn't noticed."

207

"Thank you. Channels pride themselves on controlling it."

"If you've read Andle right, things may start to break early tomorrow. Try to hang together that much longer. Zeor requires your leadership."

The channel rose and moved carefully to the farthest corner of his cage, where he sat down again, carefully, as if any sudden movement would dislodge his control. Valleroy, too, moved to the far corner of his cage, afraid to allow himself to feel a frustration that would only add to Klyd's misery.

He knew he couldn't sleep, so he was surprised when he awoke with bright sunlight in his eyes and a mob of Simes crowded around the cage bars. But the visitors weren't interested in him. It was the channel that drew them, and they showed their appreciation with taunts and jeers half of which Valleroy couldn't understand except for the intent.

Klyd was standing at the corner bars, clutching them with whitened knuckles, handling tentacles lashing about in unrestrained futility. Every few moments, an inarticulate snarl issued from the channel's lips. His body went rigid with strain. He was augmenting, trying to break the bars! But they didn't even bend under his fiercest assault.

The only results of the channel's berserk effort was an increase in the number of Simes laughing at him. But after a fairly large contingent of new onlookers arrived from the barracks, another more disciplined group marched up from the other direction. They placed a ladder to the top of Aisha's cage. Three of them mounted to the roof, and one of those three called out to the crowd below him. "Break it up! Orders are posted for Ten, Twelve, and Eighteen to move out on sweeps today. Better check the rosters!"

Every man there scrambled for running room and within a minute there wasn't a Raider in sight except the guards who were hauling Aisha up in a sling. Valleroy shouted, "Where are you taking her?"

They didn't answer until they'd carried her, biting and kicking uselessly, down the ladder. Then one of the guards came around the cage to inspect the channel's efforts with the bars. Satisfied that the pervert couldn't get loose, he paused near Valleroy and said, "Runzi always delivers merchandise cleaned and inspected . . .

208

and at the appointed moment. We'll be back for you . . . later." He cocked his head toward the raving channel. "You can tell him so if he'll listen. I hope he doesn't suicide before we can have our turn with him."

That worried Valleroy. He'd never heard of it before, but he supposed that a channel could void selyn thoroughly enough so that it would amount to suicide. But he was helpless to affect Klyd now. The mere desire to do so only attracted the Sime to the bars between their cages. But there was no recognition in his eyes.

It was at once both pitiful and frightening to watch what had been a rational human being behaving like an orangutan run amok. Safe behind three layers of unbendable bars, Valleroy wondered if he could face the channel's madness without finching. He looked into those feral eyes that no longer seemed human, and he was almost glad he wasn't going to get the chance to try.

Valleroy left his breakfast untouched.

Several times during the hours that he sat and watched what had been Sectuib Klyd Farris, the pride of Zeor, he heard the thunder of departing riders. In the back of his mind, the part of himself he'd programmed to collect every detail of their prison noted the departures and recorded the fact that he camp was now nearly empty. But Valleroy himself was too emotionally involved with the immediate agony of his friend to absorb the fact and interpret it as opportunity. He vacillated between a firm resolve to help Klyd and a bone-chilling horror that seemed not part of himself at all, but rather a sort of primeval racial memory.

When this primitive part of himself arose, it chased all rational thought from his mind. He had to begin from scratch and rebuild all the reasons why the service of the Companions was necessary, and why his service to this particular channel was both imperative and possible. In the end, it wasn't the cold, logical objective of saving Zeor, the Tecton, and the human race that brought Valleroy back into the safe frame of mind. It was the memory of the warmth he'd felt when Feleho had called him Naztehr.

With that memory came a flood of associated moments. The instant praise his work had earned at Hrel's disjunction party. The unparalleled satisfaction of finding a part of himself that responded to Zeor and pouring that vision into his Arensti design. The thrill of having that design accepted and understood by so many whose praise he'd come to value. The look on Sectuib Nashmar's face when he saw the sketch of Enam and Zinter. And finally the great, overwhelming joy that he felt whenever someone at Imil took his achievements for granted because of his association with Zeor . . . synonymous with the best in everything.

All of this had occurred within the space of four weeks, while nothing at all similar had happened in nearly thirty years of his life. He knew where he belonged. To Zeor. But Zeor depended on Klyd's skills both as a channel and as an unusually adept administrator. And, Valleroy realized, Klyd's life now depended on Valleroy's own ability as a Companion.

Time and time again, he reached the decision. Klyd's life was more important than Valleroy's own, since without Klyd there would be no Zeor and nothing to go home to. Therefore, let Klyd try to kill him, and if he died, at least Klyd would live. It was an emotional decision that agreed with the more rational factors he had to consider. But every time he was secure in that decision, he pictured himself actually reaching out to touch the mindlessly raging channel with no bars between them . . . and the primeval terror rose again to choke him.

He fought it down only by reminding himself that he was in a cage and it wasn't his decision to make.

Finally they brought Valleroy a lifting harness and hauled him out of his cage. It was the opportunity he'd been waiting for, but the cyclical thoughts of the morning left him too numb for triumph. A part of his mind recorded the number painted on the trap door of Klyd's cage, but he knew of no use for the datum. Even though free of the cage, he was not free to act.

The straps that bound him were stronger than rawhide. All the thongs joined at a point in the center of his back where a lock mechanism secured them. The four Sime guards that escorted him allowed not the slightest chance for action. So he went peacefully. He hated to admit, even to himself, how glad he was to get away from the raving channel and the dilemma he caused.

Determined to make the most of this break, however, Valleroy lashed his mind back to Aisha and her fate. The guards wouldn't answer his questions, so he kept busy exploring all the possibilities and what he could do about them. They marched him between barracks buildings, around the stables, and into the administration complex by the back door. At the far end of the building, they entered a side corridor that led to a shower room. Two guards unstrapped him, roughly undressed him, scrubbed him down with the efficiency of harried stable boys, and shoved him into a knee-length, white tunic . . . standard pen issue.

To all of this, Valleroy submitted docilely, since he didn't mind getting clean. But when they started to strap him back into the harness without his pants, he balked.

With a sudden, twisting lunge, he ripped the harness right out of the guard's hands. Two seconds later, he had one of the straps looped around the leader's tentacles. He twisted the Sime's arm in a modified hammerlock that applied cruel pressure to the laterals. The other Simes froze, ready to leap but unable to risk that particular injury to their comrade.

Knowing that he had no advantage save that of surprise, Valleroy spoke fast. "I don't mind the white tunic. Especially if you're sending me to Klyd. But I don't go anywhere without my pants, cloak, and shoes . . . and my ring. Get them now, or you'll have to get a new squad leader!" He tightened his grip and watched them all wince at his hostage's pain.

Decisively, one of them went to the corner where they'd tossed Valleroy's things and brought back the items mentioned.

After one last, brutal squeeze, Valleroy shoved the hostage into the arms of his fellows. While two of the Simes examined the injuries, the third moved toward Valleroy with the harness.

Stretching a sock between his hands, Valleroy crouched low, balancing on the balls of his feet. "You want a turn, too?"

It was evident from his confusion that the Sime had never faced a Gen who didn't fear him. The Sime had the physical advantage, and his indecision was only momentary. But Valleroy took full advantage of that moment to slip into his mud-encrusted clothing. By the time reinforcements arrived, he once more wore the Zeor crest ring proudly on his right hand.

Seven guards, hardened professionals, now surrounded Valleroy. He wasn't afraid of them, but he knew he had no choice except to go along. He went. But he went proudly, and they didn't try to take his clothes away again. He knew he looked ridiculous, but he considered that a triumph even though he was once more harnessed.

They climbed a flight of stairs, walked a short distance and entered the top, corner room of the building. It was a small cubicle but luxuriously appointed. The carpet was a silky green velvet material; the drapes were heavy enough to darken the room against full sunlight and the walls were a polished wood that seemed to reflect the soft light in spots while absorbing it in others. The only furniture was a large studio couch and an upholstered, contoured lounge.

Seated on the lounge, chained to the wall behind her, sat Aisha. She wore the traditional white tunic and nothing else. But her collar and chain were not barbed. She could move with some freedom. Her gleaming black hair was piled onto her head into a complex structure of curves that emphasized her strong jaw line and defiant eyes.

They were allowed only a moment to look at each other. Then the guards produced one of the barbed neck chains and fastened Valleroy to a metal plate in the wall of the room opposite Aisha.

The door flew open. Andle swaggered into the room surveying the scene with evident anticipation. Then he dismissed the guards, snatching the keys from the leader and placing them on a wall hook beyond reach of both Gens. "Now, get out of the building and stay clear. I don't want any crossed-field interference."

Abruptly, the two Gens were alone with the Sime. Lips pursed, he measured Valleroy's length disdainfully, noting the Gen's mixed costume. Then he turned to Aisha, pacing slowly toward her as he spoke to Valleroy. "You see, I have her as I want her, without any aid from drugs. I've granted you permission to observe my technique . . . an opportunity any Householder would seize eagerly."

Valleroy's heart began racing. "If you wished to instruct Zeor, you should have brought Klyd here, too. Or were you afraid he might seduce you into his perversion? You're halfway there already, aren't you?"

He saw the Sime's back tense at that and pressed his advantage. "I can see it in your laterals. Your glands aren't responding to Aisha at all, are they?"

He moved a step closer to the girl, who sat wide-eyed

but immobile. "Shut up, Gen, or I'll have the guards come back with a gag . . . a foul-tasting one."

"Why? Can't you trust yourself to touch me? A Companion makes an even better transfer than a channel . . . as I'm sure you've discovered. Wouldn't you rather try out my talent for this new, exotic perversion?"

The Sime's laterals flicked out along the sides of his hands, quivering ecstatically in the dual selyn field between the two Gens. Valleroy knew his field was steeper because his single forced donation had stimulated his selyn production to higher than normal levels . . . to near Companion levels. Valleroy smiled. "That's it, isn't it? You attacked a Companion once, and you liked it so much you lost your taste for the kill. Now, if that isn't perverted, I don't know what is!"

Andle moved two more paces closer to Aisha. "Shut up or I'll have you removed!"

Valleroy gauged the distance between the pair and took a wild guess. "A *real* Sime committed to a kill wouldn't be able to talk to me at this point. But it's me you want, not her. If not, why did you have me dressed up like this?"

Andle took one more step toward the girl, but when he spoke it was much more weakly. "Shut up."

"Andle, come on over *here*." Valleroy unconsciously assumed Klyd's coaxing manner, the terribly effective manner the channel had used on Hrel and the others. "Andle, I'll serve you. Willingly. Not like the other Companion you had to force yourself on. We know the pleasures of the Sime as well as his agonies. I will serve your need, if you will let Aisha serve Klyd."

The Sime stood rigid, controlled by the instinct no Sime could overcome. At that moment, Andle was incapable of testing the logic behind that statement, Valleroy knew a moment of triumph at the Sime's hesitation. It meant he was right. Valleroy switched to English. "Aisha, he can't hurt you. Remember what we taught you, and do it just the way we decided."

Without warning, the Sime sprang at the girl. Startled, she recoiled. But then she met his outstretched tentacles with willing hands. At the moment of contact, she was kneeling on the lounge. She let his weight push her over in a tangle of arms and legs. His tentacles flashed about her arms!

Valleroy saw Andle's laterals make contact. Aisha

presented him with his fifth contact . . . a pair of moist lips. Valleroy knew that Andle felt nothing feminine in those lips. Nevertheless, jealousy surged triumphantly as Valleroy yelled, "Now, Aisha! Get him!"

Valleroy remembered that awful sensation that Klyd had inflicted on him. That was the draining horror that Aisha was facing. If she couldn't overcome it for just an instant, there would never be another chance. "AISHA! Get him!"

Her hands were rigid claws pulling away from the Sime with all her strength. It was a deep-seated reflex, Klyd had said. And he ought to know. Valleroy conceded defeat. But then, those straining fingers clamped down hard on the Sime's arms, moving up just a bit and squeezing deep into the exposed flesh.

She hit the node!

As if transfixed by high-voltage current, the Sime stiffened, throat frozen against the outcry that rose from his diaphram. Andle's eyes bulged as the lids peeled incredibly far back. Valleroy could feel the Sime's death. But the corpse refused to die. It fell back onto the cushions, vibrating hideously. The mouth was locked open. The tongue had been swallowed. The death grimace was terror incarnate. Still, the body continued to kick.

Aisha was catastrophically sick all over the silken upholstery. Valleroy would have joined her, but his stomach was empty. "Pull yourself together girl, and see if you can reach the keys. We're not finished with this job yet. Andle is only the second installment in the Death Price of Feleho Ambrov Zeor!"

Fighting the dry heaves, she eased herself around the shaking corpse and reached for the keys that still hung on the wall peg midway between them. The collar chain was just barely long enough to let her catch the bottom of one key. She jiggled it until the ring fell onto the carpet. Then she used her bare feet to retrieve the keys.

It took her several tedious moments to tame her shaking hands enough to unlock her own fetters. Moments later, she had Valleroy loose.

CHAPTER FOURTEEN

Final Decision

"GOOD," SAID VALLEROY, SHAKING OFF THE HARNESS. HE tucked the white tunic into his trousers. "Where are your clothes?"

Aisha looked down at her white shroud. "They made me leave them in the dressing room down the hall." Her eyes seemed unfocused. She swayed, on the verge of fainting. Valleroy put his arm around her in support, cursing himself for taking time to notice how good it felt.

With his other hand, Valleroy grabbed one of the harnesses. It made a good weapon. "Let's go get your clothes. You can't go out dressed like that."

They found her things in an adjacent room. She dressed rapidly while he paced. "We've got to steal three of their horses and cripple the rest. Do you know where they keep that gas they used on you?"

"The crazy stuff?"

"Yes, or the sleep gas."

"Well, it was racked in the room at the other end of this building, on the ground floor."

"Good. We have to go that way to get to the stables. Let's try it."

"It's no use. They'll spot our selyn fields moving."

"Maybe. But we can't just sit and wait for them to collect us and try again!"

"I guess." To Valleroy's eye, she looked like a wilted rose that had been stepped on too many times. Her eyes were sunken bruises.

"Can you make it?"

"If I don't, you'll just have to leave me."

Biting his lip hard, Valleroy led the way down the stairs. Andle's order had left the building deserted. The room with the gas cylinders had a perfunctory lock mechanism on the door, which Valleroy broke with four shoulder-lunges. Inside he found the interrogation center of the Raiders . . . a room he knew held terrible memo-

215

ries for Aisha. He pointed her back the other way. "Go watch the front door, the one by that office down there. I'll get the cylinder."

Wordlessly, she obeyed, and Valleroy entered that chilling theater that looked so much like a hospital operating room but wasn't. Along one wall he found a rack of gas cylinders, color banded and labeled in Simelan. But the words were all unfamiliar. Vaguely, he remembered the cylinder they'd used to put Aisha to sleep. It had borne purple bands. After a short search, he found one like it on the end of the line. It was larger than the one he'd seen, and it had no face mask attached. But there was a valve mechanism he thought he could open.

With the surprisingly heavy cylinder on one shoulder and the strap-weapon on the other, he rejoined Aisha at the exit nearest the stables. She held up a bundle of keys. "Look what I found in the office!"

Valleroy snatched them, peering intently. "The keys to the cages!" He set the cylinder on the floor and searched through the keys. Each one was numbered. Valleroy had noticed the number painted on the trap door of Klyd's cage. If he could find one that matched . . . maybe . . . Three quarters of the way around the ring, he found it, ripped it off, and shoved it in his pocket. "We'll have to make a dash for it. Think you're up to saddling a horse?"

"I'll manage or I'll ride bare." She slid past him and was out the door running before he could move.

By the time he ducked into the shadowy gloom of the stable, she was in the nearest stall saddling a handsome gelding that looked lean and fast. Her hair hung down in wisps plastered to her sweating face. Valleroy was beginning to suspect she'd been burned by Andle, but there was nothing he could do about transfer shock now.

He put the cylinder down and snatched up a saddle for the stallion across the way. If there had been a stable hand on duty, they'd have been challenged before now. No sense wasting time searching the building. There were only a handful of occupied stalls. The camp was all but deserted. Nevertheless, one Sime could be the end of their escape. Valleroy drew the cinch tight, and went to the next stall. Another sleek gelding was stomping impatiently. The Runzi had some of the best horseflesh Valleroy had ever seen.

With the hackamore in place, Valleroy collected the reins of all three horses for Aisha. "Get them outside. I'll put the others to sleep. Move."

Valleroy had to boost her into the saddle. She just barely had strength to hold on. He smacked her mount's flank and then turned to the gas cylinder. After three frantic tries, Valleroy remembered the way the Runzi message tube had been sealed. He found three recessed safety buttons that had to be held down simultaneously. They were designed to be convenient for tentacles, not fingers. He had to jam them down with splinters of wood broken from a stall, but he finally got the gas to hiss steadily forth. Holding his breath, he sprayed the occupied stalls and left the cylinder half buried in the manger near the door. Then, lungs screaming, he dashed for open air.

Rounding the corner of the building, he found Aisha waiting with the two spare mounts beside her. She slumped in the saddle, eyes squeezed shut against the bright sunlight. She hadn't noticed the Sime who had just emerged from the nearest barracks building staring at them in a moment of total shock.

Without breaking stride, Valleroy swarmed onto his horse and charged the hapless Raider at full gallop, swinging the straps of his harness into the air like a lariat. A moment before the whistling tangle of straps fell over his head, the Sime gathered his wits . . . there really was a *Gen* attacking *him!* . . . and began to move. But even Sime augmented speed couldn't quite offset the advantage of surprise.

One loop of the harness settled over the Raider's neck, and behind it came Valleroy, his full weight falling from horseback height, forcing the Sime to the ground. It was sheer luck that Valleroy landed on the Raider's back where the steely tentacles could not get an immediate grip on him. He took full advantage of that fleeting instant to yank on the noose. The dull snap of the Raider's spine was ample reward. Valleroy didn't wait to watch the man die.

Disentangling his harness, he leaped back into the saddle. "Aisha! I'm going for Klyd. You get on the road south and I'll be right behind you. Don't stop for anything!" Thundering by her, Valleroy grabbed the reins of Klyd's horse and streaked for the cages, flattening himself to the horse's back. Now that they'd been discovered, speed was their only hope.

And, thought Valleroy, concentrating on speed was *his* only hope. He dared not think about what he must do next, or what might happen after that.

Plunging out of the alley between barracks buildings, Valleroy drew up next to Klyd's cage. The channel was still at the bars, scrabbling with feeble determination. Valleroy knew that Klyd was in no way responsible for his own actions. Given the slightest chance, need would drive him to a kill right then and there, regardless of the danger of being recaptured.

Leaving his harness straps dangling over the horse's neck, Valleroy stood up on his saddle and drew himself onto the cage roof. He inserted the key into the trap door's lock. Then he lay prone to peer over the edge of the roof before opening the door. "Klyd, I'm going to raise the door. Your horse is right there. Follow me, and when we're clear of the camp, I'll stop and let you catch up. Understand?"

There was no light of recognition in those tortured eyes. Valleroy uttered a prayer as he threw the trap door open. Then he leaped back into his saddle and whipped the gelding's flank. He had tried to pick the slower horse for Klyd, but that was no sure way to win a race.

Valleroy caught up to Aisha midway down the mountainside, and there he gave her horse an encouraging smack as he passed. In response, the horse leaned into the wind.

They came off the downhill trail and dove into the dense evergreen forest. Tree trunks flashed by forming a solid wall. Out of the direct sunlight, Valleroy felt the chill bite of the mountain wind cutting through the flimsy garment he wore. Klyd was gaining on them too quickly. He forgot about the cold as he lashed his horse to one final sprint for safety. As he rode, he thought ahead to what he'd have to do.

All of their luck to this moment would be for nothing if he couldn't save Klyd to rebuild Zeor. But the emotions of that morning still plagued him. He knew that his only chance for survival lay in his willingness to sacrifice his life for Klyd's. But it had to be a genuine commitment. To the hypnotic beat of the horse's hoofs, he ran over and over the arguments.

In the end, it was that one word from Feleho Ambrov Zeor that made it all real to Valleroy. "Naztehr." He'd been honored with that title. Now that time had come to earn the honor. And he really wanted to earn it.

He allowed Aisha to draw ahead. When they had come to a small clearing where shafts of misty sunlight speared the dense gloom, he had reined in without warning her. By the time she had noticed, and had turned to come back, Klyd had caught up to Valleroy.

The two horses stood lathered and blowing clouds of steam into the rods of sunlight. The arching trees above were so much like a cathedral that Valleroy thought it would be a fine place to die. Wearily, he dismounted and stood ankle-deep in fragrant pine needles, waiting for the channel.

With an augmented burst of motion, the Sime was before Valleroy, tentacles outstretched, face drawn to such a tension that any Gen would have been terrified. But in that instant, Valleroy saw not a ferocious predator intent on murder, but his partner, who had sacrificed family and reputation and who now pleaded desperately for help to avoid the final disgrace of his name . . . the kill.

Something deep within Valleroy responded to that plea, sending his own hands out to meet those tentacles He could not allow Zeor to be disgraced!

As the dripping laterals flashed about his arms, Valleroy experienced a thrill of sensation, almost like the jolt of smelling salts clearing away the fog of unconsciousness. He was scarcely aware of the bruising lip contact that followed. That painful clarity of the senses grew until, through some trick of total empathy, Valleroy himself *became* both giver and receiver in that interchange.

Valleroy's own guts churned with need, and somehow he knew it for what it was.

In response to that need within himself, Valleroy poured forth all the selyn stored within him. With frenzied desperation he fed the demand that seemed at once to be so bottomless and so much his own.

Slowly, the speed of that draw diminished. As the demand fell off, Valleroy knew a double satisfaction that soothed both halves of him, dragging him down with weariness into the deepest darkness he'd ever known.

It wasn't the darkness of unconsciousness . . . not

219

quite. It was a darkness of separation. The darkness of disunity. The darkness of disintegration. The darkness that follows a dangerously bright flash of light. He was alone, with only one self again, with only the ache of sore muscles, and without awareness of the glittering sustenance . . . selyn. The selyn nager was gone. His body no longer could sense even the strongest field-gradient. Even . . . and now he knew what the term meant . . . the selur nager was gone. He shuddered, once, sharply, severed from a higher reality that had become his norm in one brief flash.

He opened his eyes to find himself lying on the pine needles. Beside him, cross-legged, sat Klyd, gently holding his hand and frowning. The channel's face was restored to its vigorous youthful glow, and his eyes were once more lit with rationality.

Tears stung Valleroy behind the nose. "We did it!"

"We did, but I'm not exactly certain *what* we did. I've never felt anything like that before."

"Whatever it was, it didn't hurt."

"Apparently not," said Klyd, smiling so that his sharp features softened. "Can you stand?"

Valleroy sat up, surprised that he felt not the slightest twinge of the agony that had haunted his first days and nights at Zeor. "I'm fine," he said, climbing to his feet as Klyd did likewise.

As he reached his full height, Aisha came running, arms wide to embrace him. "Hugh!" She sobbed on his shoulder, letting her full weight fall against him. "I thought you were dead!"

"I'm glad you're so glad I'm not dead. I love you."

"I love you, too, you beast!"

He kissed her and she kissed back as if they'd just been married. After several moments, Klyd interrupted. "Do I take it Zeor has gained another Gen member? The Sectuib of a Householding is empowered to perform marriages, you know."

The couple parted as if just realizing they weren't alone. Something told Valleroy that the channel was feeling an even more intense awareness of Aisha's feminity that he himself was. And from what he'd learned of the Householding custom, Valleroy knew that the channel's gene was so valuable that he was allowed to take whatever woman he fancied . . . whenever he liked.

220

Strangely enough, Valleroy wasn't jealous even when Klyd put a hand on Aisha's cheek. But if the Sime had any ideas regarding her, he forgot them immediately. She fainted.

Before she'd half closed her eyes, Klyd had eased her to the ground and was conducting a very impersonal check on her condition. "She's been burned slightly," he announced. "Tell me what happened with Andle."

Valleroy told him, ending with the condition they'd left the corpse in. The channel was horrified. "No human being should be forced to suffer *that*. If he's a channel, it will take him weeks to die, and the Runzi won't know that death is inevitable because they don't have any channels to diagnose him. That the hand of Zeor could be involved in this! Will history ever forgive us?"

Valleroy actually saw tears start to the Sime's eyes. "Andle was responsible for the death of your grandfather, your wife, and your heir . . . *and* Feleho. He deserved what he got."

"No. You should have finished the job."

"I thought it was finished. I'm sorry if I besmirched the name of Zeor. But I did what I saw had to be done."

Across Aisha's still form, Klyd reached out and took Valleroy's hand. "How can you find the capacity to be angry with me . . . after what we've just done?"

Something of that deep rapport that had welded the two of them in transfer still lingered in that touch. Valleroy said, "I can't be angry."

"Then come, let's take your bride home to Zeor. I have two funerals to conduct. We'll need a marriage to remind us that existence continues. In a few years, perhaps, you'll understand about Andle."

"We can't go to Zeor with you. Stacy's waiting, and I have a small reward to collect. I think I know now what I want to do with it. Unless Aisha's hurt . . ."

"No, she'll be all right. She's really an extraordinary person. You're lucky."

"Klyd, I'm sorry about Yenava. It was my fault . . ."

"No, not at all. No more than it's my fault for having been born with the Farris genes. While I live, there is yet the chance there may be an heir. That chance we owe to you."

"I still feel that I owe Zeor more than Zeor owes me. But I think I've hit on a way to balance the scales."

Aisha stirred and opened her eyes. Instantly, Klyd was all physician and healer, soothing, encouraging, and concerned. But she brushed that aside impatiently, though not trying to get up. "Balance what scales?"

Valleroy took a deep breath. "Aisha, will you marry me?"

"Of course. I made up my mind about that several years ago. But you always were slow. What scales are we balancing?"

"I'm not sure. Justice maybe. How would you like to establish an underground link across the territory border and spend the rest of your days dodging the law on both sides?"

"I don't know what you're talking about."

Valleroy told her about the land and pension he'd been promised and about how he'd wanted to spend the rest of his life painting. "I could take those acres in border property . . . maybe even adjacent to Zeor. . . . Perhaps they'd grant a few more acres because border land is so cheap. Then we could establish a Householding of our own. I haven't chosen a name. . . ."

"How about," said Klyd, "Householding Rior?"

"What does that mean?" asked Aisha.

"Forepoint, lighthouse, beacon, or sometimes the prow of a ship, or the point scout of an army."

"Yes," said Valleroy, "I like that. We wouldn't be able to keep any Simes, but kids who could get to us could be helped across the border. Maybe in time, we'd be able to keep them from killing in first transfer. We could help Gens escaping from in-Territory to adjust to our way of life. I don't know . . . there are so many possibilities."

"Exciting possibilities!" said Aisha. "When do we start?"

"Do you think you can ride now?" asked Valleroy.

"We can't stay here all night. The Runzi are probably all over these hills."

"Not for miles around. We're free for the moment," said Klyd. "But I still wish you'd come home."

"I made my obligations to Stacy before I even knew about Zeor. If I break my word to him, what good is my word to Zeor?"

Klyd laughed, shaking his head ruefully. "And you complain about Sime philosophy!" He helped Aisha to her feet, and they gathered the horses.

Mounted once again, the channel said, "Hugh, I'm going to miss you. I hope . . . you'll visit Zeor often."

Valleroy grinned. "Especially when you're in need? You couldn't keep me away. I've *got* to see if we can do that again!"

"It *was* . . . unique." Klyd stretched his tentacles out to touch the tips of his fingers, inspecting their steadiness. "It's a date then. Make it thirty days to sharpen the gradient and we'll try it again."

Valleroy asked, "What about Denrau?"

"He'll be training Zinter."

"And afterwards? How long can we . . ."

Klyd looked uncomfortable. "We'll see. Meanwhile, Rior can purchase assistance through your service."

Valleroy inclined his head formally. "Rior thanks Sectuib Ambrov Zeor."

"It it Zeor that gains the honor of sponsoring a new Householding."

"I doubt if the Tecton will ever recognize us."

Klyd laughed, the free hearty laughter of a man who knows no ilmits. "Then you'll found your own Tecton!"

Valleroy laughed, too, unaware of the torturous path to the realization of that prophecy.

Aisha cut into a masculine laughter. "Klyd, you'll always be welcome in Householding Rior . . . as if it were your own."

"Because it is his own," corrected Valleroy. "If it weren't for Sectuib Farris, none of us would have survived to see this day. And our grandchildren would have died unborn."

"Zelerod's Doom is not yet averted, merely postponed," said Klyd. "I have much more work to do at Zeor. But I don't know how I'm going to explain your absence."

"Oh, just say I met a girl who didn't want to live in-Territory. In a few months, they'll all understand the why of it."

Klyd nodded. "Good-bye, then. Until we meet again."

Valleroy wheeled his horse around so he could ride knee to knee beside Aisha. "Good-bye, and good luck at Arensti."

"I won't require luck there. I've got the winning entry."

Horses' hoofs stirring the fragrant pine needles with a swooshing tattoo, they parted, the Gens toward Hanrahan Pass and the lone Sime toward a lonely funeral walk. The future was hidden from all of them behind veils as misty as the shafts of sunlight piercing the vaulted shadows of that open-air cathedral, now hallowed for all time by what had occurred there.